The Sloth Zone

A SWEET ROMANCE

THE SKATERS OF SEQUOIA VALLEY
BOOK TWO

TOMI TABB

First edition

First published by Pas de Chat Publications 2024 Copyright © 2024 by Tomi Tabb

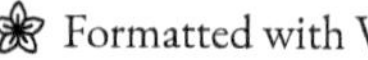 Formatted with Vellum

Gemma and Tim's World

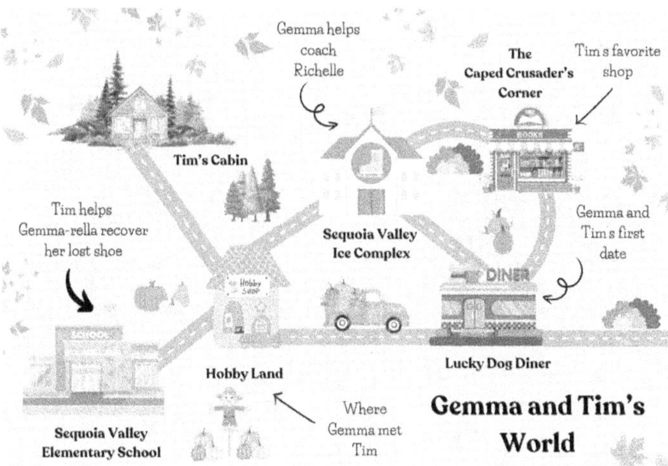

"All right, Gem, I'm ready." My best friend Frankie gives me a thumbs-up from the bar stool she's sitting on.

Taking a deep breath, I plaster a wide smile onto my face and speak directly to the camera. "Cheers! My name is Gemma MacLeod. I'm twenty-eight years old and originally from Glasgow, Scotland. I play Cinderella as a professional show skater with Dreams on Ice. For the last couple of years, I've traveled the world and performed in front of thousands of people. While it might seem like a fairy-tale job, it makes dating difficult when you live out of a suitcase ten months a year. If I ever want to get my own happily ever after and find my Prince Charming, I need help. This Cinderella is ready to trade in her skates for a pair of comfy trainers. If you're looking for your next bachelorette for *Cupid's Arrow,* look no further. You should cast me."

"Cut," Frankie says, tapping the Stop button on her phone. "That line about finding Prince Charming is great! The producers of *Cupid's Arrow* are going to eat this stuff up."

"You think so? It wasn't too cheesy?" I blow at one of the ringlets that's escaped my ponytail. I hope she's right. I'm sick and tired of being lonely.

Trying out for a reality show may be extreme, but at this point, I'm desperate. When it comes to dating, I've tried everything there is to try—blind dates, dating apps, speed dating, et cetera, et cetera—and nothing works. If I don't make it onto *Cupid's Arrow,* I don't know where I'll go from here.

"All the websites I've looked at have the same advice for audition videos—Be natural. Be yourself. That's exactly what you're doing. If you want cheesy, you can always ask my dad for his input."

We share a laugh. Frankie's words reassure me. Mr. Tomlinson considers himself to be a dating expert. Last year, when he decided he was tired of being a permanent bachelor, he read every dating book he could get his hands on.

Frankie and I teased him relentlessly about it, but it's Mr. T who ended up with the last laugh. Not only did he find a girlfriend—he married her! Whenever I see Mr. T and Suzy together, they remind me of Monica and Chandler from *Friends.* They're a couple who have brilliant chemistry, share a lot of laughs, but most importantly, they support and love one another. I want what they have.

"I can hear your dad now." I drop my voice an octave. "Gemma, it's one thing to say you play a princess, but it's better if you show those casting directors and really knock their socks off."

"You're right." Frankie lets out a cackle. "If it were up to Dad, he'd have you wear your Cindy costume and lose your ice skate in the opening shot. He'd probably push you to film it in black and white too."

My lips twitch. That isn't a half-bad idea. Anything to make me stand out at this point would be worth considering. Mr. T *will* have some great ideas, but I'm more afraid of him getting carried away. "Let's not tell him about filming this until after we've had some time to play around with the video a little more."

"Agreed." Walking over to the refrigerator, Frankie retrieves two bottles of sparkling water. "So what else are you thinking about including? You said it could be up to three minutes long, right?"

I nod, sinking down onto the living room couch. "Yeah, three minutes is the max." Accepting the cold bottle from Frankie, I pop the top off and take a long sip. "After the introduction clip, I thought I'd interview you and Suzy."

Frankie nods. "Good thinking. We could highlight the types of men we'd pick out for you to date."

I lower my voice. "You two are the people I'd pick to be on the show with me too."

Cupid's Arrow is different from other reality dating shows. The bachelorette doesn't get a say in who the bachelors will be. They're all selected by her friends. Frankie knows me as well as if she were my sister. I know she'd pick the perfect bloke for me.

Suzy, on the other hand, I haven't known long, but she's a great judge of character. Watching *Cupid's Arrow* happens to be one of her guilty pleasures. Whenever Frankie, Suzy, and I chat in our group text about the latest episode, she's had a frighteningly accurate read on all the bachelors. I'm willing to bet my skates on the fact she'd be able to do the same thing during casting.

"Aww, Gem, I'm honored. And I'm sure Suzy will be too." Frankie seats herself next to me.

"Do you think she'd be free to come over this afternoon?"

"Yes, but if you don't want Dad tagging along, we need to make it sound like we're doing something he wouldn't be interested in."

I puff out my cheeks. That's easier said than done. Mr. T is attentive to Suzy to the extreme, like the lamb from "Mary Had a Little Lamb." Anywhere Suzy goes, Mr. T is sure to follow. "How about a trip to the antique market?"

"Nope." Frankie shakes her head and opens her own bottle with an audible *pop*. "Suzy got Dad into antiquing. He'll offer to come and be our muscle for the day even though he shouldn't be lifting anything." Mr. T is in his mid-seventies and has had some health issues over the last year.

"Okay."

"You're on the right track though. Some type of shopping excursion would be perfect."

I drum my fingers against the couch arm. "What about a visit to the craft shop you took me to the last time I was in town?"

"Hobby Land!" Frankie snaps her fingers together. "That's perfect. Dad wouldn't dream of setting foot in there. Hobby Land might be the only place he hates more than going to the doctor's office."

I giggle. Frankie in a craft shop is like a sushi lover at an all-you-can-eat buffet. She wanders aimlessly from aisle to aisle looking at anything that catches her eye. I think last time we were there, we spent two or three hours exploring. We walked in planning to buy a few fake flowers for her costume, and came out with a trolley full of items that were "too cute to pass up." Needless to say, Mr. T doesn't have *that* much patience. He's a retired

Navy veteran who's used to things being run on a tight schedule.

The front door to the cabin opens and closes. "Frankie . . . Gemma . . . we're home," Frankie's boyfriend Charlie calls out in his deep voice.

"In the living room," she shouts.

He enters, puts down a bag of takeaway, then walks straight over to Frankie to kiss her. Like most male pairs skaters, Charlie is tall, with the build of a lean weightlifter. He has wavy tawny-brown locks and vivid green eyes.

"Hi, Gem," he says, detaching himself from my best friend.

"Hey." I nod in acknowledgment.

Charlie has changed a lot since we first met, thanks to Frankie's influence. He's more relaxed and less of a shy, reserved grump. We're able to have entire conversations now and have become good friends.

"Did I hear somebody say the words Hobby Land?" says a woman standing right behind Charlie. She has vibrant orange-and-purple hair, a grin on her face as wide as a Cheshire cat's, and a mischievous glint behind her eyes. They're the identical shade of green as Charlie's.

"I did." Frankie giggles, covering her mouth with her hand.

"I swear you're part canine. It's creepy how good your hearing is," Charlie mutters under his breath.

The woman rolls her eyes, ignoring him.

"Er . . . just a wild guess. Leslie? Charlie's twin sister?" I say.

"I am. You must be the famous Gemma." We shake hands. It's firm, with a strong grip. "Great to finally meet you. I was bummed you had to leave town so quickly last time."

"Likewise." It's funny how two siblings can be so opposite from one another. From what Frankie's told me, Leslie is loud and outgoing, while Charlie prefers quiet and solitude.

"So . . . Hobby Land?" Leslie rubs her hands together. "Are you guys going now? Can I tag along?"

"Les, that's a bad idea." Slipping his jacket off, Charlie tosses it blindly into the spare bedroom. "You have *way* too much junk from that place at both the rink and your place."

"It's not junk. I use all the stuff I buy." She places her hands on her hips and lifts her chin in defiance. She may be a head shorter than her brother, but her presence more than makes up for that.

He snorts. "Okay, I'll bite. What about the three bags of stuff sitting on your office desk at the rink? Have you finally run out of storage space?"

"Leave it to you to notice it the *one time* I leave stuff out." She pinches the bridge of her nose and takes a deep breath. "Those bags have stuff for your big surprise party next week. Now that the cat's out of the bag, promise me you'll still act surprised. The kids have been working hard on making you and Frankie 'good luck' cards."

"What are you talking about? What party?" He frowns at his sister.

"It's our send-off to the Skate United States competition in Colorado Springs next week," Frankie explains. "Haven't you heard the kids gossiping about it every time they think they're alone?"

Charlie's eyes widen. "Nope. It's news to me."

The women of the room collectively snort. Charlie is a fantastic coach, but off the ice, he has a one-track mind.

"Anyway," Frankie says, "would you mind picking up your jacket and hanging it up in the closet, please? We talked about you not leaving your clothes on the floor, especially when we have a guest."

He crosses his arms. "How do you know my jacket is on the floor?"

"I watched you stand here and toss it into *Gemma's room*," she emphasizes.

"Oh right. I forgot Gemma's staying in there and it's not my project room. I'll, er, be right back." Twin patches of pink appear on his cheeks.

Frankie shakes with silent laughter.

"So, Hobby Land?" Leslie asks again.

I shoot a curious glance at Frankie. Leslie is not going to let this shopping trip go.

Meeting my gaze, Frankie says, "Leslie is even worse at Hobby Land than me. She'd clean out the store if she could."

"It's true." Leslie plops down into the recliner opposite the couch. "I considered getting a job there just for the discount, but Charlie talked me out of it."

"Because if you worked there, you'd spend more money than you made," he says, reentering the room. "I can see it now. You'd join the shipment team, but instead of all the new stock hitting the shelves, you'd buy it and shove it into your craft closet at the rink." He settles Frankie on his lap.

I should've guessed based on the bright hair that Leslie is a creative person. I wonder exactly how large this craft closet is and what she has inside. "I hate to be a Debbie Downer, but Frankie and I weren't actually planning to visit Hobby Land."

Leslie's face falls. "Bummer."

"Then what were you guys discussing? Things for Gem to do while she's in town?" Charlie asks.

"Yes and no. Gem is making an audition video for *Cupid's Arrow*," Frankie says brightly.

My cheeks warm as she blurts out my news.

"Why?" Charlie frowns, his tone disapproving.

I stare at the tender way he holds my best friend in his arms as she rests her head on his chest. I lower my chin to my chest and absently run a hand up my forearm. I want a guy who embraces me like that too. "To find love," I tell him. "Not that I have much of a chance of being selected for it, but both the bachelorettes from the previous two seasons ended up engaged to the perfect guys. That's what I want."

"Gem, it's not worth it. Think about it. You'd be putting yourself out there for millions upon millions of people to see," Charlie says.

"That's great. It means a bigger dating pool," I counter.

"What about kissing your private life goodbye?"

"That's not the kind of kiss I usually go for."

Charlie face-palms. "You know what I mean."

"I do, and I have nothing to hide." I shrug. "There's little privacy as it is on tour. The world is welcome to see how glamorous being a show skater really is. We work out, practice, perform, eat, sleep, and repeat. Any free time we get, we spend resting."

Okay, that's not *exactly* the truth, but it's close enough. Frankie and I used to use our free time to go sightseeing or shopping. But it *is* true that our bodies were both exhausted by the end of the day. We'd use the downtime on the tour bus to sleep. It's hard to do something so physical day in and day out with few days off.

"If you're looking for a guy to date, are you open to a long-distance relationship? Because I'm sure that between

Les, Frankie, and me, we could find someone local you'd hit it off with. We know a lot of people," Charlie says.

Leslie fake coughs. "*We* know a lot of people?"

"Fine." He rolls his eyes. "You ladies know a lot of people."

"That's more like it." She looks smug.

"Yes, I'm willing," I answer without hesitation, hoping the desperation in my voice isn't coming through.

Frankie clears her throat. "It might help if you told them about your one little deal-breaker, Gem."

"Oh, um . . . I'd prefer not to date a guy who skates or plays hockey right now. I've tried dating guys who do both, and the last few times, the experiment has failed miserably. This time, I'd like to have a go at dating someone outside the skating bubble. Do any of you know someone like that?" My eyes rake the room. The occupants stay quiet, backed by the hum of the ceiling fan. "That's what I thought." I feel deflated.

"Don't give up yet, Gemma." Leslie scratches her forehead. "You put us on the spot. I'm sure between the three of us, we can come up with at least one guy for you. In meantime, have you asked our nan? She knows most of the people in town."

Aside from technically being Frankie's stepmum, Suzy is also Charlie and Leslie's grandmother. And she acts more like a grandmum to my best friend.

"I haven't, but that's a brilliant idea," I say.

"We'll add it to the list of things to ask her," Frankie says.

"I can call her now if you want." Leslie pulls out her mobile.

"Don't bother, Les. Nan and Mr. T were heading to the

casino in Jasper Ridge today. I doubt they'll answer their phones," Charlie says.

"I wish she'd invited me." Leslie huffs. "I could use some extra cash."

Charlie's eyes narrow. "What for?"

She pinches her lips together. "None of your business."

"It's for more junk from Hobby Land, isn't it."

"For the last time, it's not junk. There are some specific things I need for the rink at the semi-annual sale."

"Sure," he deadpans. "Just like I need four twenty-packs of toilet paper from Costco."

Frankie and I exchange glances. She rolls her eyes. If we weren't here, I'm sure Charlie and Leslie would continue their verbal sparring session. I jump in and change the subject. "Is Suzy good at cards?"

"Slot machines," the twins answer at the same time.

"She always comes back cash positive. I don't know how she does it," Leslie says.

"Well, I guess we can ask her to come over tomorrow. I just hope she's free. We're running out of time before your vacation is over, Gem," Frankie tells me.

"I know."

"Is there anything I can help with?" Leslie asks.

"Thanks for the offer, but I think Gemma had her heart set on using Suzy for her *Cupid's Arrow* audition video."

"Wait, *Cupid's Arrow*? Is that the show Nan is always raving about?" she asks.

"Yes." Frankie explains some of the ideas we brainstormed earlier.

"Got it." Leslie turns toward me. "If I were in your shoes, I'd want Nan too."

Charlie groans. "Les, you're supposed to be on my side. Gemma doesn't need to go on a dating show."

"What? There are no sides. We're one team, and that's Team Gemma. If this is what she wants, we should support her."

Frankie pecks him on the cheek. "You worry too much."

"Somebody has to." He holds Frankie tighter. "The same goes for you, Gem. I just don't want anyone taking advantage of you. You're like a sister to us."

My body floods with warmth. I grew up with an older sister. But I'd always wondered what it would be like to have a protective big brother. Now I have one. "How about this—If by some miracle the show's casting directors decide they want me, you can sit right beside Frankie and Suzy and help vet all the guys who want to have a go at dating me."

His eyes twitch. "So there's no way you'll consider not trying out?"

Crossing my arms, I attempt my best imitation of Charlie. "No. I've made up my mind."

Frankie and Leslie giggle uncontrollably.

"Are you trying to be me? If you are, you need to clench your jaw a little more and furrow the brows," Charlie says.

"Like this?" I grit my teeth, trying to pull my eyebrows down farther.

Leslie and Frankie laugh even harder.

"Er, not really . . . you look as if you're more bored than angry." Charlie rubs the back of his neck. "Maybe if you stood a little taller?"

"Charlie, nothing you suggest is going to make her look like you," Frankie interjects. "Gemma doesn't have a mean bone in her body. She's as close to a real-life Cinderella as they come."

He holds up his hands. "Fine. I know when I'm outnumbered. I'm going to start plating dinner. Les and I picked up Italian for tonight." Removing Frankie from his lap, he stands up and goes to the kitchen, leaving us to our own devices.

Leslie swoops in and steals his space on the couch next to her. "Have you ever tried out a dating app?"

"Mm-hmm." My cheeks boil as hot as water in a pressure cooker. "Nearly all the ones in the Apple store."

"And you didn't have any luck?" Leslie raises an eyebrow.

"No." I rub my hands against my forearms.

"Gem always pulls the short straw when it comes to dates." Frankie starts counting on her fingers. "There was the guy who only agreed to go out with her for a free meal. The guy who didn't date women over five-feet-two because he didn't want anyone towering over him. Oh, and my personal favorite, the guy who told her she'd have to quit skating so she could stay at home to raise their ten kids."

I grimace as she brings up each bad date. Leave it to Frankie to remember them—and in detail.

Leslie winces. "Ouch."

"The biggest problem I've had is that none of the blokes I connect with ever end up being anything like their profiles." I pinch the bridge of my nose. "After the guy who wanted ten kids, I moved on from dating apps to dating skaters."

"And what was wrong with them?" Leslie asks, hugging a pillow to her chest.

"The only thing we had in common was skating, or the blokes just wanted a casual fling." I blow out air. "Maybe I'm being too picky."

"There's nothing wrong with that. You should be. When it comes to love and guys, don't settle. You'll never be happy with yourself if you do. I stand by what I said earlier. Ask Nan."

"Diiiiiiiiinner," Charlie calls out from the kitchen.

"We're coming," Frankie shouts in reply.

We stand and head to the kitchen, and I watch as she casually slips her arms around Charlie's waist. He leans over and kisses her, whispering softly into her ear. She giggles, her cheeks coloring a light shade of pink.

I take a deep breath and turn my attention away from them, staring out the window at the colorful fall leaves. My heart aches. "I know the right person is out there waiting for me. But where are you?" I whisper softly.

Chapter Two

A few days later, Leslie, Frankie, and I decide to actually take a trip to Hobby Land. While they're keen to see the new Halloween items that have come in over the weekend, I have plans to look over the sewing section.

Frankie mentioned she's unhappy with the costume she had designed for her long program. When she tried it on, I had to agree with her. The cut and color make her appear washed out. I know she's tried contacting the designer, but they aren't budging on making any alterations without charging her an arm and a leg.

Since she's done so much for me, and I enjoy playing around with costume design, I thought I'd take a stab at seeing if I could improve what she has. I think a few sequins and an overskirt would make a world of difference. I've shown Frankie a rough Photoshop rendering of what I have in mind, and she's given me her blessing to do "whatever the heck" I want to the dress.

My eyes widen as we enter the store. "Wow," I gasp. I can see why my friends wanted to come here. I don't think I've ever seen so many Halloween decorations in one place.

To my left, there's a six-foot-tall black skeletal tree trimmed with orange, purple, and black baubles, and a string of twinkling ghost-shaped fairy lights. On my right, an entire aisle is dedicated to inflatable yard decor. I spy a black cat, witch, vampire, zombie, and mummy, just to name a few. Over the store's speaker system, a soundtrack plays haunting music, filled with the eerie howls of werewolves.

I approach the nearest plexiglass case. It contains a detailed purple-and-black Victorian manor with flickering LED lights. "Is that a haunted dollhouse?"

"Nope, but that's a good guess," Leslie replies with a chuckle. "It's a haunted house that's meant to sit out and look pretty, like those village displays people set out on their tables and shelves during Christmas. Only for Halloween."

"It still looks like a dollhouse to me." I understand buying the Christmas villages, since you can get away with displaying them from November until maybe the second week in January. But the Halloween ones confuse me. The season is much shorter. I lean forward again and study the house in closer detail. "For three hundred dollars, I hope it at least does something, like play music?"

"It doesn't." Leslie stands next to me and stares longingly at the luxury mansion. "I've always wanted to buy one for the rink, but Charlie and Uncle Jack veto me every time. They think it's impractical to have something so expensive and fragile in a place filled with hyperactive kids."

I secretly agree with them on that one. "You could always buy it for your house."

"No, my boyfriend would think it's creepy. He's not big on Halloween. A girl can still dream though."

"Oh, look at those!" Frankie exclaims, skipping over to the display of fall and Thanksgiving decor. She pulls out her mobile and snaps a few photos of a scarecrow perched on a bale of hay. "This would look amazing by the cabin's front door. I have to send a photo of this to Charlie. I was just talking to him last night about how we should decorate the porch."

As I watch Frankie send a text to her boyfriend, I'm struck by how much our lives have diverged in only a year. Last October, we were sitting in our hotel room in Marseille, France, talking about taking a vacation together to Thailand in the spring. Now, Frankie's returned to competitive skating and settled in this small town with Charlie, and little has changed for me.

I'm still single and skating as Cinderella with Dreams on Ice. It's funny, even though I'm a bit envious of what Frankie has, I know I'm not ready to trade skating for settling down. At least, not yet. DOI is my dream job, and I plan to keep doing it as long as I can. If I meet the right bloke—no, *when* I meet the right bloke—he'll have to go along with that.

That said, my contract with Dreams on Ice expires in December. A couple of months ago, I hinted to Frankie that it's the first time I've even *considered* not renewing it. Without her on tour, something's been missing. Our friend Fernando is still there, but there are certain things, like gossiping about guys and giving one another facials, that only my bestie gets.

Lately, I've been feeling a little lonely.

Leslie joins us, glances at the price tag dangling from the scarecrow's hat, and frowns. "Fifty bucks? That's too much. I can make you one that's way better looking for less than half the price."

"Would you?" Frankie says, placing her hands together in a pleading gesture.

"Totally." Leslie opens the notes app on her mobile. "What did you have in mind? How big should it be? What colors? Male or female?"

"Um, I want something medium-sized? Maybe three feet tall?" Frankie looks thoughtful. "Let's say five feet. And I'd actually like a scarecrow couple. Can you make them matching outfits? What about hats?"

"Hold on. You're going too fast for me." Leslie's fingers fly across the screen. "Five feet . . . boy and girl . . . matching outfits. OK, now I'm ready."

It'll take them ten minutes to make a list and another hour to pick out the supplies. My gaze travels back to the Halloween items. There's steam billowing from a cauldron in one of the aisles. I'm dying to see what else is on offer. "I'm going to have a wander through the costumes."

"Sounds good. We'll come find you in a few minutes," Leslie calls out absently.

"If I'm not there, I'll be near the fabrics."

"You got it, Gem," Frankie says.

I turn to my left and look over the selection of masks, wands, wigs, and other accessories, wondering if there's anything in here that I could use for Frankie's dress. "Oh, these are pretty," I say, picking up a pair of wings at random, running my fingers over the delicate glittery mesh material.

I had a pair like these when I was six. I wanted to be a fairy so badly, just like Tinker Bell. When I joined Dreams on Ice, I'd hoped that Tink might be one of the roles I'd get to play, but I'm too tall. Our casting directors only select women under five feet. Oh well. Being Cinderella isn't a bad alternative.

"If I were you, I wouldn't go for those. The quality sucks. Spend another five bucks and go for the wings made by the Glamour Company. They light up, and out of everything here, they look the most real."

My head pops up and I drop the wings. A man with dark-brown hair shoots me an amused expression. He's dressed in an untucked green plaid shirt and a pair of well-worn dark-wash jeans. His sleeves are rolled up to the elbow.

"Uh, thanks. I'll keep that in mind."

The man bends over, picks them up, and hands them to me. "Are you planning to be a fairy for Halloween? Because if you ask me, you look more like an angel than a fairy."

Does he mean that as a pickup line? Because if he does, he can do better than that. Something flutters inside of me, and my lips twitch. I can't remember the last time a guy tried to flirt with me. I'm excited to play along. "What makes you say that?"

He nods toward my outfit. "The accent, hair, and the white dress you have on."

He has me there. My hands run over the smooth cotton dress I picked up in Greece. It's white and stops just above my knees. My blond curls are also pulled into a high bun. "I suppose you have a point."

My attention travels back to the man and up to his face. He has a strong jawline with the beginnings of a five o'clock shadow, a nose that's slightly crooked and may have been broken once or twice, and cheekbones that are sharp enough to cut glass. As soon as I see his eyes, I can't look away. They're a rich hazel color with flecks of green and brown, accentuated by the green tones of his shirt.

I stare for a good ten seconds before I force myself to

look away. My cheeks sear with heat. "And, er, what are you planning to be?" I sputter.

"I was Dr. Henry Jones last year, but this year, who knows. Maybe I'll change it up a bit."

I know that name. Frankie and Charlie were talking about it a few days ago. They were streaming a movie. The question is, which one? It was a thriller with an archaeologist in it. There was a brown hat and a bullwhip. That's when it clicks. I slowly lift my chin, daring to meet the stranger's gaze again. "That's Indiana Jones' real name."

"Correct." He flashes me a cheeky smile. "If you want to get technical, his full name is Dr. Henry Walton Jones Jr."

This bloke must be really into films. Or maybe just Indiana Jones. I chew on my lip, trying my best to remember the scene it was on when I joined Frankie and Charlie. I can tell you lots about reality shows, but when it comes to the cinema, it's like trying to shoot a basketball from midcourt for a million dollars.

I know next to nothing about anything outside of rom-coms. But I can't let this guy know that. I don't know why, but I have the urge to impress him. *Think, Gemma. Think.* My mind stays blank. Ugh. Of all the times for that to happen. I'll have to take a shot in the dark. "Um . . . Indiana was the name of his dog, wasn't it?"

"Uh-huh. Impressive." The man leans his elbows against his shopping trolley, casually showing off the ridges of corded muscles in his forearms. "Very few people know that."

I shrug, trying to keep it cool despite feeling like a squirrel who just discovered an all-you-can-enjoy nut buffet. "I take it you're a fan?"

"I am. Picked that up from my parents. Who wouldn't

be? Indy's the type of hero who doesn't need superpowers to save the world. All he needs is logic and a bullwhip."

I replace the wings on the shelf, stealing another glance at his eyes. The puppy inside of me is wagging its tail hard enough to hover a few inches off the ground. "Well, if it were up to me, I think you should be Dr. Jones again for Halloween."

"You may have just convinced me." He winks. "Of course, I did agree to let my kids have the final say. Otherwise, I'd commit to it on the spot."

My heart drops. He has kids? I'd hoped—well, never mind. It doesn't matter now. Another bloke who's off the market. "Oh."

"Gemma, there you are! You have to come and see the —oh, um . . . hi." Frankie stops short. Her eyes dart from the guy back to me. "I didn't mean to interrupt you two."

Saved by the bestie. Frankie doesn't know it, but she couldn't have shown up at a better time. This conversation was about to get awkward.

I blink slowly. "It's fine. We were just discussing fairy wings." I nod to the shelf. "I'll remember to pick up the ones you recommended if I decide I need a pair. Thanks for the tip."

"You're welcome, Gemma."

Hearing him say my name causes a few goosebumps to form on my arm.

"You can call me Henry." He tips an invisible hat to me. "I'd better get going myself." Whistling the *Indiana Jones* theme song to himself, he pushes the trolley up the aisle, disappearing around the corner.

"Henry. Is that your real name?" I whisper to myself.

"Way to go, Gem. He's cute." Frankie elbows me. "Did you get his number?"

"No," I groan. "He has kids."

"So? Maybe he's a single dad. I didn't see a ring on his finger."

"Frankie. Not helping." I rub my temples. "Some men don't wear rings. You sound like your dad." I take a deep breath. It's probably for the best that nothing happened. My vacation is almost over, and I'll be back on the road touring again by this time next week. It's not a great time to start anything. Spinning around and pushing aside all thoughts of Henry, I change the subject. "What did you want me to see?"

"Oh, Les found the cutest little train set! We're going to get it and put it away for Charlie for Christmas. He's been looking for his next woodworking project, and we think it'll inspire him to build a little town for it."

"That sounds brilliant. Show me!"

Later that evening, I swirl some white wine around in my glass as I listen to the soft, soothing voice of Elvis play out from the jukebox in Suzy and Mr. T's den. It's just the three of us. Frankie and Charlie still haven't returned from their after-dinner stroll by the lake. Leslie opted to have a quiet dinner with her boyfriend.

"Dinner was delicious, as always. Thanks for inviting me over tonight," I say.

"You're part of the family, dear." Suzy sits down next to her husband, who drapes an arm across her shoulders, pulling her closer to him. He places a gentle kiss on her cheek.

Once again, I feel a yearning stir inside of me. Here's a couple who met on a dating app. Every time I'm with them,

I see the tender looks Suzy and Mr. T give to one another and watch how they make each other laugh. My throat goes dry, and I can't help but wonder if I'll ever be in their shoes. They look like they've fallen deeper in love since the last time I was here, if that's even possible.

"Frankie mentioned you had something you wanted to ask us about tonight?" Suzy says.

"Yes." I return my attention to her.

Before I can find my voice, Frankie's father blurts out, "Gem is going to ask you to be in her audition video for *Cupid's Arrow* and if you know of any single young men you can set her up with for a date."

Suzy swats his hand. "Rich! You were supposed to be *subtle* and let her ask us. Not the other way around."

"Gem knows I'm a straight shooter who likes to get right to the point."

I should be surprised somebody's spilled the beans to him, but I'm not. There are very few secrets in this family. Or if there are, they don't stay secret for long. "It's true." I double over laughing. "Who told you? Was it Leslie or Frankie?"

"Neither. It was Charlie."

"Huh. Go figure. I didn't see him as the tattletale type," I say.

Mr. T shrugs, then retrieves a folded piece of paper from his pocket. "I had a little time on my hands this afternoon and came up with a few ideas I thought would work well in your video." He slides a pair of thick black reading glasses onto his nose. "If you're going to capture the casting director's attention, you need to be playful with the camera and let your personality shine through."

"I'm afraid to ask, but what do you have in mind?"

"I think you should play a round of rapid-fire twenty

questions. Have Frankie shout things at you from behind the camera that show how quickly you can think on your feet."

Suzy smiles and rubs her husband's shoulder. "Rich, that's a wonderful idea."

"Agreed." I'm relieved Mr. T has come up with something that's doable and not too crazy. Actually, twenty questions sounds refreshing since I have no idea what my answers will be ahead of time.

"I've been known to come up with something good every now and again. That's old age for you." He smirks.

"What else do you have on the list?" I ask, cocking my head to the side.

"I think you should open the video with a cut of you on the ice mid-jump. I can't remember where I read it, but the human mind decides in the first three seconds of seeing something if it'll be interested in a topic or not. If I were in the casting director's chair, that would intrigue me."

A half-hour later, we've come up with a rough outline for the remainder of the video.

Opening Scene:
- Action clip featuring a triple toe or possibly a spiral sequence
- A clip of me sitting in a chair in my Cindy costume while Charlie's silhouette appears and attempts to slip a skate on my foot
Introduction:
- Ten rapid-fire questions (be sure to let Frankie know what's off-limits).
- Give one sentence on why I'm looking for love.
Cutaway:
- Frankie, Suzy, and Leslie each give a sentence on the type of man they'd pick for me.

- A grumpy Charlie issues a warning that he'll be watching.

__Grand Finale:__

- Call to action reminding them to cast me.

- Clip of me skating away from the camera and out of the frame to the Cinderella theme music.

"That sounds like the winning ticket, dear," Suzy says after we've finished going over everything. "I'd cast you."

"Thanks, Suzy." I click the mobile screen off and close my notes app. "Do you mind if Frankie and I film the clip of you when she gets back?"

"Of course not."

"Now, if we're done with the *Cupid's Arrow* planning, we can talk about the other elephant in the room," Mr. T says.

"Other elephant?" I ask.

His eyes twinkle. "Finding you some young men to go out with."

My mouth opens and closes. Caught up with the audition video, I'd forgotten all about asking Suzy if she knew any blokes. Leave it to Mr. T to remember. If there's an elephant in the room, it's him. His memory is as sharp as a paring knife.

"That's something I *was* going to ask, but I've been thinking it might not be such a good idea after all."

"And why not?" Suzy asks.

"The timing is poor." Henry's face flashes before my eyes, reinforcing the fact that I'm cursed. I can't even meet a bloke in the wild without having him be attached to someone. I want to enjoy the rest of my vacation, not continue to make myself miserable.

"Oh, that's too bad." Suzy walks over to the antique desk that holds the landline and removes a notepad from the top drawer. "Over lunch, Rich and I came up with a few men we thought you might enjoy meeting. But if you don't want the list. . ." She begins to set the notepad back inside.

"Wait!" I shout. My fingers itch to yank the pad from Suzy's hands, like Golem in the *Lord of the Rings* books. My head is screaming at me not to waste the opportunity. Especially if the men have been personally selected by Suzy. "If you've already put it together, I suppose it wouldn't hurt to look at it."

Suzy smiles. She takes hold of the notepad again and hands it to me. "Here you are."

There are three names listed. That's three more chances for me to find love. I read them aloud. "Dylan Conti, Brandon Webb, and Tim Lyons."

"Dylan's a veterinarian. Brandon is a yoga instructor. Tim is a teacher." Suzy returns to the couch. "Based on what Charlie mentioned, you're looking for a man who's not connected to ice skating. Well, these three are as normal as they come."

I glance in Mr. Tomlinson's direction. "And I'm guessing all three of these lads have been properly vetted by you guys?"

"Yes. You're like a daughter to me, Gem. We'd never want you to waste your time with someone who's untrustworthy."

My chest tightens in the best way. Mr. T feels like a second dad to me too. It's comforting to know he's looking out for me.

"If I had to ask which one you'd recommend contacting first about a date, it would be?"

Suzy clamps a hand over her husband's mouth. "All three men are wonderful people. You should take the time to get to know each one of them for yourself. Don't let our opinions influence you one way or the other."

Catching his wife's eye, Mr. T relaxes and nods. She peels her hand off his mouth. "What Suzy said. It's for us to know and for you to find out."

"I guess if that's the case, then I'll just have to start at the top of the list and work my way down, beginning with Dylan."

Suzy and Mr. T flash twin smiles in my direction.

"That's the spirit," she says.

Chapter Three

The moment I walk into the empty waiting area of the Grizzly Springs Animal Hospital, the scent of animals and chemical disinfectant hits my nose.

"Can I help you?" the receptionist asks, glancing up from her computer screen.

"Cheers. I'm Gemma." I approach the in-take window. "Dylan asked me to meet him here for coffee."

"Oh, you're Gemma." She sits taller and her eyes widen in excitement. "Dr. Conti is just finishing up with a patient. I'll let him know you're here." Not waiting for an answer, she pushes her chair back and scrambles through a door labeled "Private."

"Somebody's eager." I chuckle to myself. It must be a slow day. I wonder if she's been waiting to see who her boss is having coffee with. I'd be curious if I were in her shoes too.

I take a seat next to a scale for animals and my eyes sweep the room. Portraits of various cats, dogs, rabbits, and birds adorn the walls. The far corner of the room opposite the reception desk is packed floor to ceiling with cases of wet and dry pet food.

"Gemma?" A man wearing a white lab coat over a set of black scrubs walks out from the back. He's about five-foot-eight and has the beginnings of a dark beard and icy-blue eyes.

"That's me." I stand and wave, straightening my skirt.

"Glad you could make it in. I'm Dylan."

"It's nice to meet you. I'm Gemma, but you already knew that." My cheeks warm. I wish I could've thought of something more witty to say.

"I did." He chuckles. "Come on back and we'll have a coffee in my office. My clinic partner, Dr. Brown, is in the middle of doing inventory, so you'll have to excuse the mess."

"Sure, no problem."

I collect my purse, and he holds the door open for me, pausing to tell the receptionist, "Vicki, if anyone comes in asking for me, pass them off to Dr. Brown and have her get them started."

"Yes, boss." She salutes, continuing to watch us with undivided attention.

Dylan notices and arches his eyebrow. She sighs and sits back down at her computer.

We pass through an area where a woman with light-brown hair is furiously counting vials in a cabinet. Her hair is disheveled, and her white lab coat is sitting in a wadded-up ball on top a file cabinet. Dylan places a finger to his lips. I nod. It looks like she's deep in thought.

He shows me into a room with two desks, a stack of boxes, and more filing cabinets. "Sorry about that. Ava—I mean, Dr. Brown—is moody today." He closes the door. "I didn't want to set her off again." Dylan chuckles.

I'm not exactly sure what to make of his strange comment. I don't know anything about the situation, but in my opinion, it doesn't seem like anything to laugh about. For now, I'll give him the benefit of the doubt. I borrow a chair from the opposite side of the room and sit. "So, um, what types of animals do you treat?"

"We're an all-species practice. We see mostly cats and dogs. But we occasionally work with birds, reptiles, and some farm animals."

"That sounds interesting."

"Not really. Life around here is slow. It's all vaccines and annual check-ups. Things I can do in my sleep. I'm wasting my skills out here. I wish we had more interesting cases like I did back in Fort Collins."

I bite my lip. That's the second odd comment from Dylan. As a vet, shouldn't he be happy if his clients are in good health? I wouldn't wish an illness on anybody's pet. He's going to be another guy I strike out with, isn't he?

Despite the urge to give up and leave, I push myself to continue chatting with him. "And, uh, where is that?"

"Colorado. It's where I did my vet schooling." Slipping off his lab coat, he drapes it on a peg near the door and walks over to a high-end coffee machine. "I have dark roast, french roast, vanilla, and cinnamon pods. Pick your poison."

"I'll have the vanilla, please."

He inserts the cup into the top of the machine and clicks the "Brew" button. "Any creamer or sugar for you?"

"No thanks." I cross my legs.

A few moments of silence elapse, filled by the hum of the coffee machine. Dylan moves around his desk, prepping a ceramic mug for himself and a paper cup for me. What frustrates me is that he isn't trying to contribute to the conversation. He's left it all up to me. A tension headache begins to form behind my eyes. "What's the most unique animal you've ever treated?"

He faces me, leaning against his desk. "That would have to be a bison or a wolf."

I let out a long whistle. "Was that back in Colorado too?"

"Uh-huh."

More silence. His stock continues to drop. "I'd imagine a wolf is a lot like a dog."

"They are and they aren't. Modern dogs are descended from wolves, but wolves are much more cunning. Living in the wild means they haven't lost their problem-solving ability. I can't wait until I'm finally back in Fort Collins and able to start working with animals like them again."

"Oh? Are you moving back?" I blink a few times in surprise.

"I am." Dylan nods. "I've taken up a research position at the vet school for the fall. I can't wait to do something that matters again."

I internally cringe. That is the last straw for me. Everything he does as a vet, no matter how big or small, matters. The life of a dog or cat is not less valuable than a wolf. At least in my eyes.

The coffee machine beeps, and he offers me a steaming cup. He inserts a new pod into the machine and waits for his own cup to brew. So far, I've felt zero spark or connection to Dylan. He's spoken only about himself and hasn't bothered asking anything about me. I'm ready for this date to end. But I should at least hold out until I finish my coffee.

"Congrats on getting the job. What exactly will you be researching?"

"The impact of humans on the migration patterns of turkey vultures and black vultures."

"That sounds . . . interesting."

"Oh, they are." He lights up. "Vultures are my favorite animals. They've been given a bad reputation because they're scavengers, but let me give you all the reasons they're awesome."

I force a smile onto my face. "I can't wait to hear."

The next morning, I get up early and carpool to the rink with Charlie and Frankie. With three of the skating-school instructors out sick, Leslie was desperate for some extra help, and I felt like I had to offer a hand. Even if I'm not a fan of coaching.

When I turned sixteen, I was hired by my rink to help with the group classes. I assumed coaching would be a piece of cake. I'd show up to class, give out a couple corrections, and send the students home having learned something new.

Unfortunately, I was dead wrong. The group I was assigned were little terrors. All of them refused to listen. I lost control of the class five minutes in, and spent the remaining twenty-five minutes chasing them down. I had so many parent complaints. My supervisor was sympathetic and said it would get easier in my next lesson. But it didn't.

I continued to struggle. Every class was torture. By the end of my third week on the job, I had so much anxiety that I wasn't sleeping, and my skating and schoolwork started to suffer. So, I quit. The experience left a bitter taste in my mouth and made me never want to teach again. Until today.

Frankie, Charlie, and Leslie have gone out of their way

to take care of me during my visit. Helping them out is the least I can do to repay them. Even if it means fighting my past demons.

"All right, everyone, when you're skating as a group, the key to success is being able to listen carefully. Do you think that's something you can all do?" I ask the group of twelve young girls.

"Yes, Coach Gemma!" they yell out enthusiastically.

So far, today's kids have been well-behaved. But I don't want to jinx it. It's still early in the day. "Brilliant." I flash them a smile. "Then let's have a go at trying one of the first moves I learned when I was new to synchronized ice skating too—the circle."

A few of the younger girls giggle. What are they laughing at? Is it something I've said or done?

"Coach Gemma, that's baby stuff. We already know how to skate in a circle," a girl in a blue dress calls out. She's about ten years old and wears her hair in two french braids.

I sigh in relief. It's just overconfidence—that, I can handle. Skating in a circle isn't difficult, technically speaking . . . until you have a group of people all trying to do the same thing at the same time. "If that's the case, then this should be easy for you." I wink. "Go ahead. Show me how it's done."

The girl in blue huffs. "Come on, guys.'"

I skate backward, allowing the group some space. As I approach the wall, a sharp jab radiates up my hip, causing the muscles to spasm. I inhale sharply. Where did that come from? I shake my head, ignoring it. I don't have time to deal with a pulled muscle or whatever it might be. Keeping my eyes pinned on my students, I watch as the girl leads everyone out around the red circle in the corner of the rink, as if she's playing a game of follow the leader.

They perform a set of clumsy forward crossovers. I bite back another wince watching everyone skate at their own speed. From experience, I know what's coming. A moment later, two of the older and taller girls bump into one another. Another few seconds after that, another girl trips and grabs the wall. I hate having to let them fail, but it's the only way they'll learn.

I clap my hands together. Everyone stops talking, giving me their undivided attention. "That was a good first attempt. But in synchronized skating, you guys don't skate as individuals. You have to skate as a team," I explain.

The girls stare at me with a series of blank faces. I have to remember I'm working with children and not with other professional skaters. They need a visual reference. Reaching into my pocket, I retrieve my mobile and unlock the screen. "Here, it might make more sense if you have a look at this video clip."

The girls of the Intro to Syncro class huddle around me. I tap Play and the screen lights up with a clip from a Dreams on Ice practice. The skaters on the screen latch on to each other's shoulders and perform a set of backward crossovers. "Do you see how everyone in the circle is looking at one another? They're watching each other to make sure they're all skating at the same speed at the same time."

My students nod in understanding.

"Oh, I get it now," the girl in the blue dress exclaims, her eyes widening. "We need to pretend we're like Coach Frankie and Mr. C when they skate together."

"That's the right idea," I affirm, and line them up once again. "Go ahead and grab each other's hands. This time, when you get to the circle, we'll try pumping our right skates forward, just like we do before a crossover."

The girls glide over to form a circle.

"When I count off 'one and two,' pump. On the counts 'three and four,' I want you to glide."

"I'm confused, Coach Gemma."

"Me too."

I remind myself not to get frustrated. I don't need a repeat of what happened ten years ago. I exhale slowly. "It'll make more sense in a moment, I promise."

Thirty long minutes later, the class is mercifully over. I flee the ice for the safety of the pros' room as quickly as I can. Closing the door behind me, I sink onto the bench by my temporary locker and remove my skates. I survived. But barely. The students had so many questions, and stopping every two minutes to answer them was beginning to fray my nerves.

"Tough time?" Charlie's amused voice calls out.

My head shoots up. He's sitting at the end of the bench, tucking the bottom of his skating trousers over one of his skating boots.

I nod glumly. "I'm rubbish at coaching."

Charlie chuckles. "I doubt it went as badly as you think it did."

"It did, trust me." I furrow my brow. "I can't explain things properly. The children kept staring at me with blank faces. It took us the entire class to do one simple move."

"Did you yell or lose your temper?"

"No." I shake my head. That's a mistake teenage Gemma made. Adult Gemma knows better.

"Then you did just fine. Coaching is tricky, and at times, frustrating. We've all been there. You just need time and practice." He stands. "Wasn't Leslie supposed to help you?"

I rub the ball of my bare foot and set my skate beside

me. "She got called away to deal with a couple troublemakers."

I'm glad *I* didn't have to deal with them. Not having Leslie around freaked me out at first, but now that I think about it, coaching on my own ended up being a good thing. I've proven to myself I could make it through a whole class today. For me, that's like leaping across the English Channel. I'm proud of myself. Teenage me thought she'd be scarred for life.

"Got it. In that case, I'm even more impressed you made it through the class all on your own. Leslie doesn't usually let anyone coach on their own if she hasn't worked with them before. It goes to show how much she trusts you." His words fill me with happiness. "Are you done coaching for the day?"

"Yeah, that was my last lesson."

"Tell you what, why don't you come and join me."

"Join you?" I ask. "As in, *more* coaching?"

"Uh-huh. Come and see what it's like to work with a higher-level student. Not that I'm supposed to play favorites, but one of the kiddos I enjoy the most is here for a final lesson before her competition next week." He opens his locker and retrieves a puffy black coat embroidered with the name "Mr. C" on the front pocket.

"I think I'm all coached out." I stiffen. "Some people, like Frankie, are naturals at teaching. I don't have the gene."

"I bet you do. Coaching is like a muscle. You can train it to be strong. It just needs consistency and repetition." He studies me for a moment. "I'm not a natural coach either. On top of being an introvert, I had to work extra hard to learn how to not scare kids." He zips the coat up. "Between you and me, I think you're off to a better start than Frankie when she started coaching."

I lock eyes with Charlie. "Do you really think so?" I can't imagine my best friend failing at anything.

"I do."

"Thanks." I grin. "But don't think you get off the hook just because you're dating my best friend. I'm so telling her you said that."

"Go ahead." He closes his locker. "So what do you say? Will you join me? I think you'd have fun with us."

I know Charlie is right. Looking back, I think one of the reasons I failed was because I was so young and inexperienced. I never received the proper training on how to coach. I was tossed into it and left to figure things out on my own.

I survived this morning, and I've shown myself things can change. If I were put on the spot, I'd be able to coach. Shadowing Charlie and his student won't commit me to anything. All I'd be doing is watching and learning. It would be good for me. "You've talked me into it. Give me two minutes to put my skates back on."

Charlie nods. "I'll meet you out on the ice."

As he pushes the door open, a sweet high-pitched voice exclaims, "Mr. C! I've waited all week to see you!" Small arms envelop his legs in a hug.

"Hi, Richelle," he greets her.

As they separate, I hear the rustling of paper. "Look what I drew at school for you."

Charlie kneels down, accepting the paper with both hands as if it's the map to a hidden treasure. "Is that us?"

"No, silly . . . it's you and Coach Frankie. I'm standing over here in the pink."

"Ah, I see."

The door closes softly, and I smile. Richelle is adorable. I can't believe she took the time to draw him a picture. If I *had* to coach, I'd love to have a student like that. I can't wait to see how he works with her.

As I stand up, another sharp twinge shoots up my leg to my hip. Inhaling sharply, I brace myself against the metal lockers and wait a moment for the sensation to pass. "Things were going so well today," I mutter.

The door creaks open. "Gemma? Are you all right?"

I flash a thumbs-up. "Just some tendonitis I'm dealing with. I must've overdone it today."

Charlie shoots me a sympathetic glance. "That sucks. Anything I can do to help?" He stows Richelle's artwork inside his locker.

"No. The pain comes and goes." I stand up straighter. "See, it's already better. I shouldn't be too long. You go on. I'll be right behind you."

Charlie hesitates in the doorway, but reluctantly agrees and leaves me alone. I close my eyes. I hope this isn't the start of a new injury. I spent the second half of last year dealing with a cranky hip. It took months for it to go away.

We're about to go into the busiest time of year on the Dreams on Ice schedule. Between now and Christmas, we have quite a few double- and triple-show days. I can't afford to miss much time. I need my body to be in tip-top shape.

I make a mental note to talk to Mel, the DOI PT, as soon as I can. Hopefully we can start treatment and some preventative care and nip whatever's going on in the bud before it gets any worse. Until then, I push my worries aside. There's no point in speculating what's wrong. I'll only make myself mad. For now, I'll focus on enjoying the rest of my time in Sequoia Valley.

Richelle changes feet and finishes her combination spin with a blurred back scratch spin, then exits onto a sharp outside edge. I nod, impressed with her positions and speed. Charlie's done a fantastic job with her.

"That was great, tiny mite." Charlie gives her a high-five. "Promise me you'll skate just like that next weekend."

"I promise," the young skater says with a spark of determination in her eyes, approaching the area of the ice where Charlie and I stand. "Can I have my mom video call you after I skate my short program?"

"Absolutely! I'm hoping she'll send a recording of it to me too."

"Mommy always makes my big brother or sister film it. She says she gets too nervous to watch me." Richelle takes a long drink from a glittery pink water bottle. "Mr. C, I almost forgot to ask, but can you and Coach Frankie come to my school's Halloween festival? I want all my friends to meet you because you're the coolest person I know. You're like twenty years old!"

I snicker. Try thirty-something. It's always amused me how old kids think adults actually are.

"I'm a *little* older than that, Richelle, but good guess. When's the festival?"

"Um . . ." She glances to the door of the ice, where her mother stands in a thick white parka. "Mom, when's the Halloween thing again?" she shouts loudly.

"It's this Friday at four." Her mother glances at her watch. "Now hurry up, we need to go pick up your brother from judo."

Without a care that they'll be late, Richelle cheerfully repeats, "It's this Friday. Can you come?" She laces her hands together in a begging motion. "Please, please, please?"

My heart does a little somersault. With her big eyes and high-pitched voice, she reminds me of an anime character. *Come on, Charlie. There's no way you can say no to a face like that.*

He runs a hand through his hair. "Richelle, Coach Frankie and I are leaving for our own competition on Thursday."

Oh no. I'd forgotten about Skate United States! It's the first time Frankie and Charlie will be competing together internationally. They've done well domestically, but now it's important they skate well and show the international judges they're a consistent team. They don't have much of a reputation yet, and in a highly subjective sport like this one, that reputation could mean the difference in winning a medal.

Richelle's face falls. "Oh."

Charlie glances at me quickly. I inhale sharply. Uh-oh. He's not going to put me on the spot, is he?

"Maybe you could ask Coach Gemma?"

He did. Darn it, Charlie.

His eyes plead with me, saying, *"Can you do me a favor? We can't disappoint her."*

Ugh. I can't stand to be the bad guy. "I'm flying out to Austin, Texas, to skate—" I start.

She lowers her head, staring at the ice. I hear a few sniffles. "It's okay. Maybe next time."

Charlie's favorite student is tugging at my heartstrings. I know what has to be done. Quickly, I add, "But I'm not leaving until Saturday morning. As long as I have everything packed and ready to go, I think I can make it."

Richelle's head rises. "Really? You'll come?"

"Yes, I'll be there," I confirm.

"Thank you!" She smiles wide and launches herself at my legs with enough force to push us both into the wall. For someone so tiny, she's sure strong. I lock eyes with Charlie. We share a chuckle.

"I know Coach Gemma isn't me, but she's the next best thing. You'll have a lot of fun with her, and you can even tell your friends she's a real-life princess!" he boasts.

Richelle's eyes widen. "You are?" She glides back and appraises me. It's the same look of awe and excitement I see when I look out onto the audience on tour. I wonder if we have a future princess in our midst.

"Er, in a way. I play Cinderella with Dreams on Ice."

"Richelle! Let's go!" her mother yells, frustration evident in her voice. I lift my chin, looking over the girl's head at a woman in a black puffy coat with jet-black hair piled into a high bun. She glances at her watch. Her brows are furrowed. From her tone, this mom means business.

"Coming, Mom!" she calls out. "Bye, Coach Gemma! Bye, Mr. C!" Richelle waves, powering her way to the rink's door.

"It's funny how she can be so cheery with a mom like that," I say.

"Mrs. Zhang is all bark. Once you get to know her, she's a pretty nice person. She has a lot on her plate with her three kids," Charlie says as we watch Richelle's mom whisk her out of the rink toward the parking lot with the speed of a cheetah.

I return my attention to Charlie as we wait for a skater warming up their backward power pulls to cross in front of us, then start toward the exit. "Do I need to bring anything to this school festival?"

"No, just yourself. The parents and teachers are in

charge." He snaps his fingers together. "Oh, but you should go in costume. If you need something, I'm sure Leslie or Frankie can lend you one. I think Frankie was an angel last year."

An angel. I blink slowly. As Charlie prattles on, my thoughts turn back to the guy I met at Hobby Land, wondering what Henry might be up to.

"Do you and Frankie still have the *Indiana Jones* films downloaded to your computer?"

"Yeah, I think so. We haven't finished the second one yet."

"Do you mind if I watch the first one tonight?"

"Knock yourself out. You'll just need to ask Frankie for the password."

"Thanks."

Chapter Four

On Wednesday afternoon, I finally muster the courage to send a text to the last remaining man on my list, Tim Lyons. I had hopes that after Dylan, my date with Brandon would be a hit, but it was another dud.

Brandon was supposed to meet me for dinner, but he kept texting me to say he was running late. After an hour, I stopped checking my mobile and left the restaurant. Later, Suzy heard from his mother that he was on another date. I wish he would've just canceled on me. Oh well. At least I dodged a bullet with him.

Unlocking my mobile, I type:

> Gemma: Hi, Tim. I'm not sure if Suzy
> Welch-Tomlinson told you about me, but
> my name is Gemma.

I hesitate, trying to keep this casual.

Gemma: I was wondering if you might be
free to grab a coffee with me sometime
today or tomorrow. Cheers!

Before I change my mind, I tap Send. There. Now I can check that off my to-do list. If we do end up meeting, I hope this date goes off better than the one with Dylan.

I glance at the time. It's about two in the afternoon. I probably won't hear from Tim until after three, when school finishes for the day. Placing my mobile down, I shift my attention to more pressing matters. I pick up the hangers of the two costumes laid out on the bed and study them up close. "Shall I be a sloth or a peacock?"

"You know, you don't have to choose either one," Frankie says, lingering in the doorway as she runs a towel over the ends of her damp hair. "You still have time to run over to Hobby Land and pick something else up."

"I might just have to." I glance up at her. "These are fun, but neither one feels like me." I set them back down. "I wanted to ask you earlier. What happened to your costume from last year? The angel one."

"I donated it. A couple of months ago, I did a major closet clean out. Anything I hadn't worn in a year, I donated."

My stomach drops. What a shame. The angel would've been perfect. When I approached Leslie about costumes, she had a ton of things to choose from, but nothing fit. She's taller and stockier than me.

I suppose my best option now is to make do with the white dress I wore to Hobby Land and pick up some gold ribbon and the wings Henry suggested. I should have enough time to spruce it up.

"You know, I have some skating dresses you could go

through." Frankie disappears into the bathroom, reappearing a moment later with her hairbrush. "They're hanging in the armoire in the garage."

"The garage?"

"It's only temporary. Charlie is in the middle of customizing our closet for me."

"Jealous." I start toward the door. "Then you don't mind if I do a little snooping?"

"Knock yourself out. You can borrow anything you find."

"Thanks," I say, making my way over to the garage.

The door creaks as I open it. I flip on the light switch, and the hum of electricity fills the room. Considering how minimalist Charlie and Frankie are, there's a lot of stuff in here. Half the space is crowded with gym equipment and large pieces of furniture that Charlie has crafted. They look professional. Something out of a Wayfair catalog. If he ever decided to change careers, he'd make a killing selling his pieces. The remainder of the garage contains a few boxes of Frankie's belongings.

"There you are," I murmur under my breath. The armoire I'm looking for is nestled in the far corner, next to a stationary bike and weight rack. Scooting around the equipment, I make my way over to the wardrobe. "Let's see what treasures await us."

Swinging it open reveals a row of dresses, neatly organized by color. That's so Frankie. Thumbing through, I search for ones with longer skirts. I want my costume to look like a normal dress instead of a skating outfit. Most of them stop at the top of my thighs. Out of thirty possible options, I find three that might work, until I reach the selection of blue dresses.

"Oh, what do we have here?" I push the hangers

together and shimmy an ice-blue dress out of the wardrobe. I hold it up to my reflection in the mirror by the weight rack. It's a simple cap-sleeved garment with a knee-length chiffon skirt. "Once a Cinderella, always a Cinderella." I giggle.

Hopefully Frankie won't mind if I make a few alterations to it. I still have some leftover sequins and ribbon from the adjustments I made to her dress. Which she loved, by the way. If I add a belt, some bling to the sleeves and skirt, and a choker, I'll be all set for the ball—or Halloween party. I wish I had a couple of mice to lend me a hand.

Humming the *Indiana Jones* theme song to myself, I hurry back inside to show Frankie what I've found.

Whena I finally have time to check my mobile a couple of hours later, there's a message from Tim.

> Tim: Hi, Gemma, nice to meet you. When I saw Suzy, she mentioned a friend of her grandson's might be reaching out to me. Under normal circumstances, I'd love to grab a coffee with you, but unfortunately, I'm busy until Saturday. Can we do a rain check?

Frankie glances back at me from the back seat of Charlie's car. "Was that Tim?"

"Yeah." I let out a deep sigh. "He's busy until the weekend. Looks like the coffee date is gonna be a no go."

"Too bad, Tim's a good guy. I can vouch for him," Charlie says. "Maybe it'll work out next time."

I type a short reply.

> Gemma: Thanks for texting me back.
> Sorry this week doesn't work for either
> of us. I'm happy to do a rain check, but it
> may be a while before I can cash it in.
> I'm not sure when I'll be back in town.

"Oh well, it just wasn't meant to be." I stare out the window at the passing trees. Not surprised, but nevertheless frustrated that I continue to be cursed. I wish a fairy godmother would appear ASAP to help me break it.

"I can't believe you went zero for three on the dating front. Dylan was moving and a narcissist, Brandon was on a date with another woman, and Tim is busy.

"I did. Suzy felt horrid that two of the three guys on the list were washouts. But it's not her fault. Even with her intuition, you can't really *know* a person until you've spent time with them outside of work or a family environment." I return my mobile to my wristlet. "Anyway, finding a guy during this visit wasn't meant to be."

Charlie glances at me through the rearview mirror. "How's your other big decision going? Has your visit to Sequoia Valley convinced you to join us here?"

"To be honest, my mind's been on other things lately. I haven't given it much thought." I've been preoccupied with *Cupid's Arrow* and figuring out my dating life. Realistically, as lonely as I am being single and without Frankie, I can't picture myself doing anything other than skating on tour. If I quit, I'd have to have another job lined up. Coaching would be the obvious answer, but it's not something I'm mentally prepared to do. At least not yet.

"You've got plenty of time to figure it out," Frankie says. "You already know what my opinion is." She glances at her boyfriend. "Charlie . . ."

"Oh, um, right." He clears his throat. "Leslie and I want

you to know that the rink is always in need of good coaches. There's an open-ended offer waiting for you if you decide to move to the area."

"Thank you, guys." Charlie's words fill me with a warm, fuzzy feeling, like I've slipped on the world's softest pair of fleece pajamas. A big weight has been lifted off my shoulders. If the day comes that I decide to say goodbye to DOI, I have a fallback job.

Turning into the rink, Charlie parks near the front doors and turns off the engine. "I hope the kids don't make too much of a mess at the party tonight. When we had the end-of-summer party, it took three hours to clean up. I'd like to be home before midnight. We have an early flight in the morning."

"Charlie, you and Frankie are excused from tidying up," I say. "Leslie and I will take care of it."

"And don't worry about getting home late." Frankie climbs out of the car. "We'll be out by eight so you can get a full night's beauty sleep. I don't want to travel with a grump in the morning."

"I'm a morning person." Charlie snorts. "If there's anyone who's gonna be a grump, it's you. It'll take at least two cups of coffee just to get you to zombie walk to the car."

"Hey, that's not fair . . ."

"Okay, children, let's go inside." I shake my head as I close my car door. "Focus on the kids. They worked hard to decorate this morning. I can't wait for you to see it."

We approach the entrance, and I hear Leslie's voice directing everyone inside the facility to quiet down and get ready. The lights click off. Excited whispers filter out as I open the door. I take Frankie's mobile, positioning myself to film their entry into the surprise party.

Frankie clears her throat and says in a louder-than-normal tone, "Gee, I don't know, Charlie, it's awfully dark. Are you sure Coach Leslie said the staff meeting was at four?"

"That's what I thought she said." His voice booms even louder than Frankie's.

They turn past the skate rental counter. The lights flicker on, and a hundred people yell out, "Surprise!"

I stand off to the side, biting back laughter at the cartoon-like expression on Charlie's face. I don't think either one of them expected so many people to be here. That's one thing I've noticed that sets this rink apart from others. There is so much support and positivity between the coaches and skaters. The rink feels like one big family, not just a place of business.

"You mean there isn't a staff meeting after all?" Charlie pouts, planting his hands on his hips. His eyes take in the room. "Have you all been planning a party without telling me?"

"Yes," the kids shout.

One of the first students to step forward is Richelle. "We wanted to surprise you, Mr. C!" She giggles.

"You guys did a good job. I had no idea." He shakes his head.

Frankie links her arm through Charlie's. She points to the glittery banner that reads, "Good Luck at Skate United States, Coach Frankie and Mr. C!"

I pan the camera around the lobby. Leslie and the kids have gone above and beyond with the decor. Cardboard cutouts of Charlie and Frankie, with holes where their faces should be, are set up for partygoers to take photos with. Two long tables are filled with red cups, drinks, snacks, and a cake shaped like an ice skate. The walls are adorned with artwork of the couple made by the children. I wish my rink had given its skaters this kind of send-off to big competitions.

"Now that the guests of honor are here, who's ready to eat?" Leslie chimes in.

The kids all scramble to gather near the cake. I laugh.

"Mr. C, are you and Coach Frankie going to skate for us tonight too?" Richelle appraises him with her doe-like eyes.

"Oh, um . . ." He exchanges glances with Frankie. "I don't think . . . that is to say we have to leave early."

Frankie jumps in. "But don't worry, we'll skate for you before it's time to go home." Hiding her mouth with her hand, she whispers to Charlie, "I threw our skates in the trunk just in case."

Richelle cheers and hugs Charlie, then Frankie. "Coach Gemma, will you skate for us too?"

I inhale sharply and lower the camera. She wants to see me too? But I'm just a visitor. "Oh, you don't want to watch me. Tonight is about Mr. C and Coach Frankie."

"But I *do* want to see you skate. Mr. C said you're a princess." She twirls and points to her pink outfit. "My mom even let me wear my Sleeping Beauty dress tonight. See?"

"It's very pretty." I hesitate. An internal tug-of-war is taking place. I've been trying to rest my body while I can. Once I return to Dreams on Ice, it'll be six or seven days of performing in a row before I have a day off. So far, the downtime has been working. I haven't felt any pain since the last time I was here.

But on the other hand, Richelle is so excited. Her little cheeks are rosy pink and she's flashing me a million-watt smile with a few missing teeth. Charlie is beginning to rub off on me. I can't say no. "I'll do it."

Richelle cheers again and hugs me. "I can't wait."

S tanding in the hockey box, I film Frankie and Charlie's modified exhibition skate to "Can You Feel the Love Tonight." I can't believe how much speed they have. Every time I see them together, they've improved. It's as if they're sharing a hive mind and know exactly what the other is thinking. It's hard to believe they've only been partners for about a year. Any other team would take a few years to develop that type of unison.

Charlie grasps Frankie's hand and they finish their program with a centered pair spin.

"Way to go!" I shout, my voice trembling as they take several extended bows. I lower the camera.

Frankie skates up to me. "Your turn." I force a smile onto my face, and we fist bump. "Go get 'em Gemma-rella."

"Up next, we have an extra special treat for you. Cinderella herself! Let's hear it for Coooooooooaaaach Geeeeeeeeeeeeeeeeeeeeeema!" Leslie booms. The audience cheers.

I glide onto center ice, then roll my shoulders a few times, smooth down the skirt of the borrowed dress from Frankie, and pound my legs. Muttering under my breath, I remind myself to keep it clean and simple. I haven't had time to stretch and warm up. And I haven't skated in three or four days. My body feels heavy and stiff.

I exhale as I assume my opening pose from my normal Dreams on Ice program. It's a program I've skated thousands of times. All I have to do is let my muscle memory take over. Cinderella's theme music begins to play. Plastering a smile onto my face, I gather speed into a set of crossovers into my opening footwork sequence.

It's strange not to have props and the ensemble skaters that play the mice and birds around me. I'm so used to having them to interact with that I've forgotten what it's like to skate alone on the ice, even though I skated singles from the age of three until I was nineteen. I didn't learn any pairs skills until I turned professional.

Normally, at this part in the program, Fernando comes out to join me as Prince Charming. Thinking quickly on my feet, I fill the empty music with a layback spin. As I push my hips forward and stare up at the blurry ceiling, I remind myself that I need to ask one of my friends to film a couple clips of me on the ice before we go home.

So far, I've finished editing and assembling all the clips for my *Cupid's Arrow* audition video except for the opening. Aside from needing a slow-motion clip of me jumping, the video has been coming along nicely. My plan is to put together the final edit and submit it to the Connected Hearts Network before I leave on Saturday morning. By the afternoon, all my energy will go to getting through rehearsals for the Dreams on Ice holiday show. We have a few changes to the choreography of our normal tour programs for the last two months of the year.

Exiting the spin, I bend my knees, turn, and tap my left skate into the ice, vaulting myself into the air. Pulling my arms and legs in tightly to my body, I rotate twice and land. My smile widens and I begin to mouth the lyrics to the music. I have a minute left. Gliding out of an Ina Bauer, I pick up one final burst of speed and change edges.

Just as I'm in the middle of taking off for a double Axel, a sharp burning sensation shoots up my leg, as if someone had taken a hammer and whacked it across my hip. On a scale from one to ten, it's an eleven. I bit down on my lips and bail, turning it into a baby waltz jump.

Fighting to maintain my composure, only experience and adrenaline help me through the remaining twenty seconds. Every move I make is becoming a struggle. My leg is numb, like a pirate's peg leg. It doesn't feel attached to my body. But I refuse to let that stop me. If this happened on tour during a show, I wouldn't stop either. I'd never let the audience know something has gone wrong. As the final notes of the music echo through the rink, I strike my closing pose, masking how I feel with a forced smile.

Coming off the ice, I glide on my left leg, taking all the weight off my right side. Frankie hugs me. "Gorgeous, but what happened on the last jump? It looks like you slipped off your edge."

"That's exactly what happened. I slipped." I laugh nervously. I don't want my friends to know what just happened. I don't want them worrying about me. They're about to leave for a major competition tomorrow. They can't afford to be distracted. "You know how unpredictable Axel takeoffs can be. Even when you've been doing it as long as we have." My pulse races wildly in my ears. *Please accept the lie. Don't question it.*

Frankie shares a knowing glance. "You're totally right." She elbows Charlie. "He made a similar mistake in practice earlier this week—popping his Axels a couple times."

"I did." The lines around Charlie's eyes and mouth tighten. "But it didn't look like you slipped, it looked like—"

"Frankie, Charlie, you guys are needed in the lobby." Leslie bursts her way into our small circle.

Relief floods my body. Charlie's sister couldn't have had better timing.

"In a minute," he says. "I wanted to check with Gemma if—"

"Not in a minute. Now. There's a TV crew, two reporters, and a bunch of the kids all waiting to see you."

"Go on. I'll catch up with you in a couple of minutes." My voice shakes. I look away, unable to meet Charlie's eyes. I know he knows something's up. When it comes to skating, he's a technical mastermind. It's why so many of his students seek him out. He's observant and an expert at breaking down the smallest details in a jump.

"But . . ."

"I'm good. Just need to change. Go on," I urge, schooling my face so it's neutral.

"You heard her. Now let's go, bro." Leslie gently grabs Frankie's and Charlie's elbows and guides them toward the lobby doors.

As my friends disappear, I make my way to a quiet corner of the rink. Each step I take is agony. Bracing my hands against the cold concrete wall, I drop my chin to my chest. This can't be happening to me. What am I going to do?

Chapter Five

It's around ten when Leslie drops me off at Frankie and Charlie's cabin. "Thanks for staying to help clean up. I really appreciate it. It saved me about an hour or two of work in the morning."

"It wasn't any trouble at all," I manage, biting back the pins-and-needles sensation radiating through my hip as I climb out of her car.

Leslie thankfully doesn't notice anything is amiss as she fights a yawn. "My boyfriend is going to be excited that I'm home before midnight."

As casually as possible, I lean against the door, taking some weight off my leg. "Oh, is he in town?"

"Yeah, but it's only a quick stopover." She yawns again. "His hockey team is playing a series against the Jasper Ridge Jaguars. He'll be off to Seattle after this."

I nod, sympathizing with Leslie. "It must be hard to be apart for long periods at a time."

"We both knew when we started dating that being a long-distance couple meant we'd have to compromise. It's Ron's dream to play pro hockey, just like it was mine to run a rink. We find time to be together when we can. What helps is knowing we won't be apart forever."

"I'm coming to you if I have questions about dating long-distance."

"Please do." She tilts her head to the side. "You know, if you're interested, there are at least two single guys on Ron's team. I could put in a good word for you."

"I'll keep that in mind, but for now it's still a no. I'm not interested in any hockey players or skaters."

"I respect that." She nods. "If my bro or Frankie are still up, which I doubt, let them know I'll be here at five to take them to the airport."

"Of course."

"Do you have a key to let yourself in?"

I open my wristlet and hold up the key. "Right here."

"Great. I'll just wait until I see you get inside, then I'm off."

I push myself away from the car. The walk to the front door has never seemed so long. I hope the dark helps disguise my uneven gait. I insert the key into the lock, wave, and watch Leslie drive away.

Once inside, I lock the door behind me and lean against it, taking a moment to catch my breath. I close my eyes and my face falls. In here, I don't have to pretend I'm okay. A few silent tears fall down my face. I know whatever is causing the pain has to be bad. I wish I could ask Frankie for advice, but that's not an option until after their competition.

And then there's Mel, the Dreams on Ice PT. If I let on how I'm really feeling, she'll be obligated to refer me to a doctor. And that's something I'd like to avoid. Dreams on Ice is in the middle of being acquired, and with a new ownership group taking over, there's no telling what they'll do with an injured skater. No. It's better right now if I do nothing. I've had injuries before, I can handle this. All I need is a little time to rest.

L ate the following morning, I receive a message from Suzy.

> Suzy: Hi, Gemma, how are you doing this morning?

I stare at the screen. The real answer is that I ache and would love nothing better than to spend the day in bed. But I promised Richelle I'd go to the Halloween party tomorrow night. And that's a promise I intend to keep.

> Gemma: Last night took a toll on me. But I had a long lie-in and a hot shower and now I feel more like myself.

That's not technically a lie.

> Suzy: Glad to hear it.

Three dots blink. Suzy is typing.

> Suzy: Thanks for sending me your Cupid's Arrow video. I shared it with Rich, and we think it looked wonderful. I'm sure it's only a matter of time until they snap you up.

Pride swells through my body. I stayed up until two in the morning, playing with the final edits until the video felt just right. It was just the distraction I needed to block out the pain.

> Gemma: Thanks for saying so. Now it's a waiting game. I think applications are open until 31 December and they have until March to review everything. The website said successful applicants would hear something from the Connected Hearts network by mid-April. Hopefully I'll have some news by my next visit here.

> Suzy: I'm crossing my fingers for you.

> Gemma: Thanks.

> Suzy: Anyway, dear, I wanted to ask what your plans were for this morning.

> Gemma: I don't have any.

> Suzy: Are you interested in going on another date while you're here?

I stare at the blinking cursor on the screen. I'm *not* in the mood. But a part of me is curious.

> Gemma: That depends. Tell me more.

> Suzy: My granddaughter has invited a very single, strapping teammate of Ron's over for brunch. He's sitting with Rich and Leslie now. Let me see if I can discreetly take a photo of him for you.

I huff with frustration. I specifically asked her not to set me up with anyone. Especially a professional hockey player. I rub my temples. If this bloke is already at Suzy's house, I suppose I'd better suck it up and go. "I just have to look at it as another opportunity to find love," I mumble to myself.

> Gemma: Don't worry about sending a
> photo. I'll come.

> Suzy: That's the spirit. Would you like me
> to send Rich or Leslie to pick you up?

> Gemma: No thanks, I'll take care of it.
> See you soon.

S tanding safely next to Suzy, Leslie makes introductions. Her innocent look doesn't fool me. "Gemma, this is Derrick. Derrick, Gemma."

"Nice to meet you, Gemma." I lift my chin and stare up at him. Derrick is a large man with a round baby face coated with several days' worth of stubble, steel-gray eyes, and a cleft in his chin. I have to hand it to him. He knows how to dress sharply. He's wearing an immaculately-tailored black suit with a crisp white dress shirt and a burgundy pocket square.

"Likewise." We walk over to the kitchen island, and each pull out a bar stool. "So . . . you play hockey?"

"Yup." He puffs out his massive chest. "I'm a right wing on the second line."

I nod, not having a clue what that means. "That sounds brilliant."

"And what do you do?" Derrick asks, appraising me.

Suzy moves around the kitchen, pulling out a few glasses. "Our Gemma is a professional figure skater."

"Oh, a twirl girl." He snorts. "Are you free tonight? Maybe you could come down to the rink and see how *real* skaters skate." He elbows Ron.

Everyone else in the room, including me, visibly tenses. Is he being serious? I open and close my hands. Trying to keep my voice calm and facial features neutral, I blink slowly and say in a flat tone, "You don't consider figure skaters to be real skaters?"

Oblivious to his insulting words, he continues, "No. What you do is tricks and frilly spins. Real skating is stuff that requires speed, agility, strength, and solid edgework like hockey."

"We do all of that in figure skating." I cross my arms. "How else do you think we're able to do jumps that require throwing your body into the air and landing with a force that's about five times our body weight?"

"Luck. If you ask me, figure skating isn't even a real sport."

The temperature of the room drops ten degrees. Suzy and Mr. T watch worriedly as I clench my jaw. There are so many things I want to say to this arrogant hockey player. Figure skating takes just as much edge work, agility, speed, and whatever else he's claiming—and more. He's just too ignorant to see it.

Before I can make a snarky retort, Ron springs out of his stool. "Derrick, have I shown you the view of the lake? Follow me outside."

"Sure." The two teammates step through the glass door.

The tight lid I've kept on my emotions snaps open, like a coil that's been wound too tightly. "Not a sport? Not a sport! I can list fifty reasons why figure skaters are more athletic than hockey players." I pound my fist against the kitchen island. "Reason number one—Figure skating blades have a sharp, pointy edge called a toe pick. Reason number two—"

"I won't argue with you, Gem. Figure skating is a completely different sport from hockey. You can't compare the two." Leslie shifts uncomfortably, her expression tight. "Derrick was out of line. I'm sorry for foisting him on you. I'd heard that he was, um, oblivious to some things, but I didn't think he'd be this clueless."

"I'm sorry too, Gemma. I'd hoped Derrick might help break up the streak of bad luck you've had with men lately." Suzy sighs. "Once we feed him, we'll kick his behind back to the hotel."

Mr. T perks up. "Does this mean I can give the young man a taste of how we handled those who stepped out of line in the Navy?"

My lips curve up. Hearing Mr. T wanting to go into drill-instructor mode makes me feel lighter. He's acting just as my father might by showing this clueless oaf why he's out of line.

"Normally I'd say no, but in this case, I think a *small* dose of Chief Petty Officer Tomlinson would be welcomed," his wife says.

"Excellent." His eyes glow. "You're the best, Suzy." He pecks Suzy on the cheek. "Let me see if I can squeeze into my old uniform."

Here's another guy to cross off my list. And a reminder of why I'm keen to avoid hockey players. I know they're not all bad. Ron seems like a good guy. But Derrick's left a bitter taste in my mouth. At least this morning won't be a total waste. I've always wondered what Mr. T was like back in his Navy days. It looks as if I'll finally get to find out.

I check in with Frankie the next day.

Gemma: How did your first practice
session go?

Frankie: I received a lot of compliments
on my dress. There were a couple
skaters asking who my designer was.
You may have a future in dress design.

I sit up taller and smile widely. I never thought anyone would be interested in my handiwork. But maybe it's something I should consider. It could be a viable alternative to coaching, although I'd need to take some sewing classes to up my game. Everything I've learned comes from watching videos on SearchTube or through self-experimentation. I wouldn't feel right charging people money without some formal training.

Gemma: That's not what I meant.

Frankie: I know. Charlie's been struggling
with his triple Sal, and me with the
landing on the throw triple loop. We're
both nervous. We've practiced our
program a thousand times, but it's
nothing like being under the lights in
front of a big audience and judges.

"Oh, Frankie," I say to myself. "You'll figure it out. You always do."

Gemma: I have the streaming schedule
all worked out so I can watch your short
program and free skate while I'm
traveling.

Frankie: *Smiling emoji*

Frankie: I wanted to ask you too . . . Dad
said you had a date yesterday? Give me
the details!

I grimace.

Gemma: There isn't much to say. Leslie
invited one of Ron's teammates over to
brunch at your dad's.

Frankie: And?

Gemma: Wipeout.

Frankie: Bummer.

Gemma: At least I can forget about it.
I'm about to head out to the Halloween
festival.

Frankie: I'd forgotten that's tonight! I'll let
you go. Have fun, Gemma-rella.

Gemma: I will!

Chapter Six

I step out of my rideshare and stare openly. This is a school event? It looks more like something put on by professionals. There's a horse-drawn wagon carrying families through a haunted forest, a large pumpkin patch, and a maze made from towers of hay bales, with people enjoying it all while "Monster Mash" plays over speakers.

Following the signs to the school's gym, I'm greeted by the sight of a dozen game booths. I look on as children toss rings onto the neck of a grinning skeleton, aim darts at colorful balloons, and trick-or-treat through the haunted locker room. I wish I'd had something like this at my school growing up.

"Coach Gemma! You made it!"

Spinning around, I'm greeted by Richelle, who's dressed as a mermaid princess in a seafoam-colored ball gown trimmed with seashells. She stops just short of me, her eyes widening. "Mr. C was right. You are Cinderella. Do you have glass slippers too?"

"No, I have these instead." I shift my heel forward, revealing a pair of blue ballet flats covered with a hundred or so Swarovski crystals. It took me all afternoon to place them. Which in hindsight may have been foolish since a lot of the crystals will probably fall out tonight.

I would've loved to have worn heels, but there's no way my leg would've tolerated it. I'm having enough trouble walking normally. My hip hates me right now, but at least heating it for a few hours and taking some Advil has helped make the pain tolerable.

"Oh, they're so pretty!"

"Thanks."

"Richelle!" a man shouts. "You can't just run off like that without telling me where you're going!"

The young skater spins around, her body growing smaller. "Sorry, Daddy."

He catches up to us. "Just don't tell your mom and don't let it happen again," he scolds, though his stern expression soon relaxes. "Is this your coach?"

"No, Daddy. Mr. C is competing this weekend." She rolls her eyes. "This is Coach Gemma."

"Well, pardon me." He extends his hand to me. "Nice to meet you, Coach Gemma."

Richelle's dad is in his early fifties. He's dressed in a doctor's lab coat with a stethoscope draped around his neck. I have no trouble believing he might've just come from work. He has laugh lines around his eyes, and seems like the opposite of Richelle's uptight mom. I can see who Richelle takes after.

I squint at the name on the plastic badge attached to the coat's front pocket. "Cheers, Dr. Zhang. I'm your daughter's stand-in coach."

Richelle nods in confirmation. "Mr. C asked her to come so I could introduce her to my friends. Did you know she's a princess?"

"I can see that." Dr. Zhang winks. "You must be Snow White."

Richelle face-palms. "No, Daddy. She's Cinderella!"

Dr. Zhang and I share a laugh over her dramatic behavior.

"Well, now that you've found Coach Gemma, let's take her to your friends. I think your mom said you guys were supposed to meet them by the haunted hayride."

Richelle tugs at my hand. "Come on, it's right this way."

Caught off guard by the surprising strength of someone so tiny, I stumble forward, and my hand flies out of hers. The muscles in my hip spasm and send a sharp jab of white-hot pain up my leg.

As I attempt to steady myself, one of my shoes slips off my foot, and I bump into the solid body of the person passing by on the left. With the reflexes of a cat, their strong arms reach around and steady me. I squeeze my eyes shut for a few seconds, taking some deep breaths.

"Are you okay?" a familiar voice says.

"Fine. Just need a second. Thanks for catching me. I'm sorry I knocked into you," I say quickly, avoiding his gaze with a nervous smile.

"It's no problem at all, Gemma. I'm here to save the day."

My eyes open. My gaze slowly travels up from the khaki-colored shirt and well-worn brown leather jacket, locking on to the glimmering hazel eyes of the man I met at Hobby Land. He's shaven since our last encounter, revealing a set of dimples and cut cheekbones. My pulse quickens. "Henry," I whisper.

"Coach Gemma, are you okay?" Richelle asks.

"I am now," I reply, quickly breaking apart from Henry and smoothing out my skirt. My face burns even hotter.

"Richelle, what should you say?" Dr. Zhang asks.

She stares at the ground. "I'm sorry."

I force a smile onto my face. "No harm done." I glance behind her.

Henry follows my gaze and grins. "We can't have Cinderella losing her shoe, can we?"

"No." Richelle shakes her head.

He walks over and retrieves it, along with his hat, then kneels down in front of me. "Princess, let's see if this fits."

Richelle giggles.

I rest my hand on his shoulder as I slip my foot back into the shoe. "Well, it looks like this was made just for you, princess. It fits like a glove!" Henry says.

Our eyes lock for a moment, and the air fizzles around us. His hand lingers on my foot a moment longer than necessary, the light touch causing goosebumps to form on my arms. I can't believe I have so much chemistry with someone I hardly know. I almost forget he has kids. And maybe even a wife!

"Coach Gemma, are you ready to go to the haunted hayride now?" Richelle inquires.

The spell between Henry and me breaks. That's right, we're not alone. We're at the school Halloween festival. I step away from him. My body is so hot that if I were riding inside a pumpkin carriage, I might cook the darn thing. "Um . . ."

Reading us, Dr. Zhang steps in and clears his throat. "I think Gemma needs another minute or two, sweet pea. I'll help you find your friends, and your coach can join us when she's ready."

Richelle tilts her head, her quizzical expression sending me into a fit of laughter. "But she said she was fine."

"How about we walk through the trick-or-treat trail on the way?"

"But Mommy said no candy." She pouts.

Dr. Zhang blinks slowly. "It'll be our secret. We can keep it at my office."

Her arms fly around her father's legs. "Daddy, you're the best." Taking hold of his daughter's hand, Dr. Zhang winks, then leads her toward the food booths.

I could kiss him for his timely intervention. I turn my attention back to Henry. "I see you went with the Indiana Jones costume again after all."

"What can I say? Never mess with success." As he returns his hat to his head, his shirt stretches tightly over his muscled arms. I can just make out the ridges of his biceps through the thin fabric. "And I see you didn't go for the fairy or the angel route."

"No. I didn't know I'd need a costume until the last minute. It was either this, a peacock, or a sloth."

"Those are, um . . . interesting options." His lips twitch. "I personally would've picked the sloth, but I'm glad you went for the princess. It suits you."

I stand taller. "Me too."

"Come on. I'll walk you over to the hayride, so your little friend doesn't think I've turned you into a frog or something." His tone is light and playful.

"Cinderella would never get turned into a frog. A servant or a mouse, maybe."

We start strolling side by side. I take slow, calculated steps, afraid to aggravate my ailing limb even further. I hurt, but the ache has lessened to more of a constant throb instead of a sharp jab. Henry's long legs carry him a few steps ahead of me, but as soon as he sees me lagging behind, he slows down.

"Can I let you in on a little secret?" he says.

"Sure." I nod, wondering what he'd possibly want to share with me. Something about Indiana Jones? His kids?

"I don't know much about fairy tales. Just the barebones basics, like Snow White ate a poison apple and Cinderella lost her glass slipper."

The scent of freshly popped popcorn mixes with the sweet aroma of apple cider as we pass the food booths. It's a combination that makes my mouth water. I'll have to circle back here later. I don't normally eat too many sweets, but for these, I'll make an exception. "Oh, there's candy floss? That looks delicious." I stop for a moment to stare at the fluffy pink dessert.

Henry wrinkles his nose. "What's candy floss? It sounds like every dentist's worst nightmare."

How can he not have heard of it? I thought everybody knew what candy floss was. I point to it.

"You mean cotton candy!"

"Yes? Is that what it's called here?" I cock my head to the side. "I suppose it does look like cotton. Americans have such odd names for things."

"It's not odd. We just call it like we see it, unlike you people from England."

"I'm Scottish," I correct. "But whatever you say."

"Sorry," he quickly apologizes. A look of concern fills his eyes. "I didn't mean to insult you."

"It's fine." I shrug. "Scotland *is* technically part of the United Kingdom." My lips curve. I try my best to keep the conversation light. "And just for the record, I'm still convinced candy floss is the better name."

"It's funny, we both speak the same language, but

American English and British English have a lot of differences. Like using soccer instead of football."

Henry has hit on one of the big ones. I've never been the biggest fan of football, but the rest of my family are loyal Aberdeen FC fans. If I called football anything else, they'd give me a hard time. And actually, I can't imagine it being called anything else. "I hope you're not one of those people who's going to convince me that football should be called soccer," I tease.

"Nope. If it were up to me, soccer *would* be called football." Henry shakes with laughter. "It makes more sense for a game that's played with your feet." He swings his leg in an exaggerated motion, mimicking a dramatic kick. His eyes widen in mock astonishment, as if he's just scored the goal of the century. "And the crowd goes wild!" he announces, cupping his hands around his mouth to let out a ridiculously enthusiastic cheer. "Wooooo!"

Henry's energy is infectious. There's something about the way he throws himself so completely into a moment—it draws me in like a moth to a flame. "Do you have a victory dance you perform, too, when you play football?"

"Oh no. I never played soccer. My sport's baseball." He brings his hands together and pretends to hit an invisible ball. Once again, his shirt pulls tightly, teasing me with a hint of the lean, muscular body underneath.

Before I can admit my own little secret to Henry—that I know nothing about baseball—we reach the hayride queue. Richelle is waiting near the entrance with her dad, happily munching on a chocolate candy bar.

Henry glances at his watch. "Oh shoot, it's already five-thirty." He sighs. "I'm supposed to take a turn in the dunking booth. Might as well get it over with. I hope none of the students actually manage to get me soaking wet."

Why did he have to say that? My mind immediately conjures the iconic image of Henry wearing a soaking-wet shirt, clinging to his chest like Colin Firth, my perfect Mr. Darcy. I swallow hard. That version of *Pride and Prejudice* is one of my guilty pleasures. I've seen it more times than I care to admit.

"I'll let you go. It was nice chatting with you."

He tips his hat to me. "You too, Gemma." As I watch him retreat, my stomach coils in knots. He's not getting away from me this time. Feeling bold, I shout, "Henry, wait! Can I have your mobile number?"

He turns around, and I see his eyes are sparkling with mirth. "You already have it!" Then he waves and continues walking away, whistling the theme song to *Indiana Jones*.

Huh? I already have it? I scrunch my nose. What does he mean? That's not possible. We've only met twice. I'd remember asking him for it, or if he gave it to me.

"Coach Gemma!" Richelle yells, waving.

"Coming, Richelle." I sigh. I'll have to leave the unlocking of the Henry mystery until later. For now, duty calls.

I spend the next few hours with Richelle, her friends, and their parents. By the end of the night, I'm surprised by how much I enjoyed myself. I've skated in front of thousands of kids in audiences with DOI, but I've rarely spent any one-on-one time with them. They're a breath of fresh air with the carefree way they see the world.

I never thought I'd say this, but if I knew the kids I'd coach would be just like Richelle, I might consider doing it. But as Charlie has told me before, Richelle is "one of the rare ones." So in actuality, my becoming a coach is not any closer to being a reality.

"Thank you for coming tonight, Coach Gemma. I had so much fun." Richelle wraps her arms around me and gives me a tight hug. "You're almost as cool as Mr. C."

"I'll take that as a huge compliment coming from you." I know how attached she is to Charlie.

Richelle fights a yawn as she climbs into the back seat of her dad's maroon SUV. She buckles her seat belt, resting her head against the window once Dr. Zhang closes the door.

"I was worried all the sugar would keep her up, but it looks like the ride home is going to be quiet. I might even get to pick the music for a change." He smiles. "That's a rarity with the kids around."

"She's a good kid. I hope I'll get to see her the next time I'm in town."

"I'm sure she'd say the same thing." Dr. Zhang leans against the car. We lock eyes and he gives me a knowing look. "She'd also want me to make sure her coaches are healthy too. I couldn't help but notice you're favoring your right side tonight. I know athletes are tough, but it's important to remember that your body is not a machine. It needs to be taken care of. It's the only body you get."

Leave it to a doctor to notice something's amiss. As tempted as I am to ask for his advice, I don't want to make a bigger deal out of this than I need to. I fancy Mel's opinion first. Maybe this injury isn't as bad as I think it is and can be healed with some rehab.

He reaches into his pocket. "If there is anything you need, feel free to reach out to me anytime. Here's my business card. It's got my work number and email on it."

"Thank you so much." Glancing at the card, my eyes

widen. "You're the team doctor for the Jasper Ridge Jaguars hockey team?"

Dr. Zhang nods. "I am."

That's an interesting contact to have. We chat for a few more moments, then father and daughter depart.

A chilly gust of wind blows. I hug my arms to my body, wishing I'd remembered to bring a coat with me. It's too cold to linger out here. Where's that pumpkin carriage when you need it? Pulling out my mobile, I open my ride-sharing app and type in my location. "Forty minutes?" I groan. It stinks, but I have little choice, so I click "Accept." I guess I should be thankful that there are any cars available in a small town like Sequoia Valley. I head back toward the gym. I might as well be comfortable while I wait.

Inside, the cleanup has begun. Booths are being dismantled, chairs stacked, and trays of leftover food packed away. The hum of post-event chatter fills the space. Locating the bleachers, I sink down onto the wooden seats. I've been standing too long. There's a tightness wrapping from the front of my hip to my sit bones, as if I've been wearing a pair of shoes three sizes too small. I rub my hip, trying to release some of the ache.

"Gemma? What are you still doing here?" Henry says, coming to a stop in front of me. He's removed his coat and hat. Under this lighting, there's a few golden highlights mixed into his messy brown locks. The sleeves of his shirt have been rolled up to his elbows. In a few places, it's become damp with perspiration, clinging to his chest.

"Oh hi, Henry." My voice is slightly hoarse. I clear my throat. "I'm, uh, just waiting for my car."

"Not a pumpkin carriage?" he teases, flashing his boyish smile.

"Nope." I chuckle. "The carriage wasn't available."

"If that wasn't an option, they should've offered you an upgrade to a flying carpet. Or a winged horse."

"Both of those would've been nice. I bet I wouldn't have to wait forty minutes for them."

He wrinkles his nose. "Is that how long the rideshare app quoted you?"

I nod.

"I'll tell you what, if you don't mind waiting ten minutes, I can give you a ride home." He glances behind me. "We're just about done here. The rest of the cleanup, we'll do in the morning when it's lighter outside."

"Only if it's not an inconvenience to you," I sputter.

"It's not. Otherwise, I wouldn't offer."

I *would* like to spend some more time with him and see what's going to pop out of his mouth next. His unusual interests make for some interesting conversations. I want more. I'm hopeful he may be single since he's been flirting right back with me all evening.

"Then I'd love to take you up on it."

"Great. I'll be right back. I just need to sign my cash back in and lock it up. In the meantime, try not to trade your voice to a sea witch. And here"—he tosses his jacket to me—"you look like you're freezing."

Wrong princess, but at least he's trying. I'll give him points for effort. I catch the jacket and drape it over my shoulders. His warmth still clings to the fabric. There's also a hint of cedar and something spicy. It reminds me of a walk through the woods.

I pull the jacket tighter around my body, impressed that Henry is putting my comfort before his own. It seems like a quality most men should have, but don't. Take the guy from my last date. We'd just finished dinner and were walking back to my hotel when it started raining. All I had on was my DOI hoodie over a maxi dress. My date, on the other hand, had on waterproofs and carried an umbrella. Did he offer to let me use the umbrella? Or his jacket? No. I got soaking wet.

I shake my head. Pulling out my mobile, I cancel my ride request just as Henry comes strolling up to the bench. "Okay, I'm all set. You ready?"

I stand, biting back a wince. "Lead the way."

Henry opens the gym door for me. "What did you think of the festival? Did you have a good time?"

"I did, but I was surprised it was held so early. Halloween isn't until next week."

"We did that on purpose." He laughs. "The PTA didn't want to have the kids pick and choose between trick-or-treating and attending the school festival. So they moved it up."

"Oh. That makes a lot of sense."

We reach a white minivan, and he clicks the key fob. The doors slide open, and lights click on. "Fancy."

It must be for his kids. I wonder how many he has. I'm gonna guess at least two, from the amount of stuff scattered in the back. I see a few jackets, a flashlight, a sports bag, a case of water, and a few boxes of sports bars.

"Not really, but it's practical."

I climb into the passenger seat. "Is that because it makes it easier to shuttle your kids around?"

Henry closes the door, inserts the key into the ignition, and stares at me with a confused expression on his face. "My kids?"

"Yeah, you know . . . your tiny humans?" I chew on my lip. "I'm surprised. I thought they'd be with you tonight."

"Some of them were here."

"Some?"

"Yeah, I think about twenty made it."

I blanch. "Um, exactly how many kids do you have?"

Henry starts the engine. "Thirty-five."

I grip the armrest attached to the door. "Thirty-five," I sputter. Have I heard him right? He must be joking. Any second now he's going to say, "Just kidding."

"Uh-huh. A few more than average." Slowly backing the car out, he looks both ways, ensuring there's no approaching traffic, then turns out of the car park onto the darkened State Highway Three.

A red alarm blares out in my mind. That must be why he's single. Nobody in their right mind would want to attach themselves to a man with thirty-five children. Myself included. Time to cross him off the list. "I assume not all of them live with you. You'd need to have an enormous farm, and about thirty washrooms."

"Live with me? Thirty bathrooms?" His eyes widen, and he roars with laughter. Pulling over to the side of the road, Henry wipes the corners of his eyes. "Gemma, I'm not the father of thirty-five kids. I'm a sixth-grade teacher."

<h1 style="text-align:center">Chapter Seven</h1>

I want to disappear. How could I make such a huge mistake? I knew it was unreasonable, and yet my brain did not want to compute. The exhaustion must finally be catching up with me. The only word I can manage is, "Oh." I place my hands over my face.

Henry chuckles, still recovering. "As much as I'd love to be a dad in the future, one, I don't think I'd want more than three kids, and two, I'd have to be in a relationship for that to happen."

I slowly lower my hands and perk up. "You're single?"

"Uh-huh. I thought you would've picked up on the fact that I'm interested in you. But then again, I've never been all that great at reading women." He rests his hand on his stomach. "Oh, my abs are gonna be sore from laughing so hard."

"You read me right." I lick my lips. "I've been thinking about you since Hobby Land, but you mentioned having kids the day we met."

"I did?" He scratches his forehead.

"Mm-hmm. You said you were planning to let your kids choose your Halloween costume this year. Then I saw the minivan and I thought . . . well, we both know where my mind went." I hang my head, giggling to myself.

"Ah. I can see where you might've thought I had kids." His cheeky grin causes my stomach to perform somersaults.

"Everything makes sense now, except . . . I'm still confused about the minivan."

"Oh." He shrugs. "As you might've guessed from the state of the back seat, I use this guy like a closet. A normal car doesn't have as much space for stuff like my baseball gear and the supplies for my classroom."

"You didn't want an SUV?" I tease.

"I wouldn't have minded it, but the van was five grand cheaper. Five grand is five grand. Maybe next time."

The final piece of the puzzle has fallen into place. I crack my window open, hoping the air will help cool my body. A few thoughts run through my head. One, Henry is single. Two, he's interested in me. And three, this is the first time in a long time I've felt that magic spark. After having a bad luck streak, it's about time something goes right! Except . . . I'm leaving town tomorrow. Ugh. I spoke too soon.

"You've gotten quiet." Henry pulls back out onto the road and glances in my direction. "What are you thinking?"

"I'm thinking that I'd love to spend some more time getting to know you better, but the timing couldn't be worse." I lower my chin and draw small circles on my seat. "I'm flying out tomorrow."

"That sucks." He puffs out his cheeks. "I should've tried harder to meet you for coffee when you texted me. It's not that I didn't want to. I've just been swamped with stuff for the festival. It's my first time heading the organizing committee."

"I didn't text you," I say slowly. "I don't have your number. I checked. There's no Henry in my mobile."

"That's my fault." He groans. "Henry isn't my real name. I'm Tim. Or Timothy. Or Timmy. Or Mr. Lyons. I answer to them all. I told you I was Henry at Hobby Land because I thought it was a fun nod to Indiana Jones. I didn't think I'd see you again . . ." He trails off.

Suddenly, I realize I still didn't have the full picture after all. Tim was on Suzy and Mr. T's list. "I do have your number." I'm annoyed he lied to me, and that it took him this long to correct me. But I guess I should give him the benefit of the doubt. I never thought I'd see him again either. We were both having fun flirting with one another. And originally, I wasn't planning to give him my name. "Well, we have one unique meet-cute."

"You can say that again," Henry—or rather Tim— agrees.

"My friends are never going to let me live it down. This stuff only happens in movies."

"Oh, I bet—especially Suzy. She's always had an awesome sense of humor. I can hear her now. She'll say it was the universe's way of making your visit to town memorable."

"You're right. She probably will." I smile. "I'll have to call her in the morning and bring her up to speed. I wish I could do it in person, but I need to leave pretty early for the airport."

"Is your work flexible? Maybe they'd give you another two or three days if you worked your magic on them." Henry—no, Tim—wiggles his fingers. "Sprinkle a little pixie dust on their heads and *poof*. More vacation is magically granted."

Adjusting from Henry to Tim is going to take some getting used to. "Nope. I'm a figure skater with Dreams on Ice. We get five days of preapproved vacation a year. Otherwise, all my vacation time has to coincide with the days off in the tour schedule."

"An ice skater, huh?" Tim lets out a long whistle. "I have mad respect for what you guys do. I've gone skating a couple of times with Charlie and I forget every time how hard it is. I'm glad baseball is played on dry land."

We share a laugh.

"I totally get the non-flexible vacation time. It's that way with teaching too. We have subs when we're sick or if an emergency comes up, but as a rule of thumb, we can only take vacations during the summer, or during spring or winter break."

"What do you enjoy most about teaching?" I ask.

"Hands down, it's my students. I love that they're just like me. We share a lot of interests. I have the permanent mind of a twelve-year-old."

I cock my head to the side. "Like what?"

"Oh, you know, stuff like baseball, comic books, and cartoons. How about you? What are you into?"

Yikes. Not those, that's for sure. So far, it seems like we're total opposites. How much should I share with him? What if he hears what I'm into and decides I'm not worth his time? My eyes flutter. No. I can't think like that. I have to think positive. "Uh, my guilty pleasure is watching reality dating shows," I say in a squeaky voice. "I love all the drama."

"That's great." He sits up taller. "Have you seen *Cupid's Arrow*?"

Relief floods through me. "Er, yeah. That's my favorite show."

He raises an eyebrow. "You seem surprised."

"I am," I admit. "No offense, but you're not the type of person I'd picture watching a reality dating show."

"Normally I wouldn't. But it's what most of my fellow teachers are into. I had to see what all the fuss was about, so I watched a couple episodes. It wasn't what I expected. I enjoyed it. It's even given me some practical dating advice."

"You need dating advice? I seriously doubt that."

"It's true," he says, his voice softening. "My last two relationships didn't last long or end well. I'd hoped *Cupid's Arrow* could help me figure out what went wrong."

"Did it?"

"I guess so. I haven't had a chance to test my theory out."

"You can use me as a guinea pig," I offer.

He stays silent for several moments. "I don't know . . ."

"I won't judge you because I'm in the same boat. None of the guys I've dated in the past have lasted past the third date." I can't believe I've just admitted that to him. But it feels like the right thing to do. "I'm focused on my career, and a lot of guys don't want to commit to a long-distance relationship."

"Is Dreams on Ice your dream job?"

"It is. It's the only job I ever imagined doing." I picture myself as a child wearing a Snow White dress, waving wildly to the Dreams on Ice skaters as they skated around the area during the grand finale lap. Little Gemma wore that dress so much that my mum had to sneak it away from me when I finally outgrew it.

"Then you shouldn't have to give it up. You're the only

person I know that ever got lucky enough to actually live out their dream."

Hearing him say that causes my heart to skip a beat. Tim sounds like he would be open to me skating and doing something long-distance. I don't want to get my hopes up though. That would be one major win. "What's your dream job?"

"I'm living it now," he deadpans.

I raise my eyebrow. I seriously doubt that. School-aged children *never* want to be teachers. They normally can't wait to leave school. Although I guess there's exceptions to every rule. "You mean to tell me you wanted to be a teacher as a kid?"

"No. Of course not. That's what I decided I'd do when I was in college." He chuckles. "Growing up, I wanted to be a pro baseball player." A look of sadness crosses his face and his Adam's apple constricts. "But the road to the major leagues is like searching for a four-leaf clover. You have to get lucky. I think something like only three percent of Little League kids ever make it."

"I can believe that." Ice skating is the same. There are a lot of kids who start out in the sport, but the odds of making it to the Olympics are less than one percent. Great Britain isn't a powerful skating country, and usually, we only qualify to send one skater per discipline to the Olympics every four years. "So now that I've shared a little about me, it's your turn," I urge. "What's this theory you've come up with?"

"I think the, um, problem is my interests." His voice grows quiet. "Women aren't into a guy who spends most of his free time reading comic books or watching baseball."

I frown. All that sounds perfectly normal to me. "What do you think women want?"

"That's the thing, I don't know. A rich, six-foot-five hockey player?" His eyes dart in my direction. "Every time I'm in the bookstore, that's what all the book covers on the front table seem to have on them."

"Well, not me." I cross my arms. "Hockey players are another species." I know I'm not being fair. There are plenty of good guys out there, like Leslie's boyfriend. But after my recent experience with Derrick, I'd prefer to avoid them completely.

He chuckles. "I'd always wondered if there was a rivalry between ice skaters and hockey players."

"There usually isn't."

"You don't have to elaborate. I can read between the lines." He turns left and starts up the tall hill to Charlie's cabin.

A wave of relief passes through me. I'm glad because I'm not in the mood to think about more bad dating experiences with hockey players. "Anyway, if you want my opinion, I think your theory is flawed. There's nothing wrong with having a guilty pleasure, like reading comic books." I mean it too.

"Then why do I have so much bad luck with dating apps?"

"Because you haven't found the right woman to date yet," I declare. My heart begins to hammer against my ribs. I've never felt so bold or attracted to someone this quickly. There's something about Tim that's pulling me toward him, like a boat being guided into a harbor. I don't just want to know more about him—I have to. "You need somebody like me."

The car stops in front of the dimly lit cabin. Tim turns and gazes directly into my eyes. The green in his is swirling with the gold, as if there's a stormy battle playing out. He licks his lips. "I'd like to keep getting to know you."

His words send a shiver through my body. There is so much I want to ask him. I wish we could just sit here and chat all night. I'm dying to keep unraveling the mystery of the man in front of me. "If we do this, we'd have to settle for exchanging texts and video chats. Is that a deal-breaker for you?"

"No, it's not. As much as I'd love to jump on a plane and meet you on the weekends, it's not realistic on my teacher's salary." The tips of his ears turn a light shade of pink. "Video chats sound perfect. I'd, um, like to take this slow." He runs a hand through his hair. It does nothing to tame the mess. The ends continue to stick out at odd angles. "Does that, er . . . work for you?" he sputters.

It takes all my willpower to rein in my excitement. I squeeze my knees together and manage a "Yes" in my normal voice. Internally, however, I've popped a cork of champagne and am doing a happy dance and singing "Celebrate." I've finally, finally found a man who ticks all my boxes!

Well, sort of. I realize we haven't spent enough time together for me to know about ticking *all* the boxes, but my instincts are telling me I should take a chance on him. I haven't felt this confident in ages.

Unbuckling my seat belt, I force myself to open the door. "Thanks again for the ride. I appreciate it. I hope I didn't take you too far out of the way."

"You didn't." He chuckles. "And it was well worth it."

How should I say goodbye? With a hug? A kiss? A handshake? I watch Tim for cues. When he doesn't move, I climb out of the van and shut the door. "Good night, Tim," I say, slightly disappointed.

"Good night, Gemma."

Tim waits until I'm at the front door and I let myself inside before driving off. I close the door behind me and rest against it. Tonight was a good night. Although I wish we could've ended it with a kiss, I know he wants to take things slowly. When we do kiss, it'll be all the more special.

Chapter Eight

I have a difficult time keeping the cheesy smile off my face every time Tim and I exchange texts over the next few days as we continue to get to know one another.

Gemma: What's your stance on capes?
Should superheroes have them?

Tim: That's a tough one. It depends if it's more for looks or if it adds to the hero's powers. What about you?

Gemma: You didn't answer the question, but I'm all for them. Capes add to a hero's coolness factor.

Tim: Fine, if I have to pick a side, I'm team no capes. If you've seen The Incredibles, you'll know why.

Gemma: That's one of the few Pixar films I haven't seen. Is that one I should add to my must-watch list?

Tim: Yes! And when you do, look out for
Edna Mode.

Gemma: Is that a superhero mode?

Tim: *Face-palm emoji* You're killing me.
No. She's an important character in the
movie.

Gemma: I'll take your word for it.

I look up from my phone screen and giggle. Tim wasn't lying. He does indeed have the mind of a teenager. I never expected to stay up late discussing the merits of superhero capes with anyone, let alone a guy. Tim keeps me guessing about what we'll be talking about next. It's a refreshing change from every other relationship I've ever been in.

Gemma: Have a great day at school.
Send me photos of how your classroom
turns out when you finish decorating it.

Tim: I will. Have a good show in Dallas.

After saying goodbye to Tim, I decide check in with Frankie.

Frankie: Did you finally open the email
from the Connected Hearts Network???

Gemma: Yes.

Frankie: Don't leave me hanging. What
did it say?

Gemma: I made it to the next round. The
Cupid's Arrow casting team wants me to
film a short video answering a list of
questions they sent me. But I don't know
if I should.

Two weeks ago, I was gung-ho about being the next bachelorette on the show. I was convinced it was the answer to all my dating problems, but since I met Tim, things have changed. I haven't thought about *Cupid's Arrow* once. I've been focused on developing our friendship and seeing where it might lead us.

Frankie: Eek! I'm so excited for you. It's
just the nerves talking. You have to do
this. You've talked about applying for so
long. I'd hate to see you lose your shot.
Obviously, the casting team sees
something special in you—just as I knew
they would—if they picked your
application out of thousands of others
for the next round. If you want, we can
brainstorm your answers when we chat
tomorrow.

I haven't told Frankie about Tim. I usually tell my best friend everything, but for once, I just want it to be the two of us. I take a deep breath. She does have some valid points. It has been a longtime goal of mine. And I am curious. Do I have what it takes to make it onto the show?

I chew on my lip. It wouldn't hurt if I filmed another video and submitted it. I can always back out if I make it further in the casting process—and that's a big if. Tim knows I'm a fan of the show. I'm sure he wouldn't mind.

Gemma: I'd like that.

Frankie: That's the spirit. Don't give up yet. Gotta run. Talk to you later.

The following morning, Suzy texts me.

Suzy: I saw your young man Tim this past weekend. He was helping out at his father's hardware shop.

Gemma: He's not my Tim. We're just friends.

When Tim said he wanted to take things slow, he meant it. We've stuck to texting silly questions and haven't had a proper video chat yet. My schedule has been busier than ever. When I'm not at rehearsals, I'm doing physical therapy. And by the time I'm back in my hotel room at the end of the night, I fall asleep as soon as my head hits the pillow.

I hope we can find time to have a "date" soon, though, because I need an escape from my current situation. My injury is starting to wear me down. When I wake up in the morning, I dread getting out of bed and taking that first step. That's when it's the worst. But once I start moving my body, it gets better. Since I've been back on tour, the only good news is that the injury hasn't gotten any worse. Although it doesn't seem to be improving either. Mel says I just need to give it time. I hope she's right.

> Suzy: Uh-huh. Well, whatever you want
> to call it, he remembered that my first
> husband was Scottish and was asking
> an awful lot of questions about Scotland.
> He wants to impress you.

As I read Suzy's text, it's like a flock of tiny paper airplanes takes off in my chest, each one soaring at the thought of Tim taking the time to learn about my home country. None of the blokes I've dated in the past ever made that kind of effort. I should return the favor and learn more about Batman, his favorite comic hero. Maybe I can squeeze some time in tonight.

> Gemma: *Blushing emoji*

> Suzy: You've turned that boy's head.
> About time too. He's been alone too
> long.

Later that evening, I step onto the ice and push aside the dull throb at the top of my right leg. I've spent the last twenty minutes icing it. It's just numb enough to last until my next chance to pop backstage. Although it's dark, I can tell the arena is filled to capacity. The audience buzzes with anticipation. I plaster a smile onto my face as I take my starting position.

The spotlight finds me, and the opening notes of the music fill the air. My heart races. I mouth the lyrics to Cinderella's familiar theme song as the crowd watches with rapt attention. I execute a series of spirals that leave the crowd applauding wildly. I'm in the zone. My focus is on making it through each of my elements cleanly. Something that's gotten harder and harder to do.

Two hours later, it's over. I've made it through another performance. Thank goodness, I can finally relax. I have my leg stretched out onto my makeup table and my trusty heating pad plugged into the wall. A knock sounds on my door. "It's open," I call out, lifting my eye mask.

"Sorry, Gem, did I wake you?" Fernando, my skating partner, asks.

Originally from Spain, Fernando is about six feet tall and has dark-brown hair and large, expressive brown eyes. He's built like a hockey player, with an athletic frame and broad shoulders. You wouldn't know it from looking at him, but he's one of the most graceful people on the ice.

"No, I was just meditating."

"Huh, I didn't know you did that."

"It's something new I'm trying." I turn off the heating pad, lower my leg, and face him. "What's up?"

"I have a special delivery for you." He holds up a box that's about half the size of his body. "Do you want it in here?"

"Um, sure." What on earth is in there? Did I order something and forget about it?

"The delivery guy was asking for a Gemma-rella. I knew it had to be for you, so I risked my life and signed for it." Fernando rubs his hands together. "Are you going to open it?"

"Duh," I snicker.

I wonder if the package is from Frankie. She's the only person I can think of who'd call me Gemma-rella. I lean forward to inspect the box. It has several red-and-white "Fragile" stickers pasted to the side and an arrow pointing to which side is up. As Fernando mentioned, it's addressed to Gemma-rella. There's no return address. "You don't happen to have—"

"A pocketknife? I do." He whips one out of his pocket with surprising speed.

I gesture to the top of the box. "Have at it. Just be careful."

"Careful is my middle name," he says.

"Really? I thought it was Alberto."

"Haha. Very funny." Fernando makes quick, efficient work of slicing the tape. He peels the flaps open and retrieves a black envelope from the top. "You'd better read this first."

My hands tremble as I turn the envelope over. It's addressed in white block letters to *The Fairest One of All*. I don't recognize the writing, but I have a hunch of who it might be from—the same person who mixes up their fairy tales.

I pull out an orange pumpkin-shaped card and read:

Dear Gemma-rella,

Happy Halloween. I know you've been busy, but we can't have you missing out on celebrating my favorite holiday. When you open the box, make sure you have plenty of room and a friend to do the activity with. If you're up for it, let's have our first "date" tonight. I'm free any time after five.

Yours,

Tim

Kneeling, I place the card down and peek inside the box. Beneath some bubble wrap and purple tissue paper adorned with ghosts, pumpkins, and bats, my hands close around something round, cool, and smooth.

Removing the protective wrapping, I discover two medium-sized pumpkins, a carving kit, a pack of permanent markers, tealight candles, and packages of pumpkin-flavored cookies, candy corn, and gummy bugs. "I can't believe you put this all together for me, Tim," I mumble.

"Whoever sent you all this is a keeper, Gem."

"He is." I continue to stare at the pumpkin. How did Tim have the time to go shopping for all these things? And find out where to send them? I picture him walking through a pumpkin patch, looking for just the right size and shape pumpkins to send me. I swallow hard, feeling guilty that I've done nothing for him.

"There are two pumpkins. Does that mean I can carve one too?" Fernando says, his voice hopeful. "If you let me, I'll promise to do all the cleanup."

I glance at my pairs partner. "Sure. Tim told me to open the box with a friend. And by default, you know that's you."

"Aww, gracias, Gem. The feeling is mutual." He looks at the note. "Tim, huh? Which app did you meet him on?"

"None. Charlie's grandmother set us up." It feels more natural to say that than Frankie's stepmom. Which I still have trouble wrapping my head around. "When you decide you're ready to get back on the dating bandwagon, you could ask her for help finding your perfect woman."

Fernando laughs. "That's never going to happen. But if it does, I'll keep that in mind."

Poor Fernando. As long as I've known him, he's been single. I've never gotten the full story out of him, but from what I've pieced together, he's been burned by love in the past. I think staying single is his way of avoiding getting hurt again. I wish I could convince him to apply for *Cupid's Arrow*. He'd be perfect! I want him to get his happy ending too.

"We'd better get going on the pumpkin carving if you

want to finish before the next show. We only have three hours. And I'll need time to clean up."

I furrow my brow. "It can't be that messy, can it?"

Fernando snorts and gives me a knowing look.

"Oh."

He glances around the dressing room. "I'll ask the backstage crew for a couple of rubbish-bin bags. We'll spread them out across the floor and use those as our work surface. Pumpkins have a lot of guts we'll have to remove. In the meantime, your job is to figure out what you want to carve on your pumpkin."

I frown. "I was planning to make a face. You know, two triangle eyes, a smaller triangle nose and . . ." Fernando shakes his head. "What?"

"The guy who sent this to you obviously put a lot of thought into it. If I were you, I'd do the same." Fernando steps out of the room.

There I go again. Not thinking about Tim. Fernando's right. I owe it to Tim to put some effort into my carving. I unlock my mobile and start to scroll through Pinterest for some inspiration.

Chapter Nine

"Alittle higher, Gem." I shift my pumpkin so it's at chest height. "That's perfecto. Uno, dos, tres." He snaps a few photos, then returns my mobile to me as I set the pumpkin down. "How did I do?"

I skim the burst of images. "Brilliant. Do you want one too?"

"No, gracias." He waves me off. "I'll take pictures of it, but not me *with* it." He jokes.

I study his pumpkin. "Er . . . it's spirited." He claimed it's a ghost, but it looks like an abstract circle.

"You're being too nice." He laughs, the sound bubbling out of him. "Let's face it, I have zero talent for this. It looks like a blob."

I hold up my hands. "You said it. Not me."

"Oh well, I had fun carving it. Nobody except for the two of us is ever going to see it." He compiles all our rubbish in a bin bag, securely knotting the top. "I'm gonna dump this, then shower before the night show. We have about an hour. Do you need anything else before I leave?"

My eyes trace the room. We've gotten all the guts

cleaned up. He was right, it did make a huge mess. I had no idea they'd be so sticky or stringy. "No, but thanks for asking."

"When you phone your boyfriend, tell him I said gracias."

"He's not my boyfriend." *Yet*, I silently add. "We haven't even had a date. All we've done is text and talk."

"Uh-huh," he says, clearly not believing me.

"It's true," I protest.

"You can deny it all you want, Gemma, but you're flustered, and your face is as red as the Queen of Hearts."

Okay, he has a point there. My body feels like a furnace. I place my hands on my cheeks, hoping it'll help cool me down.

"Anyway, do you mind if I leave my work of art here until later?"

"No, feel free."

"Bueno." He sets it down next to mine.

"I'll meet you for warm-ups in a half hour."

Taking the bin bag with him, Fernando exits the room, closing the door behind him. I stare once more at my pumpkin. Instead of a face, I opted to try and create a bat. Tracing my fingers over the rough, uneven edges of its silhouette, I have to admit, I'm thrilled with how it's turned out. Unlike Fernando's, people should be able to tell what it is from a distance.

My mobile vibrates. Glancing at the screen, I see it's Tim. Something light and sparkly flutters in my chest.

Tim: Nice photos! The bat was a good choice! I have a soft spot for them.

I grin to myself. That's exactly the reaction I'd hoped for.

Gemma: Are you home from school already?

Tim: Not yet. I have two kids sitting in detention for chewing gum during class.

Gemma: And you're texting me in front of them?

Tim: They're busy playing on their phones. One of them has it under the desk, and the other kid is pretending to go through his backpack. They think I can't see what they're doing, but I know all the tricks.

I laugh to myself, trying to picture the scene.

Gemma: Are you going to let them get away with it?

Tim: For a moment. I'll bust them as soon as we're done.

Gemma: Then I won't keep you too long. I wanted to see if eight your time works for tonight. I should be back at the hotel by then.

Tim: It's perfect. See you then.

Covering a yawn with my hand, I wiggle my mobile to reveal the time. It's nine forty-five. I still have about fifteen minutes before I'm meant to call Tim. Setting it beside me, I throw my head back onto the fluffy mound of pillows and tuck two under my right side.

It takes some of the pressure off my side, but not much. Double show days are rough. At least I have my talk with Tim to take my mind off things.

> Gemma: Just letting you know I'm
> settled in at the hotel. We can talk
> anytime.

Getting up from the bed, I bumble over to the room's balcony and slide open the glass door. The cool night breeze tickles my face, making me shiver. I check on my pumpkin, pleased to see the tealight candle inside still flickering and casting an eerie glow. I can't wait for Tim to see it.

As I go inside, I notice the screen on my phone lighting up. I hurry over to it and slide to answer the call.

"Hey, stranger," he says. A day's worth of stubble coats his jaw. A pair of square, black-framed glasses is perched on his nose. He's giving me Clark Kent vibes. I also see some cobwebs, pumpkins, and paper bats hanging from his classroom ceiling.

"Hiya, Tim. I thought you were going home after school. And didn't you already decorate your classroom?"

"I went home for dinner, then came back. I put a few decorations up last week, but I needed some more. Tomorrow is actual Halloween. It's the only day of the year my principal allows me to fully express my creativity."

"And by that you mean?" I ask, curiosity piqued.

"Let me flip the camera. It'll be easier if you see what I'm doing."

His face disappears from the screen, replaced with his classroom. The windows are covered with yellow paper and stringy spiderwebs. His desk, also covered in spiderwebs, holds a mega-sized cauldron filled with candy and two light-up plastic pumpkins.

The back wall is concealed with cutouts of the silhouette of a tree, a full moon, white ghosts, a haunted house with eerie yellow windows, and thirty-five pumpkins, each bearing a student's name. From the ceiling, Tim has suspended flickering LED pumpkin lights, and about thirty more bats than the day before.

"Wow. You've been busy."

"I have. And I still have a long way to go." He touches the camera, returning the focus to his face.

"What else do you plan to do?"

"I have the fog machine to rig up, a witch on a broomstick to hang on this empty wall by the whiteboard, a life-sized model skeleton to assemble, and then I have all the activity stations."

I shake my head. Talk about an enthusiastic teacher. Tim is going above and beyond for his students. They're lucky to have somebody like him. "Are your kids going to learn anything tomorrow?"

"Maybe?" He shrugs. "The next two days, I consider lost causes. Halloween day, the kids are too excited to pay too much attention to whatever I'm trying to teach them. And the day after, they'll be tired from staying up all night trick-or-treating."

"Aren't they a little old for that?"

"Not when there's free candy involved." He chuckles. "The last couple of years, most of my class has gone out."

I wince. "I can see how that puts you in a tight spot."

"Uh-huh." He closes his eyes. There are dark bags underneath. I know he's been putting in some long hours lately. Now I can see why. "I wish the school district would schedule a half day on Halloween and cancel classes the day after. They could call it a staff development day and still have us teachers come in."

"My mum always says teachers are never given enough of a voice when it comes to making the important decisions."

"Is she a teacher too?" he asks, opening his eyes.

"Mm-hmm. Mum taught English literature before she retired."

"I have mad respect for her. What about your dad? Is he a teacher too?"

"No." I laugh. "He's the type of person who'd stay as far away from school as possible. He's an electrician. How about your parents?"

"Dad runs the hardware shop in town. But my mom is like yours. She was a school librarian for Sequoia Valley High School until last year. Now she's the volunteer librarian at the public library three days a week." Tim's eyes soften. "She'd probably still be working if the district hadn't had such a budget shortfall."

"Was she forced into retirement?"

"Yes and no." He frowns. "Mom was told the school could only afford to keep one librarian on staff. She had the most seniority, so she had to choose who would be let go. Mom being Mom decided she didn't want to be the reason anyone lost their job, so she took an early retirement."

"Wow. She sounds like such a selfless person."

"She's my hero. And the reason I ended up becoming a teacher."

I love learning about Tim's family. It helps me sketch his character. Hearing his mum is his role model earns him even more brownie points with me.

My gaze travels to the box on his desk labeled "Biohaz-ardous." "What's in there?"

He glances over his shoulder. "The cauldron? I have some packets of candy in there."

"No, no. The box. Is it full of snakes?" I joke, proud of myself for using an *Indiana Jones* reference.

"No snakes." The folds of his lips curve. My heart flutters. His signature look is his cheeky grin. I wish he were able to patent it. Nobody else should be able to look this handsome.

"Then what's in it that's hazardous?"

"Owl pellets."

"Are you bringing a live owl into your classroom too?" I ask quizzically, wondering how the food could be toxic. "Where are you getting one?"

As if he's reading my mind, he answers, "The pellets aren't food. They're the regurgitated parts of an owl's meal that its body can't digest."

I make a face. "Owl vomit?"

Tim's cheeks color. "I guess that's what you'd technically call it."

"What are you going to do with it?"

"It's for the day after Halloween. The pellets contain things like bones, fur, claws, and teeth. I'm planning to have my students dissect them, piece the bones of the animal back together on construction paper, and write a short report on the experience. It covers English and science all at once."

"Oh, that sounds like a fun hands-on activity."

He slides his hands into his pockets, and his henley pulls snugly against his chest. In this lighting I can't make out the exact details, but I don't need to. I've been given a preview of what's beneath. I know he has sculpted biceps and strong forearms. My imagination can fill in the gaps. Add in his signature woodsy cologne and it's a chef's kiss.

"I think so too. My classes are always so excited. They call it a 'big kid' project."

I scoot back onto the bed, sitting up against the headboard. "Can the kids be trusted not to act out?" I can just picture a couple of his students getting rowdy and throwing pieces of the pellet at one another.

"That's the beauty of this project. The kids have heard about how fun it is from my past students. If they want to participate, they know they have to behave." Tim smirks. "But on the off chance I have a rebel on my hands, I have my school principal hang out in the classroom during the setup. They'll behave when he's around. He gives them a speech on proper hygiene and handling techniques. He used to be a biology teacher at the high school, so this is right up his alley."

I eye him with a newfound appreciation. "You've thought of everything."

"Not everything, but I have a pretty good idea of what to expect." He runs a hand over his jaw. It's a nervous habit I've noticed he does when he's embarrassed. "That's the nice thing about being a teacher. Once you get over the speed bump of your first year, every class and year after usually follows a similar pattern."

"Does it ever scare you that people trust you to teach their kids?" I think back to my rough experiences coaching.

"Of course. I'd taken all these classes about how to teach, but actually doing it is another beast. When I was student teaching, I was terrified I'd say the wrong thing or act the wrong way. But I'll give you a spoiler alert. With practice, that fear goes away." He squints at the screen, adjusting the glasses that have slid down his nose. "Is that your pumpkin all lit up behind you?"

"Oh yeah." I've been enjoying talking to him so much

that I've forgotten all about the pumpkin. Sliding off the bed, I hobble over to the balcony and give him an up-close look at it.

"That's a work of art."

"Thanks." My cheeks warm. It's the first time I've ever carved a pumpkin. My handiwork isn't anything Pinterest worthy, but hearing him say that sets off a hummingbird inside my chest. "I had a brilliant time doing it. I can't thank you enough for sending it to me."

"I just wanted to make you smile," he says quietly.

"Well, you definitely succeeded in doing that."

"If we'd been on an in-person date, I would've brought you to my place to carve pumpkins."

I picture Tim sitting next to me. I can see his large hands taking mine in his and hear his deep voice walking me through step by step how to carve the pumpkin. His body would be pressed directly next to mine. I'd feel the heat rolling off of him and the gentleness of his touch. A surge of disappointment fills my body that it's something I did alone instead of doing it together with him. I wish I could be back in Sequoia Valley right now instead of on tour.

"What would *you* have carved?" I ask in a low tone.

"Something like you. A bat. A cat. Something simple. I'm not the greatest with art."

My lips twitch. "Says the man who's put together the world's best haunted classroom."

He lights up, and the spark in his hazel eyes sends a rush through my body. If he were on the ice next to me, I'd be standing in a puddle.

"You know, Gemma, when I saw you at Hobby Land, you had this look on your face while you were studying the wings. It literally took my breath away. I left the store that day kicking myself for not getting your number. All I had was your name."

"I felt the same. I don't do that for everybody, but for you, I would've made an exception." I stare at the flickering candle. "I'm glad Suzy brought us together. Talking to you is one of the things I look forward to every night."

"Me too."

We spend a little more time discussing the latest episode of *Cupid's Arrow* before Tim reluctantly says, "I had better finish this up if I hope to get home before midnight. Is the same time tomorrow okay for you?"

I run through the schedule in my head. "That'd be perfect. I'll be free after four."

"It's a date."

Disconnecting the call, I hug my mobile to my chest. *Tim, you're on your way to capturing my heart.*

Chapter Ten

Another week slips away. Halloween is over and Thanksgiving is around the corner. Everyone in the Dreams on Ice cast is counting down until the long weekend. We've been performing nonstop. It'll be the first time we have two days off in a row since I returned to the tour. Some people, like Fernando, are planning to use the time to travel home to Spain. Others, like Lisa, are planning a skiing trip.

"Should I count you in again this year, Gem?" Lisa asks as we collect our newly sharpened skates from the equipment manager.

"What resort have you guys picked?"

"Snow River Run in upstate New York."

In the past, I haven't given Thanksgiving much thought. Although I enjoy the idea of people's families getting together, the American holiday doesn't hold much meaning for me. It's not something that I grew up with. My family has always gone straight into Christmas once the calendar changes to November.

But this year's different. It's the first time I've ever

pictured myself wanting to be away from Dreams on Ice and back in California with Tim, and Frankie, Charlie, Suzy, and Mr. T. I can easily see the group of us getting together and celebrating all that we have to be thankful for together.

I never thought I'd reach the point where skating would take a back seat to my plans. But here we are. The only thing is they might already have plans of their own, and I don't want to foist myself on them. "Can I get back to you?"

"Sure." Lisa nods. "Just let me know by Friday if you want in. I need to get a final tally so I can book the hotel rooms and the rental cars."

We chat for a few more minutes before I slip into my dressing room. I spend more time pondering over my Thanksgiving plans. I could ask Suzy and Mr. T if they might be willing to host me. They've always insisted I'm a part of their extended family, but I know it isn't right to assume anything. What if they planned to travel to spend time with Suzy's children and their families? Or they're full up with family members staying with them?

Crashing with Frankie and Charlie is also out. They're training for the two most important competitions of the year, US Nationals and the International Prix Final. Their season has been going phenomenally well.

They've medaled at every competition they've entered. Talking to Frankie, I know that Charlie has been superstitious about it all. I don't want to be that person who interrupts their training routine. Even if superstitions aren't really a thing, in a sport that's ninety percent mental, these small details matter.

Then there's Tim to consider. We've been chatting nearly every night and enjoying weekly virtual dates, but we're still in the early days of our relationship. And taking things slowly, per Tim's request. Inviting myself over to his place seems like it would cross the line. No. That's not an option either.

The best course of action is probably to book myself into a hotel in the area. I could visit my friends and use it as my home base without the pressure of getting anyone to commit to anything. They could drop in on me if and when they wished.

I secure the laces on my skates, tying them tight. Yes, that's what I'll do. Sequoia Valley is where my heart is. I'll start looking at airplane tickets and checking out hotels tonight. I just hope something so last minute won't cost me an arm and a leg.

As I stand, the familiar sharp sensation shoots up my hip like a rug burn. I clench my jaw and take a few deep breaths. A few seconds later, the ache subsides just as quickly as it appeared. Unfortunately, it's become a familiar pattern. As diligent as I've been with icing it, heating it, doing physical therapy, and resting when I'm not skating, nothing is making my cranky hip better.

Until last week, I'd been in a holding pattern. I constantly hurt, but it's been the same level of pain. But after the triple-show day on Sunday, something shifted. I experience moments where my leg doesn't feel stable and I hear popping noises. I know I should tell somebody, but I'm so close to the break. If I can make it to Thanksgiving, I'll have a few extended days off where I'll be able to fully rest. I'm sure that'll make all the difference.

Pulling open the door, I step out into the hallway. Each step sends a sharp jab up my leg. A cold sweat starts to form on the back of my neck as I grab the wall for support. The ache isn't going away like it normally does. "Come on,

Gem. You can do it. It's mind over matter. Block out the pain like you've been doing."

I give myself a few seconds, then push away and try to keep moving. The hip pops and I can't take another step. It's too much. I see fuzzy gray spots in my vision. I squeeze my eyes shut and lean all my weight on the wall.

This can't be happening to me. Not now.

"Gemma, I was just coming to check on you. You've skipped the warm-up again. I've told you how important it is to your recovery," says the concerned voice of Mel, the DOI physical therapist.

"I didn't skip it by choice," I say through gritted teeth.

She places a hand on my shoulder. "Can you make it to the exam room? It's at the end of the hall on the left."

I slowly raise my head and chew on my bottom lip. The hallway has never seemed so long. I can't hide it from her any longer. "I need help," I admit.

Mel, who stands a few inches shorter than me in skates, wordlessly slips her arm under my shoulder and helps me limp along. "You know the drill. Out of ten, the pain is a . . ."

I can't lie to her. She'll know if I'm covering up when I'm like this. "It's an eight. Think walking on shards of broken glass over a lava pit."

"How long?" Mel inhales sharply.

"Weeks."

"Why didn't you say anything?"

"I wanted to skate," I say weakly.

"I have premature gray hairs from you skaters," she groans. "You guys need to tell me when you're hurt, not play the hero and cover it up. It only makes whatever is going on with your body worse." We reach the room, and she deposits me on the black padded table. "You're not going to like what I'm about to tell you."

"I know. You'll tell me I need two full days of rest." I stretch my leg out and rub the hip.

"No, Gemma. It's time for you to take two to three *weeks* off to see if that helps manage the pain and inflammation."

My jaw falls open. "Two whole weeks?"

"Even though you've hidden the extent of your hip injury from me"—she sends me a "mom" look—"we've been doing PT exercises for five weeks. If the injury was getting better, it should've responded to it. But clearly, it's not. It's time for more extreme measures like complete rest. You've been pushing yourself too hard."

Mel's recommendation is like taking away an instrument from a musician. I've never taken more than two or three days off from skating before. Even when I was on vacation and visiting Frankie and Charlie, I skated every other day. I'm an athlete. I have to move my body.

"I also think you should see a doctor independent of Dreams on Ice." She lowers her voice. "Between you and me, I'm not convinced the new doctor management sends you to is fully competent." The lines on her forehead wrinkle deeply. "I know he isn't reading my reports, and there's been a few other skaters who have had some questionable diagnoses."

Mel is usually mild mannered and Ms. Positivity. It would take a lot for her admit something like this. I swallow hard. I couldn't be more thankful to have someone like her to look out for us.

"So here's what we're going to do," she continues. "I'll delay writing up a report on the condition while you rest. There isn't any point in jumping to conclusions when we don't know how your injury will respond to you taking some time off, and we don't have an official medical diagnosis."

"Thank you, Mel. I owe you for this." I hug her tightly. "I'll do whatever you tell me to."

"Good, because starting now, I'm completely shutting you down. That means no skating, jumping, running, or anything that puts additional stress on the hip. You'll be limited to low-impact workouts, and the strengthening and range-of-motion exercises we've worked on together. After two weeks, we'll reevaluate and go from there."

"It's going to be miserable having to sit here and watch everyone from the sidelines."

"You know, you don't have to stay with DOI if you're not skating." Mel kneels down to help me remove my skates. "Why not visit Frankie? You were so happy when you returned from your last trip to see her."

"What about management? Won't they notice if I suddenly disappear from the lineup?"

"I doubt it. But if they do, I'll have a note in the system saying you're on sick leave. The new management group is more concerned with filling seats and making money than with its skaters. Elodie has been out for three weeks, and Sophie for a month and a half. Presley has been filling both their roles."

Huh. I hadn't noticed either of them was gone. There's about fifty of us skaters on the tour roster, and we're usually so focused on doing our own roles that we may not catch until later on that somebody is out.

"Who are your backups?"

"Becca and Hailey."

"You'll be fine, then." Mel nods. "Neither one will say a word about you. Especially when they'll get the chance to temporarily move up from the ensemble to a principal role."

I relax. I guess if that's covered, the only thing that's left to do is warn Fernando. Becca and Hailey will need a refresher course on partnering.

"Okay, Gem, let's see what's going on. Go ahead and lie on your back. We'll heat and massage the flexors and extensors and go through some range-of-motion exercises.

As Mel sets to work palpating the soft tissue, I bite back a wince.

"Hmm . . . you're that tender?"

"Yes," I say, short of breath.

She stops and cranks up the heat. I can tell this isn't good. "Okay, let's give your body a few more minutes to relax."

Knots churn in my stomach as I stare up at the ceiling. I wasn't freaked out before, but if Mel is concerned . . . I gulp. I'm not going to bother finishing the thought. I'll only make things worse if I ask her to speculate. Which I know she won't do anyway. I'll just have to wait and see what the doctor says.

Closing my eyes, I let the heat seep into my hip and try to stay still. I relive my latest chat with Tim. His voice helps soothe my nerves. I wish he were here with me now. I could really use a non-skating friend.

In the early afternoon, I chat with Frankie and Charlie in our group text.

Gemma: Hey, guys. Is that open
invitation to come and stay with you still
good?

I know I should book myself into a hotel instead of bothering my friends, but I did the math, and a flight and two-week stay in Sequoia Valley isn't in my budget. Yes, I'm worried I'll interrupt their routine, but I reasoned with myself that if Frankie and Charlie don't want me around, they'd tell me.

Frankie: Of course! You can cash it in
whenever you want.

Charlie: For a nominal fee.

Frankie: Charlie.

That makes me chuckle. I can just hear Frankie's voice chastising her boyfriend.

Charlie: I'm not asking much.

Gemma: What's the price?

As soon as I type that, I immediately think of Tim saying, "Just your voice." A reference from *The Little Mermaid*. I sigh. I'll text him next. He's the person I'm most anxious to see. We've talked a lot via text, but how is it going to be in person?

Charlie: Help with figuring out what to
get Leslie for her birthday.

Gemma: Done.

> Frankie: I thought we decided to just get her a gift card for Hobby Land.

> Charlie: That's the easy way out. We need a gag gift too.

> Frankie: Count me out on that one.

> Charlie: Party pooper.

I giggle. I've missed the easy banter of my friends. Even Charlie's corny jokes.

> Frankie: Not to change the subject, but is everything okay? You were just here. We love having you around, but you don't normally take any days off.

Frankie is too perceptive.

> Gemma: My hip has flared again. Mel shut me down and says I need some rest.

> Frankie: Gotcha. When's your flight?

> Gemma: I haven't booked anything yet, but I'm planning to fly into Fresno early Saturday. Could I trouble you for a ride too?

> Charlie: We're a full-service place. All transportation and meals are included.

> Gemma: *Grinning emoji*

> Frankie: Let us know as soon as you have the details. We can't wait to see you!

My next message goes out to Tim.

Gemma: Hope you don't mind, but there's been a slight change in plans. I'm going to cancel our video chat tonight.

Tim: Oh, okay. Reschedule for tomorrow?

I mentally hear the disappointment in his voice, but I have a surprise up my sleeve.

Gemma: Yes, but how about we do it in person instead?

Tim: Does this mean what I think it means?

I picture his signature Peter Pan smirk slash smile. Yes, that's the name I've decided on for it. When something excites him, his inner twelve-year-old self comes out. The fine lines around his eyes and mouth fade, and out comes his dimples. The flecks of gold within his hazel eyes sparkle like pixie dust against the emerald-green. And if you look closely enough, there's a hint of mischievousness.

Gemma: What do your superhero powers tell you?

Tim: Gemma-rella is coming to town?

Gemma: Ding. Ding. Ding.

Tim: Are you flying in? Do you need a
ride from the airport?

Gemma: Yes and no. My bestie is
picking me up. What I would like to do,
though, is cash in that rain check for a
coffee.

Tim: I'll do you one better. How does
dinner sound for our first in-person
date?

Yes. Yes. Yes. I shimmy in my seat, fighting to hold
myself in check, not wanting to appear too overly eager.

Gemma: As long as they have some ice
cream on the menu, I'm game.

Tim: And what kind of ice cream should I
be on the lookout for?

Gemma: Take a wild guess.

Tim: Pumpkin? Since you're the type of
princess who might ride in a pumpkin
carriage.

Bleh. I stick my tongue out. I can't imagine a worse
flavor.

Gemma: Brilliant skills of deduction, but
no. I'm not a fan of pumpkin.

Tim: Chocolate?

Gemma: Tim for the win. Just a nice
plain chocolate ice cream puts me in my
happy place. What about you? Are you a
strawberry man?

Tim: Vanilla.

Huh. I didn't see that coming. Vanilla is so plain. But I guess it goes with everything.

Gemma: Well, it's good to know our
favorite flavors complement one another.

Tim: It is.

Three dots blink. Tim is typing something else.

Tim: There is one thing on my mind
though. Why are you coming back so
soon? Not that I don't want to see you,
but is everything okay? I thought you
couldn't get any days off until
Thanksgiving.

"You're just like Frankie. You don't miss anything," I say to myself.

Gemma: I'm nursing an injury. I have to
take at least the next two weeks off,
starting today.

His reply pops up faster than I can type.

Tim: Gemma! Are you okay?

Gemma: I'm hanging in there.

Tim: Would a chat help?

Gemma: Yes.

A moment later, a video request pops up on my mobile. I accept, balancing the device on its PopSocket. "Hey."

Tim appears on the screen as if he's rolled out of bed. He's in a white undershirt and joggers. His hair is sticking up like somebody's taken a balloon to his head and created static electricity. The room is semi-dark, illuminated by the glow of a computer. As removes his glasses, I see his eyes are bloodshot. "Hey, stranger," he says tiredly.

"Oh Tim, I hope I didn't wake you!"

"No. I haven't been able to fall asleep." His voice is raspy.

"Are you okay? You look . . ."

"Like crap?" he finishes.

"No. You're too handsome for that."

"Thanks for the ego boost, but you don't have to sugar-coat it." He attempts a laugh, but a cough comes out. He reaches for a cup of water and takes a long sip. "I've been fighting a cold all week, and it's finally caught up with me. It's the first sick day I've taken in three years."

My cheeks warm. Poor Tim. I wish I could be there to make him some soup. Although with my cooking skills, it would have to come out of a can. My problems seem too trivial to bother him. "Get some rest. Don't worry about me. We can talk when you're feeling better."

"No! I'm feeling better already. You're the best sort of medicine," he jokes. "I can sleep later. What's on your mind?"

Even when he's under the weather, he's putting me first. He really is a special man. I pull my knees to my chest. "I'm trying to stay positive and upbeat, but I'm frustrated with my body."

"You're an athlete. It's a normal emotion to feel."

For the first time in several weeks, the tight grip I've had on my emotions is beginning to waver. "It's my own stupid fault. My hip has been hurting for a long time. I thought I'd be able to push through it, and maybe by some miracle, it would just go away. But all I've managed to do is muck it up." My lips quiver. "I've been injury free almost my whole skating career. Why did this have to happen now?"

"Our bodies aren't machines. As hard as we try to keep them in tip-top condition, they still break down." Tim stays silent for a few moments, then he says, "I've been in your shoes Gem. I understand exactly what you're going through. Like you, I thought I could ignore my body when it was sending me signs to stop playing baseball and rest. I thought if I missed a day of practice or a workout, it was the end of the world."

He holds up his elbow to the camera. There's a long silvery scar that looks like a baseball seam extending from the bottom of his triceps to the middle of his forearm. "Do you see this?"

I nod.

"And this one?" He rolls up his shirtsleeve. At the top of his shoulder, there's a few puffy pink dots and a scar that curves like a smiley face.

"Yes." I swallow hard. "What happened?"

"The round scars are from an AC joint and rotator-cuff surgery, and the elbow was a UCL ligament reconstruction."

I swallow hard. "Both of those sound awful." By comparison, my hip doesn't seem that bad. "I'm sorry you had to go through them."

"I won't lie, they both sucked. But the point I wanted to make is that even though it seems like the universe hates you right now, everything happens for a reason." He leans in closer to the camera. "In my case, if my injuries hadn't ended my baseball career, I never would've become a teacher."

I bob my head up and down, thinking about what he's saying. As angry as I am with myself, I can't change the past. I should be focusing on the present and moving forward from the injury. What can I take away from it? "I guess if I have to find something positive, it's that I'm able to spend some time with you."

"Despite the circumstances, I'm looking forward to spending some time with you too." Tim's voice is growing hoarse. I've made him speak too much. "I've missed you."

I draw a small circle on the fabric of my bedsheet. "I've missed you too." If I were able to, I'd reach through the camera and wrap my arms around him tightly. Right now, I wish I could rest my head on his chest and sit with him until he fell asleep. Even if he is sick. He's my giant teddy bear.

Tim's body shakes as it's racked with another cough. He groans and rubs his temples. Seeing him in so much discomfort tugs at my heartstrings. I can't get to town quick enough. "Is there anything I can do to help you?"

"Thanks, but no. I just need to sleep this thing off." He half closes his eyes. "I just hope I'm well enough to teach on Monday. I don't have a lesson plan ready for a sub. And we have parent-teacher conferences coming up. I need to finish writing my reports on my students."

"Try not to stress and overthink. I'm sure one of your fellow teachers would step in and help if you couldn't."

He nods, fighting a yawn. His eyelids close. "You're right, my principal is fantastic."

"I won't keep you. Rest. I'll see you soon."

His eyes open a crack. "Good night, Gemma-rella."

"Good night, Timmy."

I click off my mobile screen and set the device down beside me. Even though he's feeling under the weather, Tim still took the time to talk to me when he could've been sleeping. When I get to Sequoia Valley, one of the first things I'm going to do is check in and see if he'll let me take care of him. Like me, he's an independent person, but there has to be something I can do for him, like his grocery shopping.

Maybe if I talk to Mum, she'll be able to give me a few more ideas. I glance at the time on my mobile. If I call home now, I should be able to catch my parents before they go to bed. I go into my contacts and tap her name.

"Hi, Gemma, how's my little girl doing?"

"Hi, Mum. I'm good. Sorry I'm ringing you so late, but there's a few things I need your advice on. How much time do you have?"

"As long as you need, sweetie. Start at the beginning."

"There's somebody special I met recently . . ."

Chapter Eleven

A few days later, I'm back in California. My body may ache, but it won't stop me from making the slow walk down the leaf-covered road leading to Tim's home. All this time, he's only been a ten-minute stroll from Charlie's place. I wish I'd known sooner!

The cabin comes into view, nestled among tall pines, smoke rising gently from its chimney. I can see Tim using the cozy building as his sanctuary like a modern-day superhero. Walking up the driveway, I pass a wooden carving of a sloth, then pause in front of the entry.

I notice a few succulents sitting on a windowsill, along with an Indiana Jones Chia Pet. I lean closer to the window to inspect it. A thick layer of green shoots is growing out of the top of his iconic hat. "Where did he manage to find that?"

"It was gift from a student," says Tim in a Batman-like voice.

I jump as the front door opens, my pulse racing like a golden retriever chasing a tennis ball. A shiver of delight shoots up my spine.

Tim crosses his arms and leans against the door frame, clad in a thick green jumper. He looks so much better. His cheeks are flushed, but his eyes are bright and alert. He's had time to shave and shower. The ends of his dark locks are damp and still dripping.

"Hey, Timmy." Uncertain if should hug him, kiss him, or otherwise greet him since we haven't spent much time together in person, I opt to shove the brown paper I'm holding in front of my body. "I'm glad you're feeling better. Um . . . this is from Frankie and Charlie. I think it's pie."

"Charlie knows my weakness." He chuckles and signals for me to come inside, stopping me just as I reach the entryway. His arm snakes its way across my midsection and brings me in tightly to him. My body relaxes. The woolen fabric of his jumper is soft against my cheek. I can still smell his shampoo, a melon scent. It's just as I imagined. Being held by Tim in real life is just like hugging a giant teddy. "Gemma-rella. I'm so happy you're here."

"Me too," I say, resting my head on his chest. I wish I could stay attached to him forever, but as a frigid breeze blows in and he shivers, I'm reminded he's still recovering from a nasty cold. I let go and close the door. "I don't know what flavor this is, but Frankie bought it yesterday."

"Let's see." He peeks inside the bag. "It's the fall classic, pumpkin."

I wrinkle my nose. "Bleh."

"The expression on your face is priceless." He starts to chuckle, but it turns into a cough. He taps his chest.

"Can I get you some water?"

He shakes his head. "I have some hot tea here." He reaches for a metal thermos and takes a long sip. "Much better." He clears his throat. "Tell them I said thanks."

Tim's cabin is laid out in an almost identical fashion to

Frankie and Charlie's. The main living area is open concept. There's a kitchen, living room, and two bedrooms. I expected his home to be wildly decorated just like the classroom I've seen during our video chats, but instead, it's minimalistic.

"Hmm, there's something else in here." Reaching inside, he pulls out a plain shoebox. He reads the paper taped to the top. "A Box of Awesome?"

"It's something I made for you." I study the floor. "Go on and open it."

I hear him setting the pie box and shoebox down on the counter and the lid opening. I look back up as he starts going through everything. I've put in sticky notes, pens, highlighters, hand sanitizer, tissues, a bag of chocolates, a pack of mini doughnuts, tea bags, a bottle of soda, a baseball, and aspirin.

"According to Mum, all teachers need four things—carbs, caffeine, a couple school supplies, and hand sanitizers. I know you've been stressed out, so I thought I'd make you a teacher survival kit of sorts. I know it's not that fancy, but—"

"It's perfect," he interjects.

Internally, I start doing my happy dance. Yes! I've hit a home run with him.

"I love the name you came up with. A Box of Awesome. That's so me." He flashes me a wide grin that sends a few goosebumps up my arm. "Every time I use it, I'll be thinking of you. I'm curious though, why the baseball?"

"I thought you'd like it better than a stress ball."

"You were right. It's much better." Holding it in his hands, he adjusts his fingers over the red seams. "Catch." He tosses it to me underhanded.

I fumble and catch it before it drops too low. "Underhand?" I tease, tossing it back to him.

"I can't throw overhand anymore with my bum shoulder. But even if I could, I wouldn't do it in the house. There are too many breakable plant pots." He gestures to the remainder of the living room. Tim's antique wooden desk contains a couple more Chia Pets and a small collection of cliché coffee cups that say, "World's Greatest Teacher."

"I see that." I'm kicking myself for my last remark. Quickly, I change the subject. "Is that another sloth?"

"Good eye. It is. I have two more sloth statues on the back porch, along with the rest of my Chia Pet collection."

My mouth drops open. More Chia Pets?

"I have a Yoda, a Darth Vader, Thing from *The Addams Family*, an Oscar the Grouch, a llama, and Baby Groot from *Guardians of the Galaxy*."

"Those are all from your students?"

"Most of them. Word got out that I enjoy them, and since then, it's become the go-to teacher appreciation gift." He shrugs.

I shift my weight from one foot to the other. My eyes squeeze shut for a moment as a sharp twinge jolts my leg.

"Gemma?"

My eyes flutter open. "I'm okay. Just a little achy."

"Did you walk here?"

I nod.

He presses his lips together. "I bet sitting on the plane for a couple of hours didn't do you any favors." Tim's forehead creases with worry. "I should've picked you up in my van."

I choose not to comment on the plane. The two connecting flights from Miami and seven hours of traveling left me so sore, I had a hard time standing up straight when

I landed in Fresno. But a hot shower, a few hours under the heating pad, and a good night's sleep have helped the muscles loosen. Thankfully, Frankie and Charlie didn't ask for too many details. Yet. I know Frankie is dying to. "Walking is good for me. It's on the approved list of exercises from my PT."

"Still, I feel horrible for not thinking of it." His shoulders droop. "When you texted me that you wanted to come over, I was focused on cleaning up."

"Tim, this place looks like a military barracks. It's spotless." I reach for his hand. "I don't know what you consider a mess, but this is cleaner than my flat would be if I owned one."

"I appreciate it, but I still have a sink full of dirty dishes, a pile of laundry, a—"

I press a finger to his lips. "If I can't see it, the mess doesn't exist."

He holds up his hands, resigned to letting me win the argument. "Let's get you off your feet." We take a seat on the sofa. He pushes a button on the arm and the foot pops up. I stretch my legs out and sigh in contentment. "While we're at it, we should crack open some of the goodies from the Box of Awesome. How do some doughnuts sound about now?"

"Aren't we going to dinner soon?"

"Yes, but it's a whole twenty-minute drive. And we may have to wait to be seated. I don't know about you, but I could definitely use a sugary pick-me-up."

"They're *your* goodies. Do what you want with them," I tease.

"Don't mind if I do." He stands and walks over to the box, plucking out the doughnuts. The plastic wrapping crinkles as he rips it open. "I wish I had my sense of smell back. I'm sure they'd smell delicious. I can't remember the last time I had a doughnut."

"Oh." My face falls. "I didn't know what type of desserts you liked besides pie."

"I love all desserts! Especially doughnuts. I'd eat them for every meal if I could, but I don't have as much time to spend in the gym these days. So I try not to keep too much stuff like this in the house. Otherwise, it's too tempting. I'd eat the entire package in one sitting."

Tim jokes about the lack of gym time, but he's still in very good shape. He could get away with passing for a high-level athlete. He has the lean physique of a swimmer, and from what I've seen through his shirts, defined muscles in his chest and arms. I don't doubt he also has some very sexy abs.

I take a doughnut for myself and let the sweetness melt on my tongue. "Mmm . . . brilliant. Chocolate is the best."

"Can I get you anything to drink? I have water, coffee, tea, orange juice, and a couple protein shakes."

"Just water, please. I'd love a coffee, but it's too late in the day for me."

"It's a good thing you're not a teacher, then." Tim picks out a glass in his kitchen and turns on the tap. "On school days, I usually have my last coffee around four."

"Really?

"Uh-huh. I need that jolt of caffeine to get through grading papers. Some of my students have horrible handwriting, and it's a mental workout trying to decipher what they've written."

"It can't be worse than a doctor's handwriting."

"Oh, it is. I have a couple essays sitting over there to prove it." He nods toward his desk. "Here you go."

"Thanks." I take hold of the glass and nibble on the

remainder of my doughnut. Tim sits next to me and sips from his tea. As my eyes travel the room, I can't help but notice he has a sloth-shaped lamp on his end table and a sloth-shaped clock on the wall.

An alarm bell sounds in my head. Up until now, Tim has seemed like the perfect guy. But now that I'm in his place and seeing all these sloth things, I can't help but wonder if he has a weird obsession with them. Is that going to be the thing that causes us to break up?

I pinch my lips together. I remind myself to calm down and not jump to conclusions as I might've done in the past. There has to be a good explanation for it. All I have to do is ask him. "Hey, Tim?"

"Hmm?"

"Why do you have so many sloth things?"

"So you've noticed them." He chuckles and sets his thermos down.

"I have. You've got a large collection."

"I do," he agrees. "There's actually two reasons—baseball and Costa Rica." Rolling up his trouser leg, he exposes the tattoo of a sloth wearing a green baseball uniform holding on to a baseball bat. "This guy here is the logo for an exhibition baseball team called the Scottsdale Sloths. I played three seasons with them out of college."

My forehead wrinkles. "I thought you injured yourself in college."

"I did. The Sloths aren't a normal baseball team. They're a performing team."

"I'm confused. What's the difference?"

"Think of what would happen if baseball and a musical comedy and had a baby. It'll make more sense if I show you."

Tim clicks on his smart telly and opens the SearchTube

app. Typing in the words "sloth ball," he loads a video onto the screen with baseball players in the same neon-green uniform as his tattoo.

Over the next five minutes, I watch in fascination as the Scottsdale Sloths perform a Rockettes-style kick line, sing classic nineties pop songs, and assemble a cheerleading pyramid, all while playing a game of baseball.

I lean forward in my seat. "How have I never seen this before?" I haven't had the heart to tell Tim that I find baseball boring. However, this exhibition baseball is a game changer. It's something I could get into.

"When I played for the team, it was still up-and-coming." Tim fights off another cough. "We played mostly in the Scottsdale area, but now, thanks to social media, the Sloths are growing in popularity. They went on their first national tour last year."

"Wow! And you played for three years?"

"I did. They were some of the best years of my life too. The Sloths gave me the second chance I never thought I'd have."

"Because of your injuries?"

He nods. "After I tore my rotator cuff, I was told by the doctors that my shoulder was one of the most messed-up ones they'd ever seen." He reaches for his mobile and swipes through his photos until he finds a black-and-white MRI image. "This is what a normal shoulder looks like . . . and this one is mine."

"Uh . . ."

"The white is bone. And the semi-white stuff here is cartilage." He flips back and forth between the two images.

"Oh." In the second image, the bones are sitting right against one another. They don't have a layer of cartilage acting as a cushion. "That's not good," I say slowly.

"It isn't," he confirms, setting his phone down and staring at the telly blankly. "I was told the joint is fragile and the risk of reinjury high. I was also informed I'd likely develop early onset arthritis. At the time, retiring was one of the toughest decisions I ever had to make."

I reach for his hand and stroke it with my thumb. I can only imagine being told as a teen to give up the sport you love. If I were in his shoes, I wouldn't have given up ice skating without a fight. "Tim, you don't have to talk about it if it's too painful."

He takes several deep breaths. "It's an important piece of my past." He brushes a stray lock of hair away from my forehead. His touch sends a shiver through my body. "I want you to know."

A fluttering sensation fills my stomach. He's ready to share an intimate part of himself with me. To this point, everything's been all fun and games. We've had a surface-level relationship. Am I ready for something deeper and more meaningful with this man before we've even had our first real date?

I swallow hard. All the other guys I've dated in the past, I've found reasons to run away from. For all my talk, I've never wanted a relationship I'd have to commit to. Tim is different. He's in my thoughts. In my dreams. He makes me smile when I read a text from him. And he's the man who's gotten me to start thinking about my life after skating.

I blink a few times. What is there to even have a think about? Of course I want more! "Tell me."

Tim's leg brushes against mine. I respond by resting my head on his shoulder, continuing to draw circles on his hand with my thumb.

"I was nineteen when I received the news about my shoulder. A year before that, I'd torn the ligament in my elbow. Having back-to-back injuries then being advised to retire seemed like the end of the world." He takes a deep breath. "I hit a downward spiral. I stopped going to my college classes and spent my time lying in my bed in the dark. I didn't see a point in doing anything."

I inhale sharply, placing a hand on his knee. This may have been in his past, but I still feel the need to remind him I'm here.

"I'm lucky. My college roommates called my parents and told them something was off. They made me come home and made sure I got the help I needed."

"It must've been a long road to recovery."

He nods. "It was more difficult than any physical injury. You don't know what to expect and there's no set recovery time." His face turns serious. "I still have some days where sometimes things get too heavy. They're rare, but they happen."

He stiffens. I can feel an intense energy coming from his body like a bolt of lightning striking a tree. His gaze locks with mine. The intensity of his stare asks me the silent question, "Is that a deal breaker?"

I take a few moments to compose my thoughts. "Tim, if you do have a bad day, I don't know what I'm supposed to do. I haven't had to deal with something as serious as depression. However"—I pivot my body so I'm facing him —"if you tell me how I can help you, you can count on me to be by your side."

He exhales and slides his hand up my arm, squeezing my shoulder. "Thank you," he says softly.

"It's a no-brainer. You're important to me."

He stares at me for several long moments. The Adam's apple in his throat bobs up and down. "You're important to me too."

He wraps his arms around me and hugs me tightly. Pressed against him, I feel completely at ease, like a cat napping on a soft rug in front of a roaring fire.

He excuses himself for a few minutes to refill his thermos and put away the doughnuts. I relax deeper into the couch and close my eyes. I meant every word I said to him. He's become a priority to me.

I've spent so much of my adult life living out of a suitcase and visiting a different city every few days. It's been an adventure that I've enjoyed every moment of. But if I had the chance, I wouldn't hesitate to trade all of that to be with Tim.

The future I see for myself isn't with Dreams on Ice. It's a future that revolves around me sitting next to Tim here on the sofa watching telly, snuggling into his chest, and spending hours talking to him about everything that pops into our minds. "I'm falling for you hard and fast," I whisper to the empty room.

When Tim returns, he's back to his animated self. He sits back down next to me and drapes an arm around my shoulders. Just as I'd imagined a few minutes ago, I use his body like a human pillow.

"Where were we?" he asks.

"You were about to tell me where the Sloths fit into this."

"Right, the Sloths! That happened in the spring semester of my senior year of college. One of my roommates saw a flyer in the student union looking for people to audition for a theatrical baseball team. They signed me up as a joke, thinking it would be hilarious to watch me sing and dance." His chest rumbles with laughter. "Well, I got the last laugh. My audition turned out to be answering a couple of questions over the phone. The team only wanted to know if I had some baseball skills and could teach others how to play. When I graduated, I had a job lined up as a designated hitter playing for the Sloths."

"Hold on." I frown. "How could you play if you were supposed to retire?"

"I did. My shoulder wouldn't be able to handle it. When I played for the Sloths, my job as a designated hitter meant I didn't play in the field. I only took at-bats."

"Oh, I see." I'm still confused, but I'll google what an at-bat is later. "It sounds like a dream scenario."

"It was, but there were a lot of challenges that first year." He rubs his temples. "Only half the guys on the Sloths roster had any baseball experience. The other half were actors or dancers. It was trial by fire. We had to learn how to work together to develop the skills we were missing, and quickly. Our games started six weeks after our first practice."

Spending so much time with such a tight-knit group of people can either be a good thing or a bad thing. In Tim's case, the excitement in his voice tells me all I need to know. "They became your second family, didn't they?"

He nods. "They're still the best friends I have."

"I know the feeling. How long did you play with the Sloths?"

"Three seasons. I loved every moment of it. And I got to scratch the itch of what it would be like playing professionally. But by the time I turned twenty-five, my gut instinct told me it was time to move on. There were other things I wanted to do with my life, like become a teacher. When you know, you know."

Hearing how Tim instinctually knew he was ready to close the door on his baseball career makes me wonder if it'll be the same for me when it's time for me to hang up my skates. Or will my body make that decision for me? There is so much about my future I don't know.

Sometime later, I yawn and stretch, still sitting on the couch. My pillow moves underneath me. "Gah! Did I fall asleep on you?" I squeak.

Tim removes his glasses and puts down his book. "Yes."

Covering my face with my hands, I shake my head and detach from him. "I'm so sorry. I didn't mean to trap you. I guess I was just so tired from traveling and you were so comfortable."

"Gemma, you don't have to explain it. I could tell you're exhausted. Plus, I liked it. You remind me of a baby sloth. They hold onto stuffed toys kind of like baby koalas."

"Baby sloths?" I rub my eyes. My brain is not computing. "Did your baseball team have a real sloth as a mascot? Is that even allowed?"

"I have no idea if that'd be legal, but it would've been awesome." Reaching for his mobile, Tim unlocks the screen and opens the photo app. "No, the baby sloths I'm talking about live in Costa Rica. After I stopped playing with the Sloths, I taught English there for a year. My host family rescued and rehabilitated them."

"Are the sloths why you went to Costa Rica?"

"No. It was just a coincidence. Anything sloth related just has a way of finding me."

We share a laugh. I take hold of the phone. My heart wants to melt at seeing the oversized eyes and cartoon-like expressions on the fuzzy baby sloth faces as I swipe through his photos. "They're so precious."

"They really are. I miss working with them."

I return his mobile to him, but not before I text myself one of the photos of a baby sloth hugging a teddy bear next to a shirtless Tim. "What's the strangest thing you learned about them?"

"Believe it or not, sloths only do their business once a week."

My eyes widen. "You're joking."

"Nope, definitely not." He slides the mobile back into his pocket. "Sloths digest their food slowly. A lot of the plants they eat are poisonous. Their stomachs have evolved over millions of years to be able to break down the toxins—the result is a once-a-week poop."

"I'm learning more about sloths than I ever thought I would." I shake my head. "They're definitely unique animals."

"Totally. It's why I love them. They're just like me, but in animal form."

He's got that right. Tim has a quirky personality and interests that are unlike any bloke I've dated. It makes him interesting. It's one of the qualities I'm most attracted to.

Standing up, Tim stretches. "It's seven-thirty—a little later than I'd planned for dinner. Are you still all right if we go out? I've been waiting to spoil you, Gemma-rella, and I thought we might wanna do something a little more special for our first in-person date. If not, we can postpone and order some takeout and keep things low-key. I have the patience of a sloth."

My pulse quickens at the word "date." It's finally happening. A shiver of delight runs up my spine. "I'd love to go out with you. Are you feeling up to it though? You know, since you've been sick."

"I'm tired, but nothing can keep me from missing our

date. Not an evil stepsister, a sea witch, or even a poison apple."

My lips twitch. That's what I'd hoped he'd say. "I guess this means we're officially moving from the friend zone and into the sloth zone."

"The sloth zone?" he asks.

"Uh-huh. The sloth zone," I repeat. "Nothing about our relationship so far has been traditional. We've been doing things at our own speed and in our style. Like sloths."

He chuckles. "When you put it like that, I guess we are."

"Have you ever been to a classic American diner before?" Tim asks a half hour later as he parks the car in front of the Lucky Dog Diner.

"No. This is a first."

"This is one of my favorite places in the area. I can't wait to bring you here in the summer. They host weekly drive-in movies."

"That sounds amazing." I have a flash of us sitting in the boot of Tim's van, enjoying burgers and chips.

I close the car door and follow him to the entrance. The building's brick walls are adorned with vintage soda-pop advertisements and hand-painted murals depicting scenes of life in Sequoia Valley. My eyes, however, are drawn up to the roof, where there's a statue of a giant dachshund dressed in a chef's hat and a bow tie.

"What is the story with the large dog?" I ask.

"That's Zippy, the mascot of the place." Tim holds the front door open for me. "When the diner opened in the forties, the real-life Zippy used to greet customers as they walked in. He'd wear a little hat and tie, just like the statue."

"Is there still a Zippy?"

"I wish. The current owners have huskies. They don't allow dogs inside unless they're service animals."

Entering the restaurant, I'm enveloped by the scent of brewing coffee, sizzling bacon, and freshly baked pies. The air hums with the lively chatter of customers seated at the counter facing the cook. Retro big-band music plays softly in the background. It's like walking onto the set of *Grease.*

"Hey, Steve." Tim waves. The chef nods in acknowledgment. A few of the customers at the counter swivel their seats around and also exchange greetings with him. He must be a regular at this place. Everybody seems to know one another.

We take a seat in one of the red vinyl booths in the back corner of the diner. Large windows look out onto the darkened pine forest. "The Lucky Dog has the best burgers, fries, hot dogs, and milkshakes. I used to come here as a kid every weekend with my dad after fishing on the lake," Tim says. "I know this might not have been the type of restaurant you were expecting." He hands me one of the laminated double-sided menus situated on the table by the ketchup and mustard. "So if you don't see anything you like, we can go to Millie's Steakhouse or somewhere else."

This place is special to him, and I'm honored he wanted to share it with me. He's not trying to impress me by taking me somewhere expensive. He's being his authentic self. I place a hand on top of his. "No. This place is perfect." A few moments of silence pass between us as I stare at the menu. "Just remind me when I order to ask for fries instead of chips."

"Um, sure . . ." His eyes dart back and forth in confusion.

"Back home, it's what we call American fries." I glance over the top of my menu. "Last time I ordered some, I forgot they're called fries, and I ended up with a plate of crisps. What you call potato chips."

"Oh. I've always wondered why fish and chips are called fish and chips and not fish and fries. I should've made the connection," Tim says.

"Now you know." I scan over the menu one more time. "Hmm, I know I want a burger. I'm just debating between onion rings or the chips. Which one would you go for?"

"You can't go wrong with either. Everything is made from scratch." Tim leans back in the booth. "How about if we order one of each and split them?"

"Deal."

I watch as Tim waves to the chef again. He nods and taps a bell. A couple of moments later, a server in a red-and-white checked uniform roller-skates over to our table and takes our order. We both opt for the old-fashioned burger.

"This place has a lot of memories. It's where my parents had their first date, and where I celebrated my high school graduation." Tim rests his elbows on the table. "When you mentioned coming back to Sequoia Valley, I knew I had to bring you here."

Tim has celebrated so many milestones in his life here. And now, that includes our first date. Should I take this as a sign of where things could be headed? How Tim feels about me?

I swallow hard. Originally, I was only open to having a long-distance relationship with him, but now I don't know if my heart would be able to handle being apart from him for so long. Ugh. What does this mean for me?

There are so many questions floating around in my head. I can only hope this trip helps me figure them all out.

Chapter Twelve

A few days later, I take a few moments to catch my breath and stretch my leg out in front of Tim's cabin. I probably shouldn't have taken the short walk up the hill. I hang my head. I'm frustrated at being so weak and unable to do something as normal as taking a ten-minute walk.

I've been diligent in resting and doing my PT exercises every day, but I don't think it's making a difference. There's still a constant ache and flashes of shooting pain. At least I have Tim to help distract me. Standing upright, I rap my knuckles against his cabin door.

"It's open," he calls out from inside. I turn the doorknob and let myself in. Tim stands in the kitchen, watering the last of his plants on the windowsill. "You're early. I didn't expect you until noon."

I've been ready and awake for hours, eagerly waiting to see where Tim plans to take me for our date today. I couldn't sleep last night. So many scenarios ran through my head. He hinted that it would be some type of picnic, but if

I know Tim, he has something else planned. Just like his personality, everything he does is over the top. "I wanted us to maximize our time together."

"Good to know you find me irresistible."

He puffs his chest out, and I stare for a moment longer than necessary, drinking in the sight of him in his black henley and jeans. My cheeks warm as I consider what he'd look like in a kilt. It'd be the perfect clothing item to show off his long, toned legs. Add in my family's hunter-green, red, and yellow tartan and he'd be irresistible. Green, after all, is his color.

I quickly look away, putting down the blanket I borrowed from Frankie. "What's on the agenda for today?"

"It's a surprise."

I lean against the wall, taking some of the pressure off my leg, and bat my eyelashes at him. "If I ask nicely, can I have a hint about where we're heading?"

He chuckles. "It's somewhere on the coast."

"That doesn't help." I pout. "California has a long coast."

"That's all I'm willing to say for now, except that it's about a two-hour drive to our picnic spot." Picking up his car keys from the nail by the door, he gestures to a wicker basket on the kitchen island. "Can you manage that?"

"Yes. It's my hip that's bad, not my arms." I flex and pose like a bodybuilder. "See, this skater is strong." He stares for a moment, causing me to second-guess myself.

His neck and the tips of his ears flush red. "If you ever join me at a Comic-Con, you'd make the perfect Captain Marvel," he says, his voice slightly hoarse.

Is that a good thing? Is Captain Marvel a man or woman? I wrinkle my nose. It has to be a woman. What kind of hero is she? "I've never heard of her. Is she a friend of Batman? We could go as a couple."

"No, she's in the Marvel universe."

I tilt my head. "OK?"

"She's friends with Thor, Spider-Man, Iron Man, and the Hulk."

As he explains more about the difference between the various superhero universes, my mind checks out. I'm getting better at this, but it's still too much information for me to process. It doesn't help that I'm distracted by how animated he is as he talks. I pick up the basket, taking purposefully slower steps to mask my discomfort.

"Before she was a superhero, Captain Marvel was an Air Force fighter pilot." Tim wheels a cooler behind him on our way out. He locks the door, then heads to the car. "Not only is she wicked smart, but she has some awesome powers like flying and the ability to absorb and manipulate energy."

We get in the car. "You had me at flying. That's the one power I've always thought was the best. It reminds me of Tinker Bell," I tease. "What about you? What would your superhero power of choice be?"

Tim backs the car out of the driveway and onto the main road. "I wouldn't want anything that's too flashy. I think I'd like to be able to breathe underwater or control the weather."

"You know, with power over the weather, that means you could wield thunder, lightning, hurricanes, and all of nature's most powerful forces," I counter.

"Fair point." His eyes crinkle. "In that case, I'd just be happy to be able to make it rain or be sunny at will."

"Going back to what you said earlier—you mentioned going to comic conventions? Do you do that often?"

"Not as much as I'd like. I try to get to LA Comic-Con during my spring break. If I'm lucky with the ticket lottery for San Diego Comic-Con during the summer, I'll go to that one too."

"What do you do when you're there?" I imagine a room full of people, with lads about Tim's age swapping comic books and trading cards. The adult version of things you'd do on a playground. But how do they make a full day out of it?

"For me, the biggest draw is hanging with other people who like the same stuff I do—comics, anime, sci-fi films, et cetera. But there's other stuff to do like attending panels with different actors, writers, and graphic artists, autograph sessions, shopping, and costume contests too."

Okay, that makes a lot more sense. "Do you wear a costume when you go?"

"Take a wild guess," Tim challenges.

I blink slowly. "Of course you do."

"It makes the experience more fun. Why limit dressing up to Halloween?"

"Who do you dress as?"

Tim begins to hum the *Batman* theme song. I envision him in Batman's mask, body armor, and long flowing cape. Something that strikes me suddenly is that all these superhero costumes are formfitting—Batman included.

If his outfit included a bodysuit, it'd hug his body like a second skin. I'd be able to see the defined ridges of his biceps and triceps. His sculpted pecs and the other muscles of his chest. And the legs. I haven't gotten a peek at those yet, but if I superimpose what I imagined they'd look like earlier when I fantasized about him in a kilt . . . I fan myself with my hand.

"You hot, Gem?" Tim asks, glancing in my direction. "I can turn on the air if you want."

"I'm brilliant," I squeak. "Just forgot to remove my jumper. Car rides always make me overheat."

"Do you want me to pull over so you can take it off? I don't want you being uncomfortable."

"No," I say quickly. "I'll be fine once my body adjusts."

"Okay. Just let me know if you change your mind."

"I will." Little does he know what's actually making me hot.

The landscape stays relatively the same for the first forty-five minutes of our drive. We're still surrounded by dense forest. State Highway Three seems to wind around the same mountain for miles and miles. The constant popping of my ears, however, tells me that we've changed elevation several times.

Then the trees began to thin out, and as the road descends, I spot towering sand dunes and the beach. Pelicans, seagulls, and other seabirds circle overhead. Waves break against the soft-looking white sand. "I'm surprised there aren't any people on the beach."

"The area we're passing through is all a protected part of the national seashore. There's a lot of seabirds that can only nest here."

"Got it—so no people allowed." The water sparkles like turquoise jewels under the expanse of a clear blue sky. "I'm glad. It's beautiful. I'd hate to see it change."

"Agreed. It reminds me a lot of Costa Rica." He turns the minivan down an unmarked road surrounded on both sides by yet more trees. It bumps along until coming to a stop in a deserted clearing. "Here we are!" He glances at the clock. "Right on time too. The midday heat makes them the most active."

I unlatch my seat belt. "And what would 'they' be?"

"You'll see in a couple of minutes." We climb out of the car. "We'll come back for the picnic supplies after our hike. For now, all you'll need is your jacket."

My heart drops, and I dry swallow. "Um, Tim, how far are we going?"

"Not far, maybe a half mile."

"Uh, is it all uphill?" I chew on my lower lip. Should I tell him how sore my hip really is? I look his direction. He's whistling as he zips up a puffer vest and slips a pair of binoculars around his neck. I shift my weight from one foot to the other. No, I don't want to ruin this. I want to enjoy our date and see whatever it is we've come to see. If I walk slowly, I'll be able to manage. I hope.

"Don't worry, Gem. The path we're taking is all flat," he reassures me. His eyes lock on to mine. "If it's too much for you, I can carry you or give you a piggyback ride."

I'm trusting you, Timmy. "Mmm-kay."

The dirt path may be flat, but it's not completely even. We take a cautious sloth-like pace and carefully avoid the exposed tree roots. Every step is like having a rock inside my trainers. I attempt to block out my discomfort by focusing on the stunning surroundings. The fresh scents of pine and mud. The rays of sunlight filtering through the trees.

We walk in silence for a few minutes. There's only the sound of pine needles crunching under our feet and the odd bird call. Tim's eyes scan the tops of the pine, eucalyptus, and cypress trees until he holds up his hand for us to stop.

"Ah-ha, got you," he mutters under his breath. "Okay,

bear with me here. Do you see that long orange-and-white thing that resembles a party streamer?"

I stare in the direction he's pointing. I see leaves and branches, but no streamer. "No."

Taking hold of my hand, Tim gently repositions me to where he stands. He hands me his binoculars. "Look again and try these. I forgot I had them on. They're nestled near the top. There's about a thousand of them."

He points to a long, flowing ribbon-like structure swaying in the breeze. Pressing the binoculars against my nose, I gasp. "Are those . . ."

"Monarch butterflies. Beautiful, aren't they?"

There are indeed hundreds and hundreds of butterflies with black, orange, and white markings clumped together. I discounted them a moment ago as a branch, but now that I know what to look for, there's no mistaking them for being a part of a tree.

"They migrate and go dormant here for the winter. The trees along the coast are the perfect shelter from the cold, and any storms or rain."

It's like we've stepped into the pages of a real-life fairy tale. I can't stop grinning. "Can we get closer?"

"Yeah, as long as we stay on the path. We don't want to disturb them."

Our voices grow to a soft whisper as we step carefully, mindful of any flying insects that might be resting on the ground. Tim points out more groupings of butterflies as we approach one of the trees they favor.

This area of the path is bathed in a patch of warm sunlight. My eyes widen with wonder. I can't believe he's brought me here. This is as close as you can get to an enchanted forest. The butterflies flutter and almost dance around me. I reach out my hand, and one lands on my palm, its tiny legs tickling my skin. I watch, mesmerized, as it flaps its wings.

My attention shifts to Tim. Looking up at him through my eyelashes, I watch as he holds his arm out in front of him. No less than twenty butterflies flock to him.

"Sugar water," he whispers. "They think it's nectar. Do you want some too?"

"No, I'm happy to just watch."

Every single date I've ever been on pales in comparison to this. Tim's planned our outing from his heart. He wanted to give me an experience, not just spend time together. My breath catches in my throat.

I've searched high and low, long and hard, for the right bloke for me. From my thundering pulse to the magnetic pull my body experiences when he's nearby, all the signs are telling me that I've finally found him.

"Gemma?"

"Hmm?"

Tim shakes his arms, and the butterflies take flight. "You look like a nature sprite," he says, licking his lips.

Our eyes lock. His are wide with lust. He *wants* me. I've been itching to kiss him since the night of the Halloween Festival. "At home, we'd call that a fae."

My pulse takes off like the speed of a hummingbird's wings, beating several hundred times a minute. The butterfly on my hand takes flight. I carefully close the distance between us.

Our bodies are pressed close now. We're breathing the same air. Heat rolls off him. He nuzzles my neck. I turn my head to the side. Slowly, he plants a soft trail of kisses leading up to my mouth. The stubble of his facial hair rubs against the tender skin of my cheeks.

"You're so beautiful," he whispers. Moving my hair out

from around my face, he traces my lips with his thumb. "I'm going to kiss you just like the butterflies here drink nectar from a wildflower."

True to his word, his lips brush against mine, and alone in the estuary, with the company of the butterflies, we share our first kiss.

Chapter Thirteen

The remainder of the weekend passes all too quickly for me, and before I know it, it's Monday again. I lament that Tim is back at work. I can still feel the way he held me and the lingering warmth of his kiss upon my lips.

"Which date are you reliving?" Frankie teases, joining me at the kitchen island with a cup of green tea.

"The butterfly picnic." I smile into my cup of coffee and take a long drink.

Frankie sighs. "I have to hand it to Tim. He's a genius at coming up with unique dates."

Charlie huffs as he opens the fridge and pulls out a protein shake. "And I'm not?"

Frankie and I exchange glances.

"You are in your own way," she says diplomatically. "You took me hiking and to Millie's Steakhouse. Those were places that were special to you. I love that. It allowed me to see your sparkling personality and your heart."

"That's better," Charlie says, still frowning. "You know, Frankie, I was thinking . . . we've been training really hard.

How would you like to take a day off Wednesday to go out on a sunset boat ride on Lake Wakahanra, or we could do something like go horseback riding?"

My friend perks up with interest. "Do you mean that, Charlie?"

"Yup. In fact, why should we wait until Wednesday? Let's go tomorrow. There's a ranch on the far side of the lake that does half-day rentals. I'll give them a call now and see if we can reserve two horses."

Frankie and I giggle as he disappears into his temporary man cave, the garage. Once again, I've taken over his normal space in the second bedroom.

"Charlie is so adorable when he's jealous. I would've said something about Tim earlier if I'd known it meant he would take me horseback riding."

"Now you know for future reference."

We giggle again.

"You look so happy and relaxed, Gem. I'm thrilled things are going well with Tim. Does this mean you're going to pass up *Cupid's Arrow* if they call you again?"

"We both know it's not going to happen. But if it does, yes, I'm gonna tell them I'm not interested anymore. We haven't been together long, but I have a good feeling about him and where our relationship could go."

"Oh, I hope this works out." Frankie hugs me tightly. "We should plan a double date after our next competition."

"I'd like that." Changing the subject, I ask, "What time are you guys heading back to the rink for your second training session today?"

"Not until one. Are you planning on joining us? Richelle's been asking about you. Charlie has her at three today."

I set my coffee back on the table. I still haven't told

Frankie and Charlie the real reason I'm in town. Neither of them have asked or said anything, but I'm sure they've picked up on the fact that I haven't been skating once since I've been here. "You know what, I think I will. I've been dying to see how your program is coming along in person. And I'd like to see Richelle too."

"Good news, Frankie." Charlie reenters the room with a cocky swagger in his step. "I snagged the last pair of horses. We're all set for tomorrow."

"Eek. I'm so excited." My bestie smiles as she walks over and kisses him. "Thank you!"

My gaze turns to the window as I watch the branches of the pine trees surrounding Charlie's cabin sway in the breeze. I wonder what Tim's up to right now. Is he sitting in the teacher's lounge munching on his lunch? Reading a comic book? He mentioned he had big plans for us this weekend. He's going to have a difficult time topping the butterflies.

I dream of us standing under the canopy of trees again. Goosebumps form on my arms as Tim wraps his own arms around me and cradles me against his chest. The soft cotton of his shirt brushes against my cheeks, and when I reach up, I—

"Earth to Gemma." Charlie clears his throat.

I snap my head in his direction, folding my hands on my lap. My cheeks sear with heat. "Er . . . yes?"

"Suzy just sent a text reminding Charlie to find out if you wanted to join us for Thanksgiving next week," Frankie says, resting her head on his chest. "That is assuming you're planning to still be around."

"Oh, I'm invited?"

"Gem, why would you ever think you wouldn't be invited to join us?" Frankie's eyes widen. "It's just like when

I talked you into canceling that hotel room across town the last time you were here. You always have a standing invitation."

"I didn't want to assume." I stare at the ground. "It's your first Thanksgiving with Charlie and your dad with Suzy. What if you wanted it to only be family?"

"Gem, you *are* family."

"Ditto to what Frankie said. You're just as much a sister to me as Leslie," Charlie emphasizes. "Nan would be insulted if you didn't show up to dinner. She loves you."

"And so does my dad," Frankie adds.

"As long as you're sure, it's a yes from me."

"Let's end it here, Frankie," Charlie says, glancing at the clock. The large red numbers on the hockey scoreboard read two-thirty. He releases Frankie's hand and helps her up from the ice. The ending pose of their program involves them kneeling in one another's embrace.

"Sounds good to me." Frankie brushes off her skating trousers and skates over to the hockey bench where I'm sitting. "How'd we do?" she asks, taking hold of her water bottle.

"Brilliantly, although I still prefer your *My Fair Lady* program from last year."

She nods, replacing the cap on the bottle. "I don't think anything will ever top that program."

"Why'd you decide to change it? Lots of skaters keep the same program two years in a row."

"We were planning to keep it," Charlie says, glancing to Frankie.

"Until the American Skating Union coaching staff strongly advised us at the summer preview to go a different direction," Frankie finishes.

"Ah." When your national federation gives you a recommendation to follow, you do it. Otherwise, it sends the signal to the national staff that you're difficult to work with and not team players. It could cost you funding and international assignments.

Although Frankie and Charlie may be highly experienced skaters, as a team, they're still brand-spanking new. They don't have enough clout for their opinions to matter yet. But I don't think that phase will last too long. They already have the highest score this season of any American pairs team.

"Anyway, I'm gonna head over to the pros' room and change. I have Richelle in twenty." Charlie pecks Frankie on the cheek. "You joining me, Gem, or are you heading back home with Frankie?"

"I'll stay for a little bit," I reply.

Charlie nods. "We'll be on the other rink. I'll meet you there." He gathers his jacket and bottle, and skates off toward the exit.

Frankie takes her time putting on her jacket. Getting up from my perch, I stretch, biting back a sharp wince. I walk out of the sitting area and step onto the ice. I know I shouldn't be wearing skates or be out here, but I'm only an observer today. There's no way I could fall and get hurt.

"Are you and Tim going out again tonight?" Frankie asks as we glide toward the exit.

"No. I don't want to keep him out late since he has to be up early for work tomorrow. We'll probably order takeaway and watch a film."

Frankie giggles. "Five bucks says it's a Batman movie."

"Nope, I'm not making a bet. I'm sure you're right." Tim started my Batman education with some of the "classic" films this weekend. We binged *Batman Begins* and *Batman Forever*. Like the James Bond films, I never realized there are so many different actors who have played the caped crusader. It's been an eye-opening experience.

Frankie smirks.

"Do you think I should—" My skate blade suddenly hits a rut. I fall forward, slamming my knees against the ice, and slide forward as if I'm an Olympic skeleton athlete.

"Gemma!" Frankie shouts, rushing over to me. "Are you okay?"

"Fine," I bite out automatically, lying still. "Just need a second." I'm actually far from fine. My legs are on fire. Falling on the ice is basically hitting concrete, except it's colder and wetter. I groan as I slowly push myself up to a stand, reaching for the wall. Frankie grabs my waist and helps lift me. My right leg buckles. I take several deep breaths.

I continue gripping the wall hard enough for my fingers to turn white. The only thought that goes through my head is how dumb and reckless I've been. I hope I haven't royally set myself back with a fall like this. "Can you help me get off the ice? I don't think I can do it on my own."

Chapter Fourteen

Gemma: I hate to do this, but I need to
cancel date night.

Tim: Whatever you need, Gem. Is
everything okay?

Gemma: Sort of.

I debate how much to tell him as I recline on Charlie's sofa. My eyes travel to the bags of ice on my knees. Removing the one on my "good" leg, I roll up the edge of my pajamas and take a peek at the damage. It's a spectacular shade of dark purple, red, and a sprinkling of light green.

I inhale sharply. I can't even make out the edge of my kneecap because it's so swollen. I'm sure the right is just as bad. And over the next twenty-four hours, it'll get even worse. If I hope to see Tim in the next few days, I won't be able to hide my latest injury. Walking is going to be H-E-double-hockey-sticks.

I continue typing

Gemma: I had a freak fall at the rink
today.

Tim: But I thought you weren't supposed
to skate.

Gemma: I'm not. And I wasn't technically
skating. I was watching my friends.

I know it was a stupid decision. I should never
have tempted fate and stepped foot on the ice, but it's
too late to change what happened. I've learned my
lesson.

Tim: What can I do to make you feel
better?

Gemma: Spend time with me tomorrow?
I could use some TLC from you!

Tim: You've got it. If you need anything
in the meantime, I'm only a call or bat
signal away.

My lips twitch.

Gemma: Thank you. *Heart emoji*

The following day, I spend all my time in the lead
up to my date with my legs elevated and wrapped
with Ace bandages. I'm stiff to the point that I
walk like a zombie. There's so much fluid in my knees, they
don't bend very far. My hip has also chosen to retaliate

against me. I can't stand without using furniture as a crutch.

I debate canceling again on Tim, but I'm dying to get some fresh air and see his handsome face.

Gemma: *Bat emoji*

Tim: Yes, Gemma-rella?

I tuck my chin to my chest as I type.

Gemma: I can't make the walk to your place. I'm going to need a ride.

Tim: I'll be there in ten.

Gemma: Thank you. And I'm sorry for being an inconvenience.

Tim: Don't be. I'll see you soon.

I manage to make it to the porch swing out front. Tim double-parks his van in the empty carport. I stand and hobble in his direction. The driver's door opens and closes, and he sprints over to me. "Gem, you should've told me it was this bad."

"It's not," I say through gritted teeth. Tim slips his shoulder under my arm and takes most of my weight. "It's just a couple of bruises. I've had worse."

"Bruises can be just as painful as a broken bone." He opens the passenger door and lifts me into the seat, careful not to jostle me. I don't bother fighting him. I'm relieved not to have to attempt stepping up into the car. "I'll always remember the time I got hit by a pitch right on my bicep. The pain was up there with tearing the UCL in my elbow. It took a solid three weeks for it to feel normal again."

I grimace. "I hope my knees recover before then. I already have a bum hip and walking is a struggle."

He closes the car door and hops into the driver's seat. "I noticed you were limping the other day. Every time you thought my back was turned, your face was filled with tension. Fighting the pain." Turning on the engine, he reverses and starts down the street to his home. "You can't go on like this, Gem."

I hang my head. "I know," I whisper. "I'm scared of what the doctor is going to say." A few stray tears run down my cheeks. "Skating is my life and my identity. I've been doing it since I was three. I'm not ready to give it all up."

"I know, Gem, I know."

We pull into his driveway. He comes around to my side of the car, takes me in his arms, and holds me. "Let it all out."

I sob into his chest, unable to stop once I've started. The salty tears run into my mouth. For the last few weeks, I feel like I've been trapped inside a bottle, watching events unfold outside of it. I'm exhausted. Nothing I do has made a difference in healing my hip. All I want is to go back to normal.

"Not knowing what's going on is scary. But it'll be okay. I'm living proof of that." Tim starts to rock me. I curl up against him, as if he's my lifeline in a stormy sea. His chest rumbles and he begins to sing the Beatles song "Let it Be" softly in a deep, rich tone. For a man who claimed he can't sing, he hits all the notes without any issue.

By the time I've calmed down and we make it inside his living room. It's completely dark outside. Tim lights the wood burner. The fire crackles and flames dance over the logs. He gives me a bowl of chocolate ice cream topped with hot fudge and drapes a thick blanket over my legs.

Although I'm reluctant, I bring him up to speed on my hip and Mel's treatment plan.

"If you want my opinion, I think the sooner you see a doctor, the better. You're only going to prolong the agony both physically and mentally the longer you wait." Tim sits down next to me, munching on his own vanilla and hot-fudge dessert. "Playing the what-if game is torture. It's why you're so frightened. Because you don't know what's going on."

Tim's right, of course. The dread has been like a swarm of termites eating me from the inside out. It's time for me to get an answer.

"I had my shoulder surgery done at the UCLA Medical Center. I still keep in touch with the doctor who treated me. He's a top orthopedic surgeon. I'd be happy to reach out and see if he has any appointments open while you're here," Tim offers.

"Thanks, but no." I shake my head. "There's another doctor in the area I want to get in touch with first." I take a bite of my ice cream. "Do you remember Richelle's dad from the Halloween festival? Dr. Zhang?"

"Uh-huh."

I'd forgotten until now that I still have his card in my wristlet. "He's the team doctor for the Jasper Ridge Jaguars hockey team. He knows how a figure skater's body works. He's my first choice." I make a mental note to call his office in the morning.

Tim lets out a long whistle. "That's a handy connection to have."

"If he can squeeze me in, do you think you could come with me?" I ask.

"Of course. Give me the time and date and I'll be there. No matter what." His eyes gleam with determination.

My heart flutters. He's here to take care of me. I'm continuing to fall deeper and deeper in love with this man.

On Friday, Tim and I arrive at the headquarters of the Jasper Ridge Jaguars.

"Thanks for taking the day off to come with me. But I hope you're not going to get in trouble for it." Throughout the entire car ride here, my pulse has been racing. His support means the world to me, but I know it wasn't easy for him. Tim took three sick days less than two weeks ago when he was getting over that nasty cold. And I remember him saying that as a rule of thumb, taking time off is frowned upon.

"You're important to me." My stomach performs a few backflips. "And arranging for a substitute was a no-brainer." He opens the lobby door for me. "It's a minimum day. School's out at eleven. All the kids are doing is watching a movie. Their minds are in vacation mode since they're off all next week."

"They get a full week? I thought you'd only get two days."

"That's how it was when I was a kid, but times have changed."

Entering the building's lobby, I spy the team's logo, a fierce orange jaguar jumping out of a circle with a hockey stick in its mouth, painted on the wall behind a reception desk manned by two security officers.

"Can I help you guys?" one of the officers asks.

I shift my handbag from one shoulder to the other. "Hi, I'm Gemma MacLeod. I'm here to meet with Dr. Zhang at ten-fifteen."

"Do you have your IDs with you?"

Tim reaches into his back pocket for his wallet. My hands stay glued to my handbag strap. "Um, no. I didn't think I'd need my passport." I blink twice. "I have a photo of it on my mobile. Will that do?"

The security officer stares at his computer screen and types in a few things. "If that's all you have, I guess we don't have much of a choice." He copies some information from the documents and issues us temporary visitors' badges. "Dr. Zhang's office is on the fourth floor, suite number 405. Keep this visible at all times and don't forget to turn them in when you depart."

We step into the lift and press the button for four. I wipe my palms against my trousers. My breathing grows shallow.

Noticing my discomfort, Tim places a hand on the small of my back. "It'll be okay, Gem. We're here to get some answers."

A few moments later, there's a ding and the doors open. Dr. Zhang greets us. He's dressed the same as he was the night of the festival, in a blue dress shirt, gray trousers, and a white lab coat with his name embroidered on it. "Gemma, nice to see you again. The front desk just alerted me that you were here."

"Hi, Dr. Zhang, the feeling's mutual. Thanks for fitting me in on such short notice. I'm not sure if you remember him, but this is Tim Lyons."

"I remember." Dr. Zhang chuckles and shakes hands with Tim. "You actually had my son Zaden two years ago."

"Zaden?" Tim strokes his chin. "Oh, Zaden! I remember him! He was the tallest student in his class and my best speller. How's he doing?"

"Zaden's good. He's shot up another couple of inches,

believe it or not. At thirteen, he's even taller than I am. We have no idea where his height comes from, but hey, genetics work in mysterious ways."

Dr. Zhang leads us down the hall to his office. It's filled with all different types of top-of-the-line gym and medical equipment. He sits behind a large desk and gestures for us to do the same. "So tell me, Gemma. What's been going on with your right hip?"

I mentioned some information over the phone, but didn't go into detail. "I started having some pain a couple of weeks ago."

"And is this something you've had before?" he asks.

"Yes." I nod. "On and off for the last six months. The last doctor I saw diagnosed me with tendonitis."

"Uh-huh." He scribbles a few notes onto his tablet. "And how did they treat it?"

"With physical therapy."

Dr. Zhang arches an eyebrow. "No rest."

"No," I say, folding my hands on my lap. His forehead crinkles as he records a few more notes. I glance over at Tim, whose lips are pressed together.

"And how is your pain right now?"

"An eight out of ten." If he's going to help me, I need to tell him everything. "It was about a six last week, but I took a tumble at the ice rink on Monday. Since then, it's been buckling when I overexert myself, and aching constantly."

I answer a few more questions for Dr. Zhang. Tim continues stroke my hand, although from how he's fidgeting in his seat, I can tell he's becoming agitated. And I have to admit, I am too. Dr. Zhang is not one of those doctors who's able to mask his thoughts very well. His deep-set frown and the number of notes he's writing give him away. It looks like Mel was right. The last doctor I saw didn't do a proper job of treating me.

"Thanks for bearing with me. We're almost done." Dr. Zhang clears his throat. "I'd like to give you a quick examination before we pop down to the MRI machine."

"You have an MRI machine on site?" Tim's eyes widen.

"I thought you'd send us somewhere for a scan."

"No, we have one downstairs." Dr. Zhang chuckles. "The Jaguars' ownership group hasn't spared any expenses when it comes to their players' medical treatments."

"Huh. That must be nice," Tim muses.

"It is and it isn't. I'm able to diagnose my patients quickly, but it's rare that I have a week where I don't have to use it."

We make our way over to the exam table. Dr. Zhang asks me to demonstrate a few different exercises, looking at the range of motion in my leg. Then he palpates the area. He's quick and efficient, but still takes the time to explain everything he's doing and what he's looking for. My stress levels drop. I'm reassured I made the right decision coming to see him. He's clearly very experienced and has seen injuries like mine before.

A couple of minutes later, I'm once again seated at his desk. "Based on your history and my own examination, I'd say that the muscles and ligaments in and around your hip have been inflamed for a long time."

Not a surprise given the amount of physical activity I'd usually do daily—an off-ice warm-up, an on-ice warm-up, followed by our show. On days we have double and triple shows, you can multiply all this by two or three. When you consider that we're lucky to get one full day off a week, you have the perfect recipe for a chronic overuse injury.

"This is the MRI of your good hip." He loads a black-

and-white image on his tablet and spins it toward Tim and me. "This area here, where the head of the femur meets the acetabulum, is where we have what's called the labrum. It's a ligament that acts like a cushion between the two bones."

"Uh-huh." The human body is an amazing piece of machinery. Every muscle, ligament, tendon, and bone has a specific purpose. It's fascinating to see what they look like up close.

"When we move to the image of your right side, you can see that we have all sorts of fraying." He enlarges the image. It reminds me of the split ends of a rope that's started to unravel. It's hard to believe that something the size of a paperclip could be causing me so much misery.

Dr. Zhang continues. "That's where the instability you've mentioned is coming from. The labrum on this side is partially torn."

I inhale sharply and scoot to the edge of my seat. It's the worst-case scenario come true. I feel like a bride receiving the news that her dress has been lost the day before the wedding. "Torn?"

"I'm afraid so," Dr. Zhang says calmly, folding his hands together. "But what you need to know is this is a common injury for figure skaters and hockey players, and it's completely repairable with surgery. Give it six to eight weeks for rest and recovery and you'll be back on the ice before you know it."

"Surgery?" My fingers coil tightly around the arm of the chair. "Six to eight weeks." I pause for a moment and swallow hard. The news is sending shockwaves through my system. My head has been buried in the sand. All I can hear is the muffled words "tear" and "surgery" repeating over and over again.

"Dr. Zhang, would you mind if we took a moment?" Tim says. I turn my head and stare blankly at him.

"Sure. I need to grab my charging cable anyway. I'll be right back." He stands and exits the room, giving us a moment of privacy.

"Gem, take a deep breath." Tim places a hand under my chin and gently raises it. His eyes lock onto mine. "I know this is a lot of information to process, but Dr. Zhang sounds confident you'll be able to recover from this and skate again just as well as before the injury. That's good news."

"But it's surgery," I sputter.

"Yes, it is." He nods. "From experience, I can say a lot of injuries to tendons and ligaments don't heal well on their own. Surgery is a necessary evil."

I understand what he's saying. But it still doesn't soothe how I'm feeling right now. "I'm scared," I admit.

"Come here." He assists me out of my chair and slides me onto his lap, his arms encircling me in a comforting hug. My head rests on his chest. I feel each rise and fall as he breaths and take in the clean scent of his woodsy cologne. My tense muscles slowly relax. "What you're feeling is totally normal. Especially when it's an experience you've never had before. I've had surgery three times now, and I was still nervous each time."

"You were?" I murmur.

"Uh-huh." He nods, rubbing the back of my neck with his thumb. "But you know what? I knew that one, my doctors were experts and had done the surgery a ton of times before. And two, the sooner the procedure was done, the sooner I could be pain free and start the healing process."

My mind is still like a snow globe that's been shaken up.

As the pieces of snow fall, I'm beginning to wrap my head around it all. As much as the thought of having my body sliced open freaks me out, the notion of being pain-free again is enough for me to push those fears aside and seriously consider going through with the surgery. There hasn't been a day in the last few weeks where I haven't been hurting. Even when I sleep, I toss and turn for hours. I'm mentally and physically exhausted.

Tim cups my cheeks. "Let Dr. Zhang know how you feel. Ask him questions. And don't forget, I'm here for you too."

"Okay."

He kisses the top of my head. "That's my Gemma-rella."

Dr. Zhang reenters the room. I scramble to climb off Tim's chest and back into my seat. The doctor's eyes dance in amusement.

"Did you find your charger?" Tim asks, buying me a moment to gather my thoughts.

"I did. It was in my car. My son borrowed it to charge his phone on the way to school." He fixes his attention on me. "Well, Gemma, do you have any questions for me?"

Like a lantern cutting through a thick layer of fog, Tim's pep talk has helped focus my thoughts. "I know surgery is probably the route I'll take, but are there any non-surgical treatment options for labrum tears?"

"Mm-hmm. There are. If that's the route you wanted to take, we'd focus on treating the symptoms of your injury. You'd continue with physical therapy and rest." He shoots me a pointed look. "Which means *no* skating. Or being on the ice."

"That's what I'm doing now." Well, what I was trying

to do. I run my fingers through my hair. "The rest seemed to be helping before my, uh, latest setback."

"Mm-hmm. Being off the ice was likely allowing the inflammation in your hip to subside."

This sounds too good to be true. What am I missing? There has to be a catch.

"If that's the case, could Gemma get away without having any surgery?" Tim asks.

"That depends on your goals. The labrum is a ligament that doesn't heal on its own. Without any surgical intervention, you wouldn't be able to continue skating as you currently are. You might be able to coach, but competitive or show skating would be out of the question due to the stress loads on the ligament."

Oh. That's why he said treat the symptoms. It's not a cure. PT is only patching me up with a bandage and buying me more time. "If I had surgery, how would it work?"

"The surgery is done by arthroscope." Dr. Zhang scoots his chair back to a cabinet behind his desk and pulls out a long thin instrument with a tiny light and camera attached to the top. "I'd make a few small incisions about the width of a pencil around your hip with this and tie the torn parts of the ligament back together. These days, it's an outpatient procedure. You'd be walking out of here on the same day."

Tim turns the arthroscope over in his hands. "I wish they could've used this on my shoulder."

"Hmm, I'm surprised they didn't. Most shoulder injuries can be scoped," Dr. Zhang says.

"I had a full tear. Wasn't an option."

"Ah, that makes sense."

Tim passes the instrument to me. I don't understand how something so small can do the repair, but hey, I'll take it. One of my major concerns, being on bed rest, has been alleviated. Dr. Zhang has made the procedure sound like a trip to the dentist's office. I'd be in and out on the same day *and* walking. "What's the total recovery time?"

"Bodies all heal at different rates. On average, return to full activity from a labrum repair tends to take about three to four months. Patients start with six weeks of PT, three times a week, and adjust accordingly. You could be on the ice in as little as a month if you're hoping to coach as you recover. Of course, that would be no jumps, spins, or anything risky until I fully clear you."

"I'd be a model patient," I deadpan.

"I'm not worried about you. Unlike my hockey players, figure skaters are more patient patients." Dr. Zhang chuckles at his pun. "They understand that recovery can't be rushed."

My eyes dart over the side-by-side images of my good hip and my injured hip. I'm due back on tour in a week, and I'll be expected to skate. From now through New Year's, we're going into our busiest time of the year. That means triple-show days four times a week.

Even though I'm injured, it's an all-hands-on-deck situation. Being down even a single skater hurts. It means somebody will have to forego their day off. With the amount of illness and fatigue that goes around, you depend on it to survive. "How soon would I need the surgery? If I continued with a non-surgical treatment plan for the present, could I continue skating on tour?"

Tim shoots me a "you can't be serious" look and clenches his jaw. I ignore him and focus on the doctor.

"I'd highly recommend you consider doing it sooner rather than later. We don't want the ligament to tear any more than it already has." Dr. Zhang sighs. "However, if you can handle the discomfort and limit the amount of stress you're loading onto the joint, I don't see why you can't skate."

I bite my lip. I'll be doing the opposite of all that, but maybe there's a way I can find a happy medium. What if I gave up jumping? I'm sure that would be enough just to get me through to January. After that, I can take some leave and have the procedure done.

"Do you have any other questions?"

"Not right now. I think you've answered them all. Thank you, Dr. Zhang."

"Gemma, you can't seriously be thinking about skating with your hip like this? You can barely walk," Tim says, helping me into the passenger seat as we leave Dr. Zhang's office.

"That's only because my knees are bruised and full of fluid. That injury should heal in a couple of days." I stare out onto the road, watching the passing scenery. "As for going back to Dreams on Ice, I know it's less than ideal, but the company needs me. We're a family. Everybody is counting on everyone else to be able to pull their weight. If I go out on injury leave, everybody else pays the price. I only need to hang on until January. After that, I can have Dr. Zhang do the surgery."

We pull out of the car park and head onto State Highway 3.

"That's a lot to ask of your body. What if the tear worsens because of all the extra skating?" Tim says.

"It could happen, but Mel's a fantastic physical therapist. She'll keep a watchful eye on me and make sure I'm taking care of myself."

"But Gemma—"

I cut him off. "Tim, I know your heart is in the right place, but I won't change my mind about this."

He glances in my direction. "You know yourself best." He sighs, thankfully letting the matter drop.

Deep down, I know he has a lot of valid points. But Dreams on Ice has always taken care of me. I owe it to them to at least try to make it through the next few weeks. All athletes are trained to push past pain. I can do this. At least I think I can.

Chapter Fifteen

The week flies by, and on Saturday morning, I'm shocked when Tim announces with a gleeful grin that he's taking us to Fresno for the day. The timing is good. My knees are just about back to their normal size and my hip has started to feel better too. I'm in good enough shape to be able to walk around today as long as the pace is slow and steady. We've gotten an extra early start on the road. It's nearing seven forty-five in the morning.

"And what are we going to find in Fresno this weekend?" I've only ever passed through as a passenger at the airport. There hasn't really been any reason to explore the mid-sized California city—until now.

"There are two things—sloths and more sloths." Tim glances at me with a wide brimming grin. "You look so confused."

"I am. Where are we going to find sloths in Fresno?" As the car turns the corner, a sign welcomes us to the Fresno Zoo. Everything suddenly clicks. "Oh, of course! The zoo!"

Excitement fills my body. I can't remember the last time I was at a zoo.

We share a laugh.

A few minutes later, Tim laces his fingers through mine, and we stroll up to the ticket booth. I can't think of a better way to spend the day. I just hope my hip will hold up. This might involve more walking than I'd planned for. Hopefully I won't have to rent one of the electric wheelchairs.

Leaning casually against the window, Tim says, "Hello. We're here to check in for the . . ." He lowers his voice so I can't hear. Just what does he have planned?

"Got it. What's the last name?" the zoo worker asks.

"Lyons. Party of two."

The worker pulls up the reservation and prints the tickets. "Here you go. Just wear the badge on the outside of your shirt. Your guide this morning is Judy."

Peeling the backing off the sticker, I stick it onto my blue jumper. We linger near the entrance, my heart pounding wildly. He's done it *again.* "Tim, did you book a tour? Because if you have, you've already spoiled me to death."

"I did." He flashes me a cheeky smile. "It's the best way to see the zoo when we're on a tight schedule. Plus, we won't have to deal with all the families that'll overrun the place once it opens."

Hmm. The mystery continues. If we're on a schedule, what else does he have in store for us? Rising up onto my toes, I lean forward and peck him on the cheek. "Thank you."

He sighs contentedly and rubs the spot I've just kissed. "A guy could get used to this."

A woman in her mid-forties wearing a khaki-colored

jacket, trousers, and a button-up shirt approaches. "Hi, guys, I'm Judy. You two must be my visitors this morning. If you follow me over to the golf cart, I'll take you around back to a couple of places the public doesn't normally get to see. Since the sea lions are barking up a storm, we'll start with them."

"Is it just the two of us?" I glance around, but there's nobody else.

"You're our VIPs."

I open and close my mouth. A private tour must've cost him a small fortune. And on a teacher's salary! "Tim . . ."

He plays ignorant and tugs my hand toward the cart. "Let's get this party started."

Over the course of the morning, Tim and I toss fish to the herd of greedy sea lions, look in at the baby tiger cubs inside the zoo's nursery, and feed heads of lettuce to the Masai giraffes. Just as I think one experience can't top another, we arrive at the sloth enclosure.

"We have two-toed sloths here at the zoo," Judy says. "This enclosure is home to a fella named Roger. He's about four years old."

Tim rubs his hands together. "I'm dying to meet him."

The humidity of the air rises sharply. The lens of my mobile's camera fogs up. It's like walking into a sauna. Small beads of perspiration drip down the back of my neck as I tie my hair up into a messy bun. Tim's hair is also damp. He runs a hand through his thick brown locks, reminding me of a shampoo commercial. If I saw him on the telly, I'd buy whatever he's selling in a heartbeat.

Judy unlocks the exhibit and signals for us to follow her inside. The room contains a waterfall and about ten different branches of varying heights. Birds and monkeys chirp inside the neighboring enclosures. Roger is easy to spot, hanging upside down near the far side of the room. Two legs hang on to different branches, and his arms hug a third. His long claws rival that of a dinosaur's.

"I thought I'd have you guys feed Roger, then help me with his training session."

"What do they eat?" I ask.

"All different types of leaves, flowers, fruits, and insects. Today he'll be getting some fruits, veggies, nuts, and hard-boiled eggs."

"I was about to ask what you used to supplement their protein." Tim explains that he has experience working with rehabilitating wild sloths, and they also used eggs in Costa Rica.

Judy brings out a cup and removes its top. The noise seems to wake Roger up. He opens his eyes and studies us quizzically upside down. I have to admit, he's adorable.

"Who wants to feed Roger first?"

Tim isn't shy about stepping forward. With confidence, he approaches the sloth and places a few nuts inside his mouth. His big expressive eyes study Tim as he scratches the top of Roger's head with two fingers. "You like that, big guy, don't you?" he says.

Fine lines appear around his mouth and eyelids. His grin is a mile wide. But it's the way he's glowing from the inside out that makes him so handsome. I snap a few photos of him. And may or may not set that as my wallpaper.

When it's my turn, my hands shake. I know sloths are gentle, but up close, he's larger than I thought he'd be.

"He won't bite." Tim chuckles.

I shoot him a nervous smile and offer Roger some berries. He opens his mouth, and I toss them inside. He chews slowly, watching me, almost appearing amused. Remembering how Tim pet him, I run two fingers down his back. It feels wiry like a hairbrush. "Huh. I thought you'd be soft."

Tim laughs. "Nope. His fur has to be water repellent since it rains so much in Costa Rica."

I continue to stroke him. My anxiety returns when I realize that Roger has stopped moving. I gasp. "Is he okay? Did I do something wrong?"

Judy takes a couple of steps closer. She snorts. "Oh, Roger's fine. He's asleep."

"In the middle of eating?"

"Yeah, it happens all the time. He'll wake up in a couple minutes."

I splay a hand on my chest. "That's a relief."

Judy picks up her bucket. "Come on, I'll take you two over to the public-facing side of the enclosure to see Esmeralda, our female sloth. She's recently become a mom."

Inside a room that resembles a rainforest, Judy points to her lips in a shushing motion, then to a sloth a little smaller than Roger who's asleep sitting on a branch like a koala bear. Esmerelda's bundle of joy rests its little head against her chest, a patch of fuzzy hair poking up.

Tim drapes an arm over my shoulder. His long fingers lightly brush my bicep, and my body hums in delight. "He's so precious," I whisper. Slipping out my mobile, I snap a few photos. "This is the highlight of the day so far."

"For me too." He kisses my neck. His lips are silky soft. I wish we were alone. I'd love nothing more than to kiss him senseless right now. I sigh. I'll just have to wait until later.

After we ask a couple more questions about the sloths, we walk out to the golf cart and Judy drops us back at the zoo's entrance. Families with strollers have lined up outside the front gate, chatting excitedly. It reminds me of the line to enter Disneyland at park opening.

"I guess the zoo is the place to be this morning." I giggle. "I'm glad we had the place practically to ourselves. It made the visit all the more special. Thank you for spoiling me." I nuzzle my nose against Tim's and peck him on the cheek.

"You're welcome." He glances at his watch. "We have about a half hour before we need to head out. Are there any other animals you'd like to see?"

"The elephants!" I clap my hands together. "They're my favorite animal."

"As my Gemma-rella commands." He bows and offers me his arm.

As we arrive at the stadium where the Fresno Flying Squirrels minor league baseball team plays, there's a queue several hundred people long snaking around the facility. Adults and children alike chat animatedly. Many of them are wearing neon-green shirts and yellow hats.

"That's a lot of people," I say wearily. We might have to wait several hours before we'll make it inside to what I assume is a baseball game. "It looks almost as long as the Wimbledon ticket queue. You usually have to camp overnight to make it in, and that's only if you're lucky."

My shoulders hunch. "I, er, might have to wait here in the car and have you save our spots in line until we're near the front." I hate that I'm even having to admit that to Tim when he's bouncing with excitement. But I might as well be honest.

"Lines are for the rookies." He grasps my wrist, and we saunter up to the entrance. "I have connections."

"Are you friends with one of the Fresno players?"

"Nope." His lips twitch.

"A coach?"

"You're getting warmer . . ."

As Tim has a short conversation with one of the security guards, my eyes travel to the family standing closest to us. I squint at their shirts and blink a few times. It's a brown sloth hanging from a baseball bat, the same design as the tattoo on Tim's leg.

I pivot around and take a closer look at the people in the queue. I see jerseys with "Sloths" and "Scottsdale" embroidered in gold. A few kids carrying stuffed sloths. And there are even some people wearing stuffed sloths as hats. "Are we here for a Sloths game?"

The security guard waves us through, and we enter the stadium.

"It's better than that! We're here to watch today's open auditions for the team! Surprise!" The enthusiasm in Tim's voice hits a twenty out of ten. "It'll be just as much fun as watching an episode of *Cupid's Arrow.* They're three rounds to the auditions." He starts speaking a mile a minute, gesturing wildly with his hands as he launches into a detailed explanation of what each round entails.

I shake my head and hide a giggle with my hand. The energy he's putting out right now is like a star on the verge of a supernova. Tim is fully in his element. I've never seen him happier. He's literally bouncing as he walks, and smiling so wide, I hope it doesn't break his face. And boy, is it sexy. I may not have been too thrilled about being here a few minutes ago, but now I am. Tim has let me into his world. I get an up-close look at how my man ticks.

I shade my eyes as we walk out toward the pristine emerald-green field to the lowest level. Tents have been erected with stages in three different areas of the field, labeled with white banners. There is one for registration, one for costume pickup, two for dancing, two for singing, and one that says "Trick Showcase." I'm especially curious to see what the last one means.

"Let's see if we can grab seats near the front before the gates open," Tim says.

"And what time would that be?"

"Ten."

"Timmy!" somebody shouts.

We turn and watch as two blokes in green shirts and white baseball trousers vault over the barrier between the field and the spectator area to join us. I step to the side as they mob Tim like children opening their gifts from Father Christmas.

"The Flaming Bat is back in the house! Why didn't you tell us you were coming?" one of the players asks. "We could've had a mini team reunion at dinner last night."

Hmm, the Flaming Bat? Is that a nickname Tim used to have?

"Because, Brett . . . Timmy has an *actual* job."

"I knew that!"

"Pfft, I doubt that."

"Guys!" Tim exclaims. "There's someone I'd like to introduce you to."

They freeze, release him, and both turn to stare at me. I hold up my hand and wave it in amusement. "Hello."

The guys immediately clear their throats, their expressions sheepish. "Hi . . . sorry, we didn't see you there," the taller of the two apologizes. He stands about six feet tall and has ash-blond hair. His beard extends below his chin.

"Yeah, we're really sorry. Normally we're better behaved than this." The second guy has a shaved head and a scraggly red beard shorter than the blond bloke. He's about five-foot-eight and boasts the beginnings of a beer belly.

Tim lets out a laugh, clearly amused. "Guys, this is Gemma. Gemma, meet Joe and Brett."

"It's nice to meet you two."

"Likewise," says Brett, the redhead. We all shake hands.

Joe clears his throat. "We'll catch up with you later."

The guys hop back over the fence, leaving Tim and me alone. I wonder if they've changed much from their days playing for the Sloths together. "They're nice."

"I swear, Brett and Joe normally have better manners than cavemen." Tim rubs his temples.

"Were they the chaps you were closest to on the team?"

Tim nods. "Two of the three. Our other friend, Eric, couldn't be here today. He lives in Hawaii."

He's clearly known about the auditions for a while. I'm surprised he didn't want to come down and spend more time with them while they're here. Brett—or was it Joe, I've already forgotten which one is which—mentioned a team dinner last night.

He could've gone to that, but he didn't. He spent the evening with me. We had dinner at the Lucky Dog, then went home and watched another Batman film. As I see how important the Sloths are to Tim, it's not lost on me that I was his priority. My heart flutters.

We walk down the steps and take two seats in the middle of the second row. Tim explains that if we sit at the end, people might be asking us to get up every time they want to pass us. He worries about my hip. I appreciate his thoughtfulness. It's tightened up since we left Sequoia Valley.

About ten minutes before the gates are due to open, Brett. . .at least I think it's Brett. . . jogs up the steps and removes his hat. "Er . . . Timmy, Gemma, sorry to barge in on you guys, but we have a big favor to ask you."

Tim's forehead wrinkles. "What's up?"

"Mike was supposed to be our third judge today, but his flight was delayed, and he isn't going to be able to make it until late afternoon. Would you be willing to fill in for him as one of the judges?"

Tim hesitates and glances at me, then to Brett. "I can't. It wouldn't be fair to Gemma."

"I told Joe it was a long shot. We understand."

I pull on Tim's forearm. He turns to look at me. "Tim, it's okay. Go. Be a judge today. I know how much the Sloths mean to you. Choosing the next generation of players is important. There's nobody better suited to the task than you." I know judging is something he wants to do. He's been so generous to me. It's my turn to return the favor.

"Gemma, no. Today is supposed to be a date. If I go down to the field and judge, I'll be there all day. I don't want to leave you alone."

"You're such a sweet man, especially when you're trying to be a hero. You always try to please too many people. I'll be fine. I'm a big gal." I playfully push his arm. "I'll see you afterward. In the meantime, if I have questions, I'll text you."

"Are you sure?"

"Positive. Now crack on with it already," I urge.

"Thanks, Gemma. We'll take good care of Timmy today. I promise," Brett says.

I grin. "He's among Sloths. I know he's in good hands. Or should I say claws."

The guys chuckle. Tim collects his jacket and glances one more time at me before heading down to the field.

"You're a lucky guy, Timmy. Why didn't you tell us about your smoking-hot girlfriend before?" I hear Brett ask.

"I'm selfish. I don't like to share."

He called me his girlfriend! Me! We've taken things slow per his request. I've been hoping the boyfriend-girlfriend stage was where we'd be headed when we left the sloth zone, and we have! I fan myself. I never thought this day would come. It's been months of looking for the right guy, and waiting to hear from *Cupid's Arrow*, but none of that matters anymore. At long last, Gemma-rella has found her prince.

A few other guys in green Sloth shirts come over to greet Tim once he's at one of the tents. It's clear he's a popular person—the man of the hour.

A few minutes later, the gates officially open, and a trio of women claims the row ahead of me, chatting about Tim, Joe, and Brett.

"I can't believe our luck. Did you see who the judges are on this side? We have the Blockbuster, the Maverick, and the Flaming Bat! Talk about an all-star lineup. Everybody is going to be flocking to this tent once they find out."

There it is again—that nickname. The Flaming Bat. Curiosity gets the better of me. Leaning forward, I tap the woman with long brown hair and a denim jacket on the shoulder. "Sorry, I couldn't help but overhear you. If you don't mind me asking, what's so great about these three gents?"

"They're legends! The Blockbuster used to have the most spectacular catches on the team. The Maverick would come up with the craziest skits and dance numbers, and the Flaming Bat . . . well, he's the team's all-time home-run record holder and the only guy ever to take an at-bat with his bat literally on fire."

Tim has the home-run record? And can hit with a flaming bat? How does that work? I make a mental note to look it up on SearchTube when I have a moment. "I see, thanks for sharing." I settle back in my seat just as an announcer comes over the PA system.

"Ladies and gentlemen, boys and girls, welcome to this year's Fresno Sloth Ball Tryouts. We're thrilled that you've given up your Saturday to join us. Please direct your attention to the scoreboard in center field for a short video introducing this year's judges."

As I watch the video with clips from past seasons, with Joe, Brett, and Tim walking out onto the field imitating sloths, I realize just how little I know about Tim's time with the team. Just as I'd thought I was getting to know who Tim is, another mystery appears.

Chapter Sixteen

Just when I could've sworn I've seen everything at the trick showcase—a guy performing with his trio of trained dancing puppies, a lad flipping on his mini trampoline, and a man riding into the tent on a unicycle—a bloke attempts to enter the dance tent on a pair of towering stilts. He wears a neon-green suit and top hat and has painted his face to match. As he bends his head, it's clear that he's too tall. Brett, Joe, and Tim get up out of their seats and walk outside to greet him.

"Welcome in . . ." Joe glances at his tablet. "Sterling. I see you've put a lot of thought into today's audition."

"I have." Sterling nods.

"Great. Then let's start the timer and show us what you've got." Tim clicks a remote and a country tune begins playing.

Sterling taps his foot and starts off with a line dance. A couple of seconds later, the music changes to "I'm Too Sexy." He steps over the fence and parades up and down the front row with his model walk. I join the other spectators in clapping to the music.

Shrugging out of his green suit jacket, he swings it above his head and tosses it to the crowd. Underneath, his well-defined body is painted with the Sloths' logo. The music changes one final time to "The Greatest Show." Sterling continues to dance and ends in a split. "Wow!" I say.

Everyone around me jumps to their feet. I place my fingers in my mouth and let out a shrill whistle, then clap so hard the palms of my hands grow numb. He'd better make the team with a performance like that! If the Sloths want someone who can put on a show, it's him.

Sterling gets to his feet, bows, blows a few kisses, and climbs back over the fence. Brett, Joe, and Tim huddle together in a circle. A few moments later, Tim scribbles the word "Scottsdale" on the back of a piece of paper. "Sterling, that was something else. I speak for all the Sloths' staff when I say, we'll see you in Arizona."

The crowd cheers again, attracting the attention of those sitting in other areas of the stadium. Sterling nods in gratitude to the judges and power walks, still in the stilts, over to a middle-aged man and woman, who I guess might be his parents.

The public address announcer comes on the speaker. "We'll be taking a forty-five-minute lunch break. Now is the time if you haven't already visited the Sloth Shop—make your way up to section number . . ."

I tune out the rest. All around me, people stand and stretch. Taking out my mobile from my handbag, I notice a message from Tim. Perfect timing because I've been dying to touch base with him. I glance at the field and frown when I don't see him.

> Tim: Are you enjoying it so far?

Gemma: I am. If this is how the auditions
are, I'd love to make it to a game!

Tim: *Grinning emoji* We can go
anytime. Do you have a favorite moment
so far?

Gemma: The stilts bloke!

Tim: Agreed!

Three dots blink as Tim types.

Tim: This is top-secret classified
information, but us too. I can't remember
anyone ever getting sent directly to
Scottsdale before.

I let out a long whistle.

Gemma: If there had to be a first,
Sterling deserved it.

Tim: Agreed. Now I have a question for
you. Would you like to come down to the
field during the break?

Gemma: Yes! Yes! Yes!

I can't think of a better way to pass the time.

Tim: Come down to the fence, I'll be
waiting for you.

Gemma: *Thumbs-up emoji*

As if I'm fighting a current to swim upstream, I get out
of my seat and turn my body sideways as I push past the

fans making their way up the steps to the concession stands, heading down toward the field instead. I move slowly. My hip is cranky after sitting in some uncomfortably hard seats for a few hours.

A few fans linger near the railing, attempting to catch Tim's attention.

"Yo, Lyons, can we have your autograph?"

"Mr. Flaming Bat! Can we get a picture with you?"

"Of course." Tim's cheeks flush pink, and he shoots a quick look of apology in my direction.

I watch as he reaches over the railing and signs a hat, T-shirts, and a few programs, stopping to pose in between for some photos. I'm struck by how attentive and engaging he is with the fans, treating them as if they're his long-time friends. It's no wonder he makes such a good teacher.

When he finishes with the last child, I hear him say, "The rest of the team and players will be signing out front after tryouts."

"Thank you!"

I laugh, unable to help myself. As the assembled group disappears, I take my own spot on the railing, right in front of my boyfriend. I still can't get used to saying that word. "You're Mr. Popular today."

"Sorry about that." He rubs the back of his neck. "It's weird. I've been retired from the Sloths for a couple of years, but I'm more popular now than I was back in the day with everyone watching our early videos on SearchTube."

Hmm, I wonder if they sell jerseys with Tim's name and number on it. What was his number? That'll be one of the next things I investigate. If I find one, I'm buying it and having him autograph it.

Placing his hands on my waist, he lifts me over the fence and kisses me on the cheek. The sensation sends a hum of electricity through my body. Tim's stronger than he looks. If he ever took a few ice-skating lessons, I wager he wouldn't make a half-bad pairs partner for me. "You were so good with those fans just now."

"We wouldn't be here if it weren't for them. Sloth Ball was created to build lifelong fans, not just to play games and make money. It's our motto—fans first. Wherever we can, we try our best to give the people who come watch us a memorable experience and be accessible to them."

Lacing his hand through mine, Tim leads me to home plate. "There's something special I'd like you to see." Hand on my shoulder, he spins me around. "Look behind you."

From this vantage point, I can see just about everything in the stadium. "What a view," I whisper. There's a carpet of pristine green grass extending to the outfield, flags waving in the wind, and a few players playing catch. As I glance up into the stands, I see people moving up and down the rows of seats like ants, and members of the media perched inside the press box. This is his playground. Just as the ice rink is mine. "Does being out here make you miss it?"

"Yes." He flashes me a sad smile. "There's nothing like playing in front of a big, energetic crowd hyping you up when you're about to take an at-bat."

I walk my fingers up Tim's arm. "How did you get the nickname the Flaming Bat?"

His neck flushes a deep shade of red. "By, uh, setting my bat on fire when I was at the plate."

I dip my chin to my chest. "Seriously? I thought it meant you were just a consistent hitter." I think back to what I heard about Tim holding the Sloths' home-run record.

"No, I'm completely serious. Looking back, it was one

of the most foolish things I could've done. Who in their right mind lights a piece of wood on fire when you play on a grass field? There are so many things that could go wrong."

"And the team's management didn't care?"

"No. They were more invested in the performance aspect of the game than safety. They used to tell us, 'The bigger the trick, the better.'" He runs a hand through his hair. "We operated on the mantra that it's easier to ask for forgiveness after the fact."

"Oh no." I shake my head.

"Anyway, are you okay with eating catering from the truck the team ordered? It's burgers and fries from BBQ Shack."

"Sounds brilliant." We grabbed a light breakfast before leaving town, but that was hours ago. The intoxicating scent of barbecue has never smelled so good.

We join a short line of people queuing in front of a food truck parked on the edge of the dirt track in the outfield. Another video of Tim taking an at-bat appears on the giant video screen. I watch in awe as the orange flames dance across the wooden bat. I have to admit, it looks unreal. And I have to know, "Who came up with the idea for the flaming bat?"

"You're not going to let the flaming bat go, are you?" he teases.

"Nope."

"It was a team effort." He sighs. "Brett and I were in Vegas for one of our buddies' birthdays. I don't remember if it was day or night, but we were walking down the Strip back to our hotel when we saw a street performer light his batons on fire. I'd seen it on TV before, but when it's in person, it's even more impressive."

I nod.

"That image stuck with me for a couple weeks. Brett and I wondered if there was a way we could do something like that on the baseball field."

"How exactly do you get the fire effect on the bat? Is it hollow, with a candle or some other mechanism on the inside?"

"No. Nothing that fancy."

"So . . ."

"Now remember, we were dumb, just-out-of-college kids."

"Okay," I say slowly.

"What we did was, uh . . ." Tim makes a sheepish face. "Dump kerosene on the bat and let it go."

My eyes widen. Have I heard him correctly? "You what?"

"We soaked the bat in lighter fluid and lit it up to see what would happen. We thought the bat would stay ignited for a few seconds. And it did."

"I hope you at least wore fireproof gloves and had a fire extinguisher nearby."

"Yes to both of those." I breathe a sigh of relief, even though his days of being the Flaming Bat have long since passed.

Over lunch, Tim runs into a few more former players and introduces me to more of his enormous extended Sloths family. Everyone is kind, and unsurprisingly, has a larger-than-life personalitiy. I can see why Tim enjoyed his time on the team. I'm reminded of one of those fraternities you see in American films.

"I wish everybody had name tags. It would be easier for me to keep them straight. I've met Joe, Brett, Jorge, Casey,

Dirk, Felipe, Greg, Will, Alex, and . . ." I scrunch my nose, not quite able to put my finger on the last name.

"Al," Tim adds.

I face-palm. "Al. How could I forget Big Al? He's a literal giant." As I learned from Tim, Big Al was the player who pioneered the use of stilts in a Sloths' game.

"Don't worry, you're doing great. I'm impressed you've managed to remember all those people." Tim tucks his rubbish onto his tray. "Are you all done?"

"Oh yeah."

"Perfect, I'll take those."

I add my rubbish to his. Brett finds us just as he stands. "Timmy! Look!" He holds up a plastic bag from a hardware store.

Tim grimaces. "No."

Brett's face falls. "You don't even know what's in here."

"I don't, but I have a good guess." Tim deposits the trash into the closest rubbish bin and wipes his hands on his trousers. "I'll say it again. The answer is no."

"Come on, Timmy . . . It would be an amazing way to engage the crowd and hype them up for the last part of the day."

I stare in confusion.

"I'm not going to change my mind." He crosses his arms.

"Not even for your girlfriend?" Brett nods toward me. "I bet she'd love to see the Flaming Bat work his magic in the flesh."

He rubs his temples. "Look, Brett, even if I wanted to, I don't have the gloves or the—"

The words die on his lips as his friend pulls a fire extinguisher and gloves from the bag. "Come on, where's your sense of adventure?"

"It was replaced by common sense when I became a teacher."

Joe joins the group, coming to stand beside them with a goofy grin on his face. "Mike's excited and—"

"He said no," Brett interrupts.

Poor Tim, his friends are putting him on the spot! I'm proud of him for holding his ground, but it's all over his face, he wants to do it. I chew on my lip. On one hand, the rational side of me doesn't want to see him putting himself in any danger. But on the other hand, I'm morbidly curious and would like to see one of these famous flaming bats at least once. Ugh. Should I encourage him?

"Uh . . ." Joe's cheeks redden as he looks from Tim to Brett. "We already told some of the fans."

Tim throws his head back and groans.

"Tim, I think you should just do it. As long as there are safety precautions in place, it would be brilliant for the fans to see, and if I'm being honest . . ." I walk my fingers up his arm. "I'd like to see the master at work."

He takes a deep breath. "There's no way I can get out of this, is there?"

"No," we all say at the same time.

"Fine. I'll do it, but if this goes sideways, it's on you two."

Joe and Brett high-five one another.

I rise up onto my toes and peck Tim on the cheek. "I believe in you."

"Hey, Sloth fans! Do we have a real treat for you! He's best known for being our record holder for hitting the most home runs with his fiery bat, and today, he's agreed to give a demonstration of how it's done just for you all. Let's welcome the man, the myth, the legend . . . the one and only Flaming Bat himself . . . Tiiiiiiiiiiiiim Lyyyyyyyyyyyyyyyons!"

The crowd roars so loudly that I'm halfway tempted to poke my fingers inside of my eardrums. Standing near the visitors' dugout, I look on as Tim appears at the lip of the home dugout, now dressed in a neon-green uniform. Giving a quick wave and tip of his cap to the crowd, he adjusts his gloves and takes a deep breath.

I lick my lips. Seeing him like this puts his Indy costume to shame. The top few buttons of his jersey are undone, exposing a flash of tanned skin and defined pecs. Veins are bulging in his arms as his sculpted muscles expand and contract when he adjusts his grip on the bat.

"Light her up," he mouths to Joe.

Flames engulf the wooden bat almost immediately as Tim approaches home plate. He adjusts his stance and nods to the pitcher. I nibble on my nails nervously, watching the orange flame dance from the top of the bat down to the nub.

Tim digs his feet into the ground and bends his knees. He lifts the flaming bat just above his head. Small drops of perspiration drip down the side of his face. Shifting his weight from side to side, he remains laser focused on his target. The pitcher releases the ball toward him. He swings, and every head in the stadium watches the ball sail high into the air and over the wall in the farthest part of the field. The adrenaline in my heart pounds as their roar reaches a decibel equal to that of being at a rock concert.

"It's going . . . going . . . gone! Another home run for the Flaming Bat in the record books!"

Tim's eyes widen, then a brimming smile crosses his face. Flipping the now-extinguished bat with a charred rim, he sets off at a light jog around the bases and waves to the crowd, bowing as his feet make contact with each base.

I slow clap, shaking my head. As I watch the fans, staff, ex-team members, and everyone else in the stadium cheer for him, I realize not just anybody would be on the receiving end of a reception like this. Whether it's a friend or a fan, everybody we've seen today has wanted to stop and talk to him. Tim isn't just a former player; he's a Sloths' legend.

Taking one final bow, he waves his cap to the crowd, then walks up to me. "How did I do?" he asks with a cocky grin.

"You knocked it out of the park," I tease, proud of myself for coming up with a witty baseball pun.

I wrap my arms around Tim, and he pulls me in close to his hot body. I smell the scent of his spicy deodorant and smoky wood. The fabric of his shirt is damp against my skin, causing goosebumps to appear. Bubbles float to the top of my stomach. Around us, I hear the encouraging buzz of thousands of people chanting, "Kiss, kiss, kiss."

"Well, we'd better give the people what they want," I say in a raspy voice.

Our lips touch. My body relaxes into his. It's not gentle, but a kiss of longing and desire. He's the only thing keeping me standing right now. I'd melt into a puddle if I could.

Tim breaks the kiss. "With a reception like that, maybe I *should* consider coming out of retirement," he whispers.

I whack him on the bum. "Stick to the judging, old man."

"Old man? Ouch."

"I'd miss you too much if you played on the road all the time."

"Don't worry, I'm pretty sure my playing days are over." He rubs his shoulder. "That took a lot out of me."

My expression softens. "Are you going to be okay?"

"Today, yes. Who knows about tomorrow."

"We'll just take things one day at a time."

He kisses my forehead. "Sloth-zone style."

Chapter Seventeen

As the day's auditions come to a close, the remaining people in my section pack up their belongings and chat excitedly about what they've seen. I stay seated, uncertain of what to do next, and send a text to Tim.

> Gemma: Not sure if you need more time, but do you want me to wait for you in the stands, on the field, or at the car?

Setting my phone onto the seat's armrest, I slide my newly-acquired Sloth hoodie over my replica of Tim's jersey and listen to the trio of women from earlier chat. They're an excellent source of gossip.

"I hope the Sloths do a national audition tour every year. Today was so much fun! I can't wait until the team is back here this summer," the woman with brown hair says.

The blond woman grins. "Totally. I can't wait to see another dance with Stilt-Walking Sterling. He's a shoo-in to make the team. I bet it won't take him long to gain a big fan following. Especially with his looks."

The woman's friends bob their heads up and down in agreement.

"I'm more curious about who the team's next manager is going to be." The redhead of the group checks the time on her mobile, then slides it into the side pocket of her backpack. "The Sloths always promote internally, so it'll have to be a former player. My money is on the Maverick."

"Haven't you heard? It was all over the Sloths' fan forum this morning. Someone leaked that the job has been offered to the Flaming Bat!" the blond exclaims.

I freeze. Have I heard them right? I preen my ears.

"What?! The Flaming Bat? No. Way." The redhead fans herself. "I'm hot just thinking about him in that uniform again! If he manages the team, I may just have to move to Scottsdale."

The brown-haired woman snorts. "Your husband would kill you."

"A girl can dream." The redhead sighs. "I hope the rumors are true. I thought he said he'd retired from baseball for good."

"That's what everyone on the fan forum thought too, but apparently the source believes it's a done deal. Think about it—if he weren't serious about the job, he wouldn't be here."

As the trio stands to leave, they wave to me. I offer them a weak smile. My chest grows tight. Has Tim lied to me about why we're really here today? Was it really so I could see what the Sloths are like, or did he have an ulterior motive the whole time? If he accepts the job as team manager, what happens to us? His teaching? His life in Sequoia Valley?

My mobile chimes—speaking of Tim.

Tim: We have a meeting in the clubhouse
that's going to be a half hour, then the
team owner has also asked if we could
have a quick one-on-one chat. Is that
okay? I don't want to keep you waiting,
so I can tell them I'm not available if
you'd rather get going.

Gemma: Take the meetings. I'll wait in
the car.

Tim: I think we'll be about an hour, tops.
If you want, feel free to take the car and
explore Fresno. You still have my keys,
right?

Gemma: I do, but I won't be driving
anywhere. I can't. You Americans drive
on the wrong side of the road, and it's
something I can't seem to get used to.

Tim: Gah. I'm sorry, Gem. I'll be there as
soon as I can.

I shuffle with the last couple of stragglers out of the
stadium to the car park. It isn't difficult to spot Tim's white
minivan. There are only a few cars remaining. Outside, the
sky has taken on a ghostly pale-blue hue. A thin layer of fog
lingers near the lamps, spotlighting the vehicle. It's only six
p.m., but the winter days are short. I'll be more than happy
once it's summer again and it's light until nine.

Pulling the passenger door open, I climb inside and
lock the doors. My pulse races—I'm still trying to process
what I've heard. Tim being the new manager could be a
rumor, but why else would the owner ask to see him alone?
The more I think about it, the stronger the sinking feeling

in my stomach grows. I hear the woman's voice from earlier echo inside my head. *"It's pretty much a done deal."*

I massage my temples. Let's say Tim did get offered the job and was on the road with the Sloths from April to October—theoretically, it would be similar to how it was before my injury. There'd be a lot of texting and video chats. And probably fewer chances to see one another. It sucks, but we'd keep making it work. Of course, nothing is certain yet. I need to talk to him about it. Continuing to play the what-if game will only upset me more.

Adjusting my mobile so the PopSocket balances on the dashboard, I open my Hearts Connected Network app and scroll through the list of shows until I locate an unwatched episode of *Cupid's Arrow.* A voice-over fills the car. "Previously on *Cupid's Arrow* . . . tempers flared as Jane and Liz realized that Lydia had attempted to seduce Bill."

Pulling my hood over my head, I recline my seat and allow my body to relax.

A tapping on the car window immediately causes me to jump in my seat. I glance to my left and spot Tim with his face pressed to the glass, looking in. I reach for the unlock button.

"Thanks. Sorry to wake you, but I didn't have another way to get inside." He slides into the driver's seat and quickly closes the door behind him. "I swear, I never ever thought I'd be this long. I sent you a text, but you never responded. I was worried and got out of there as fast as I could."

"Sorry I didn't reply. I fell asleep." I scrub my eyelids with my hands. "What time is it?"

"It's nine. You must be freezing and starving!"

"I'm not cold. I stole your blanket from the back seat. But I am hungry." I frown. I can't believe his meeting lasted three hours. Was it because he was ironing out his contract with the Sloths' owner?

"I'll get you something right now. It just won't be from the Little Blue Caboose Bistro." He dips his chin to his chest. "We were going to have a romantic dinner inside this old, restored train car that's down the road, but that plan's shot." The muscles in his forehead crease. "Are you okay with fast food?"

"Sure," I say.

"What are you in the mood for?"

I stretch. "Maybe some tacos? Or a burrito?"

"Got it. There are a couple hole-in-the-wall places I know of down toward Fresno State." Tim reaches for his seat belt and grins at me. "You know, having the keys might help."

"Oh yeah." I fumble for my purse, pull out the Sloths' keychain, and hand it to him. "Here."

He turns the key in the ignition. The lights and radio flicker on, but the engine remains silent. "Aw, come on, don't do this to us. Not now." He turns the key again. Silence. Resting his head on the steering wheel for a moment, he groans, "I think the battery is dead."

"Oh," I manage. I sit taller, now fully awake. "Do you have roadside towing?"

"No," Tim grumbles. "Dad will never let me live this down once he finds out. He kept bugging me to take care of it and I didn't. I guess it's a lesson not to procrastinate. I'll see if I can sign up now." He starts typing on his phone.

I reach for my mobile and take a moment to text Frankie.

Gemma: Heads up, we'll be home later
than we thought. Tim has a dead
battery.

Frankie: Bummer. Do you need us to
come and pick you guys up?

I glance in Tim's direction.

Gemma: I'll pass the offer along, but I
think he's got it sorted out.

Frankie: Okay, let me know if you need
anything.

Gemma: *Thumbs-up emoji*

"Okay, I just put in a towing request through the app. It looks like it's going to be about an hour." He leans his head back against the seat and blows out air. "Gah. I really screwed this up."

"These things happen. There isn't much you can do about it," I say empathetically.

"I just hate letting you down." Tim sits back up. He unlocks his screen again. "Tell you what, while we wait, I'll order some tacos for delivery. Do you like chips and guacamole? What type of salsa? Soft or crunchy tortillas?"

My stomach growls. I place a hand on it as heat sears my cheeks. I guess I'm hungrier than I thought. "Yes, mild, and soft."

Tim types for a couple of minutes. "Okay, the app says twenty minutes." He places his phone on the dash. "I'm sorry again for the nightmare tonight is shaping up to be."

"It wasn't bad until now. I had fun at the zoo and watching the tryouts." I draw my hoodie tighter around my body, fighting off the chill. I'm fully awake now. And all I can think about are the rumors. Are they true? I have to find out. "So . . . how did your wrap-up meeting with the lads go?"

"It went well." Tim relaxes. "We have a short list of ten contenders from here, but it sounds like they'll be taking a lot more people than that to Scottsdale. The Sloths' owner is planning to create an expansion team on the East Coast."

"Oh, that sounds exciting. Did the owner have anything else to say to you?" I play with the hoodie's drawstrings. "I mean, it's rather curious that he wanted to meet with you alone."

"Who, Mike? Nah, he's already met with the rest of the guys. He just wanted to touch base on a couple of different ideas with me for the new team, the Bridgeport Banana Slugs, but we ended up spending most of the time talking about my teaching."

Is he telling the truth? Purposefully omitting details? Or did they not discuss anything about the job? "He must really value you."

"We've always had a good working relationship." Tim stares out the window. "Mike is a good guy."

Suddenly, a pair of headlights start to drive toward the car, temporarily blinding us as it slows. We shade our eyes.

"I'm just going to see who it is," Tim says tensely. "Lock the doors just in case."

I nod, wondering who it could be. My pulse begins to race as I touch the lock button with an audible click.

Chapter Eighteen

I breathe easier as I watch Tim clap a guy in a neon-green satin bomber jacket on the back through the front window.

Tim circles back to the driver's side and I unlock the doors. "It's my pal Frank. He offered to give us a jump, but I'd rather wait and try to replace the battery now. Is that okay with you?"

"Oh yeah, that's fine." I unlatch my seat belt. "I'll get out and come meet him properly."

"No, it's freezing out there. And you already met him earlier. He'll be fine if you just wave through the window."

"Are you sure?" I glance out the window. "I don't want to be rude."

"Positive. Frank would say the same thing."

"Do you need a jacket?"

"I have one in the back seat." Tim slides open the back door and retrieves his own matching Sloths jacket. "If you need anything, just yell or text me." He pecks me on the forehead, slips the garment on, and closes the doors.

I decide to rewatch the end of the *Cupid's Arrow*

episode I missed when I fell asleep. I unlock my mobile screen and see a red number one glowing under voicemails. I frown, wondering why I didn't hear my mobile go off earlier. The sound's been on the entire time. Tapping the voicemail button, I click the speaker button and let the message play.

"Hi, this message is for Gemma MacLeod. My name is Ryan Gilcrest. I'm one of the casting directors with the Connected Hearts Network, and I was hoping that you might be able to give me a call back at this number as soon as you get this to discuss your *Cupid's Arrow* application. It's about eight-ten. I'll be in my office until nine. If you don't reach me tonight, leave a message and I'll get back to you on Monday. Thanks!"

I stare at my phone. I didn't even think I was still in the running for the show. I submitted my second-round audition video a couple of weeks ago, but I never received any sort of acknowledgment from the network. And that's after I sent two unanswered follow-up emails. I know they're busy and probably get thousands of applications, but the least they could've done was send me an auto reply.

Now, out of the blue, I've received a personal call from a casting director. I replay the message. From the guy's tone, it sounds like I've made it past another round. I shake my head in disbelief. I very well could be the next bachelorette, but it's not something I want anymore.

Tim's captured my heart. Our relationship might still be new, but every bone in my body is telling me it's something special. I've never been happier—and dare I say in love. I want to give us every chance at finding our happily ever after.

Grabbing my mobile, I check the time. It's eight-forty. If I call Ryan back now, I might still be able to catch him and tell him I'm not interested anymore. I click on the number in the voicemail.

Ring. Ring. Ring.

"Hello?"

"Hi, Ryan? This is Gemma MacLeod. So sorry I missed your call. I just got your message."

"Gemma, great to hear from you. Just give me a second here." I hear the shuffling of a few papers in the background. "One of my kids got sick this week and now I'm playing catch-up with my work."

I give a nervous laugh. "Of course."

"Ah-ha. Here's your stuff." He clears his throat. "Like I mentioned in the message, I'm one of the casting directors for *Cupid's Arrow*. The reason I called is to let you know you're one of three women moving on to the final round of casting for next season."

"Wow." My breath hitches. I had my suspicions, but hearing him say I'm one of three finalists is surreal.

"Your videos for the first two rounds stood out to us. We love that you're an ice skater, and your accent. It'll make marketing you a breeze—if you're chosen, that is."

"Um, thanks, but I—"

Ryan cuts me off. "We also loved your friend Frankie and her boyfriend Charlie. Are they the two people you were planning to have on the show with you? Or were you planning to use Suzanne? Because she seems nice, but she's too old."

I clench my fists. How can he be so rude about Suzy? "I was thinking about Frankie and Charlie, but—"

More papers rustle. "Good, good. We loved their chemistry. The team and I think the millions of people who watch the show will also fall in love with Charlie. He's perfect for our female demographic."

The longer he speaks, the more disgusted and angry I grow. Charlie isn't a piece of meat the producers can use to toss to a savage pack of hungry female viewers. He only volunteered himself to help me out so I wouldn't be taken advantage of.

"Anyway, here's a quick rundown of how the next round works. After the holidays, we'll fly you out to L.A. You'll do a few promo shoots, and then we'll have you spend about three days living in the *Cupid's Arrow* house with some of the men we've cast for the season."

"But I thought my friends would be the ones who got to choose the blokes," I sputter.

"No. We edit in some footage from our open casting call to make it appear that way. We need to keep the show entertaining and make sure the guys who make it are attractive and have the right type of personality. This isn't just about finding love—it's also a numbers game. If we want to keep the show running and our sponsors happy, we need to make sure we hit all the network's ratings targets."

I knew some of the show was scripted, but not to this extent. What exactly does the network consider the right personality? Would it be somebody like Tim? Probably not. They want guys who look like underwear models and start fights, causing drama. It may be great for the audience, but that's not for me.

I look through the foggy windshield. My eyes settle on Tim chatting animatedly with his friend. He's the only man for me. And there's nothing Hollywood about our love story. "Ryan, I'm flattered you guys are considering me for next season's bachelorette. Being on the show has always been a bucket-list item for me. But the thing is, I've met someone. I actually called you today to ask you to take me out of the running."

Ryan sighs on the other end. "Are you sure? Once you decide to pull out, you won't be eligible to apply for any of the other Connect Hearts Network family of shows for another year."

"Uh-huh. I'm a hundred percent positive."

I hear him muttering something on the other end. "I'll tell you what, I'm going out on a limb here, but as a gesture of goodwill, what if I pulled a couple of strings and snuck your boyfriend onto the show just like we did for our first season's bachelorette, Yvonne."

Huh. I never would've guessed Yvonne was like me. She'd already met her perfect match before going on the show too. A part of me is tempted to say yes to him, but knowing Tim, I highly doubt he'd want his private life splashed all over social media. Especially as a teacher. "The answer is still no." My tone is curt. "I don't want Tim to have anything to do with this."

"All right, then. I'll make a note and close your file." Ryan's tone suddenly turns cold and professional. "Thanks again for taking the time to chat with me tonight."

I can't say the same is true for me, but I'll be polite. "Likewise. I hope your kid feels better soon too."

He grunts and hangs up. Feeling slightly sickened, I let the mobile drop onto my lap and rub my temples. What a jerk.

"Gemma?" Tim's voice suddenly gets my attention. "Who was that?"

My head snaps up. I didn't realize Tim had come to the car or heard part of our conversation. He's looking down at me through the open driver's door, holding a brown paper bag in his hands. I smell the enticing scent of meat and spices. My gaze travels up to his face. His jaw is clenched, and his eyes are shining dangerously.

I swallow hard. "It was one of the casting directors for *Cupid's Arrow.*"

He slides into the car. "You applied to be on *Cupid's Arrow*?" His voice comes out strained.

"Yes. But it was before I met you," I add quickly. He knows the show is my guilty pleasure. If I applied to be on it, it shouldn't come as such a huge shock. It's not like I said yes.

"Okay." He shifts his gaze out the window. "And what did this guy want?"

"He . . . they . . . the casting team invited me to Los Angeles. The call was to let me know I'd been short-listed as one of three finalists for next season."

"Then you've spoken to them a couple of times?" His brow furrows into a deep V. His gaze is boring a hole in the window. "How long have you known they were semi-interested in you to be the next bachelorette?"

"A few weeks," I say quietly.

"And you didn't think to tell me?"

"No. There wasn't a point. I didn't think I'd ever get this far," I huff.

"But you did." My head slowly rises, and his eyes meet mine, reminding me of an unruly sea in the midst of an approaching storm. They're a mixture of anger and sadness. "And now you're going to dump me so you can go run off and fall for some guy from the show."

What?! "Tim, no, it's not like that at all."

"Was I only meant to be your fallback guy?" He chucks the food bag onto the console between us. "You know what, don't answer that. I don't even want to know. I thought this relationship would be different, but clearly, I was wrong." He gets out of the car and starts to walk away. "It's just like last time."

My own level of frustration is growing. How could he think such a thing? Doesn't he see how deeply I've fallen for him? Or feel how strong the connection is between us? He didn't even give me a chance to explain. He just assumed the worst.

I throw my door open and jump out, ignoring the white-hot searing pain radiating up my hip. I limp after him and put a hand on his shoulder. "Tim, I'd *never* do that to you. You're supposed to know me better than that."

"That's the problem, Gemma." He looks me up and down. "I don't know you as well as I thought I did. I don't know if I can trust you."

I snap like a rubber band stretched too far. "What about you? Are you planning to join the Sloths as the next manager? I'm not the only one holding things back."

His eyes widen. He takes a step back. "What—where did you hear that?"

"It doesn't matter. Is it true?"

"They did offer me the job."

"And are you considering it?"

"Of course I am. I'd be stupid not to. It's a dream job." His voice is raw and strained.

"Were you ever planning to tell me?" The corners of my eyes are moist. A few tears threaten to fall.

Tim doesn't answer.

"I'm not the only one who was keeping things hidden."

"But this is completely different."

"How is it different?"

"Mike only offered me the job as I was leaving the stadium. You've known for weeks." Tim glares at me. "I would've discussed it with you."

"Would you have? Because from where I'm standing, it

doesn't seem like you trust me very much." The tears are now free-falling.

"Darn it, Gemma, what do you think?" Tim's lips quiver. His brow furrows again, and he throws his hands wildly into the air. "Of course I would've talked things over with you. You matter. We matter. I don't make decisions that are going to affect both our lives lightly."

"I don't know what I think anymore!" I cry. "You know, our problem isn't that we don't understand one another. It's that we're too much alike."

"What are you saying?"

"I'm saying we're *so* alike. We're the same kind of stubborn, the same kind of scared." My vision is getting fuzzy, obscured by tears. Nothing makes sense to me anymore. "It means we'll never work out. We might as well save ourselves the effort and call it quits now. You were ready to walk away from me earlier. Well, I'll make it easy for you . . . go ahead. I can't be with a person who doesn't believe me or trust me."

I slide into the car and slam the door shut. I cover my face with my hands, my body racked with sobs. My heart is shattered into a billion tiny shards. I never want to ever hear or see anything about *Cupid's Arrow* or love ever again. It's nothing but trouble! All it leads to is pain and heartbreak. I'm better off alone. I can't trust anyone.

When I met Tim, I felt so giddy and full of hope. I thought that maybe he was the one. He treated me like a real-life princess. Memories flood my mind. Carving a pumpkin. Seeing his haunted classroom. Dinner at the Lucky Dog. Standing in his arms watching thousands of butterflies take flight. Our first kiss inside the forest, I felt like I was floating on a cloud just like Cinderella and Prince Charming. Where did it all go so wrong?

I cry harder, hugging myself, until there are no more tears remaining. I dry my eyes using the back of my sleeve. My face feels like someone has taken a sheet of sandpaper and rubbed it raw. Everything is dry and swollen.

The last time my relationship failed, it was because I wasn't giving enough of myself to it. I've been trying so hard to do small things for Tim to show him how much I care. Yet here I sit, a failure once again. Maybe I should've told Ryan yes after all.

Chapter Nineteen

A week passes. My mood is black. That night, we drove in silence the entire way home. Well, my pretending to be asleep didn't help the situation along. I couldn't face Tim after I'd told him it'd be best if we called it quits and broke up. I regretted yelling it to him the moment the words left my lips, but I couldn't find it in me to take them back. Since he dropped me off, I haven't heard one word from him. So I guess I know where we stand.

Today's Thanksgiving, and while I'd much rather sit in my room and be alone, I put on my big-girl trousers and plaster a smile onto my face. Even though I feel dead inside, today's a day to celebrate friends and family. I won't let my crappy mood spoil the holiday for everyone else.

I look at all the steaming dishes sitting on the sideboard at Suzy's house. There are fluffy potatoes, marshmallow-topped candied yams, soft veggies, cornbread, jellied cran-berries, stuffing, and a massive twenty-five-pound turkey. I scoop a small amount of everything onto my plate.

I sit down in the middle of the table, which has been set

for nine, even though there's only eight of us. The men—Mr. T, Charlie, Leslie's boyfriend, and their uncle Jack—linger in the kitchen, chatting over drinks as they wait for the space to clear up around the food.

A pang of sadness hits me. I'm the only one here alone, except Uncle Jack. I wonder what Tim's up to. Is he having dinner right now with his family too?

"I can see why you told me to wear stretchy trousers." I laugh.

Frankie is focused on lathering her potatoes, turkey, and stuffing with gravy. "Uh-huh. Suzy outdoes herself every year."

"Stop, Frankie, I can't take credit for everything. Your father and Charlie did a magnificent job with the turkey, potatoes, and dessert," Suzy says.

Frankie sits beside me and leans over to whisper in my ear, "Charlie did all the cooking. Dad only peeled the potatoes."

I force a laugh.

"Gem, what do you think of Thanksgiving so far?" Leslie asks.

I gesture to my plate. "I'm excited to try everything. Turkey is a nice change from the foods we eat for Christmas at home. Mum usually makes a roast or a ham."

Leslie takes a seat across from me. "Roast sounds good. Maybe that's what we should make for Christmas this year, Nan."

"What do you normally have?" I ask.

"The same spread as Thanksgiving. All this."

I nod.

"What are your plans for Christmas, Gem? Are you going home?" Frankie pours herself a glass of sparkling apple cider.

"I'm going home after New Years." I lower my chin, staring at the table. "We only have two days off."

"You didn't answer my question, Gem. What about on Christmas?"

I wince, hoping she wouldn't pry. "I'll probably do what I did with you and Fernando last year. Dinner at Denny's followed by binging *Elf* and whatever other holiday films are on Netflix."

"Can I talk you into coming back here? Fernando said he'd come!" Frankie says.

I appreciate her offer, but I'd rather be far, far away from here. If I spend Christmas here, all I'll be thinking about is Tim. And I have no desire to make myself miserable on my favorite holiday. I shake my head. "Thanks, but no. I need some time to myself."

"I understand," Frankie says, eyeing me with sympathy.

"**D**oes anyone have any room for dessert? Or should we wait an hour and digest?" Suzy asks. Everyone around the table groans.

"We don't have any room left, Nan," Charlie says.

Frankie pokes him in the arm. "And whose fault is that? You didn't have to eat three helpings!"

"Nan, I'll go out on a limb and say we should wait." Leslie stands and starts collecting everyone's plates and utensils. "Does anyone feel up for a nice walk by the lake?"

Frankie, Charlie, Ron, and Jack eagerly agree.

"It's a no for Rich and me. We want to get a head start on putting away all the leftovers," Suzy says.

"And I'm staying behind to help with the washing up," I say.

"Gem, you're our guest. You shouldn't have to do the dishes," Frankie tells me.

"I don't mind. Besides . . ." I rub my hip.

Frankie nods in understanding. Getting up from around the table, everyone helps bring the remaining dishes into the kitchen, then grabs their coats for their walk. I straggle behind them, slowly meandering into the kitchen. I'm a coward. My hip isn't that bad today, and a walk around the lake sounds lovely. I just don't want to watch Frankie and Leslie coupled up with their boyfriends.

"Suzy, are you okay without me for a few minutes? There's something I need to take care of in the den," Mr. T says.

"Go on, Rich, I'm fine."

He kisses her cheek, then exits the room. I sigh, wishing I had what he and Suzy have. When my heart heals, maybe I'll have Mr. T set up my next dating profile for me. He obviously knows what he's doing. *Cupid's Arrow* loved the edits he suggested for my audition video. And he found true love on his first try—well, second, if you don't count his first marriage. Maybe for me, the second time will be the charm.

I return my attention to Suzy. "Where would you like me to start?" I ask, placing my hands on my hips. I survey the room. There are a mountain of leftovers taking up every available inch of space on the kitchen island. We have enough food here to serve another two or three days of meals.

"If you wouldn't mind pulling some Tupperware containers from the cabinet on the right, that would be great."

I retrieve the containers, then assist Suzy. The rhythm of running the water, soaping the dishes, rinsing them, and loading the dishwasher relaxes me. I relish the quiet. As I stare out the window into the darkened forest, I think about meeting "Henry" at Hobby Land and our second meeting at the Halloween festival. It was on a night just like this one. What would've happened if I had never flirted back? Would we have encountered one another at the festival? Or would our first meeting have waited until I was able to cash in that coffee date with him? Would we still be in the same situation we're in now?

"Gemma," Suzy says, tapping me on the shoulder.

"Hmm?"

"The dishwasher is full and ready to be run." She gestures to the appliance.

My cheeks warm. "Oh, um, right." I turn off the tap and dry my hands on a dishcloth.

Suzy closes the door and pushes the "Start Cycle" button. "Rich has been gone an awfully long time. I wonder what's taking him so long. Would you mind checking on him?"

"Oh sure."

I walk down the hall to the den. The Elvis song "Walks Like an Angel" is playing from the family jukebox. "Mr. T?" I ask, tapping on the door frame.

"In here, Gem."

I push the door open and gasp. The lights have been dimmed under the soft glow of twenty candles. The coffee table has been moved to the side of the room and replaced with a carpet of rose petals.

"Gemma, I've been waiting for you," Tim says as he steps out of the shadows, wearing a crisp white dress shirt, skinny tie, and fitted black trousers that remind me of a man straight out of the 1950s.

My hands drop to my side. My heart is jackhammering

against my chest. Here's the man who's been haunting my dreams for the last week. Seeing him in person reminds me of just how much I've missed him. I openly stare. "Tim," I whisper. "How? Why?"

"I'm here to apologize, Gem." His eyes dart to Mr. T, who nods in encouragement. "I've never been more ashamed of myself for losing my cool and taking it out on you. I never wanted to hurt your feelings or ruin our relationship. You're one of the best things to ever happen to me, Gem. Allowing you to walk away from me is one of the biggest mistakes I've ever made. I let you go without a fight, and I've been kicking myself every day since."

He takes a deep breath. "I know it'll be a tall order competing with the guys that'll be on *Cupid's Arrow* with you, but I'm hoping you'll find it in your heart to forgive me and consider giving me a second chance at winning your heart."

Cupid's Arrow? Does he still think I'm going to be on the show? "Tim, I forgive you." I take a step closer, soaking in the ginger and lemon scents of his cologne. "You have no idea how much I've missed you too." I reach up and brush a stray hair out of his face, running my fingers down the side to his jaw. "But you don't have to compete against anybody on that dumb show. I won't be on it because I turned them down. I told them I'd already found my dream man. You."

The volume of the music increases. Mr. T sneaks wordlessly out of the room, a knowing grin on his face. The door swings shut softly behind him.

"You did?"

I nod.

"I thought I'd made it clear when I told you that you'd never be my fallback guy. But maybe I should've just told you point blank." I explain how everything I thought I knew about the show has been a lie. It's not about people going on to find love. It's about entertaining the viewers and making money. "It hurts me to think that you believed I'd toss you aside. I've done my best to try and show you how much I care about you, but now I feel like a failure. I didn't do enough to—"

"Gemma, you're not a failure. The problem is me." He lowers his chin, staring at the floor. "Since my last relationship, I've been afraid to let anything go too far, or anyone grow too close. It's why I wanted to take things slow with you. I had to be sure about you. My last girlfriend only agreed to date me to get back at her ex. She never had any real feelings for me. When she dumped me, it crushed me and took a long time to get over. I can handle physical pain, but emotional pain is ten times worse. I felt like my heart had been thrown into a paper shredder and ripped apart."

"Oh, Tim." I reach up and wrap my arms around him tightly, burying my head against his solid chest. I can't believe somebody would use Tim like that. It makes my blood boil. "You are definitely not the problem. You have a heart of gold." I raise my head and meet his gaze. "If your ex was too stupid to see that, her loss is my gain." I place a hand on his lips. "You're not the only one with regrets. You're the man I've fallen for. And the one I've come to love."

As the words escape my lips, Tim squeezes me tighter to his body. We're pressed up so close to one another that I can hear his breathing quicken and the rhythm of his heart attempting a world record for drumming beats per minute.

"You love me?" he whispers.

"I do."

A smile tugs at the corner of his lips. "I love you too, Gemma-rella."

If you've ever seen one of those classic black-and-white Hollywood films where the heroine is literally swept off her feet by a dapper man in a tux at the end, that's exactly how it feels when we finally kiss. My eyes flutter closed. Tim lifts me so I'm level with his mouth and greedily plants his lips on mine. With that one action, I know just how much he's missed me. I wrap my arms around his neck and return the kiss with equal force. We have a whole week of lost time to make up for, and I'm determined to make sure I get my dues.

Later, Tim and I sway side to side in a slow dance to "Walks Like An Angel," which has been playing on a loop. Being back in his arms, I'm filled with bubbles and fuzziness, as if there are adorable baby bunnies hopping around inside my tummy.

"You've been holding out on me."

"I have?" he says with a hint of fear in his voice.

I poke him in the chest. "You're a brilliant dancer."

He relaxes. "Not really, but thanks for saying so." He lifts his arm and twirls me. "I have a small confession to make."

"Oh?" I arch an eyebrow.

"Suzy and Mr. T gave me a crash course on how to slow dance."

I giggle. "Don't worry, I won't tell anyone."

"I owe them a lot for helping me figure out how I should apologize to you."

"You could've just picked up the phone," I say softly.

"I almost did every day this past week."

I wrinkle my nose. "Why didn't you?"

"I was scared you wouldn't give me another chance," he admits, a sheepish expression crossing his face. "I knew you were angry with me over the Sloths' job and I thought you'd dumped me to be on . . . well, we both know what I thought."

"Phones work both ways. I could've been the one to call you too. Only I thought that since I hadn't heard from you, you'd decided you didn't want to be with me anymore." I take a deep breath. "What a pair we make." One simple conversation between us could've cleared all this up, and we'd have avoided being miserable.

"Well, I'm glad the air has been mostly cleared between us," Tim says.

"Mostly?" I pop my head up, blinking in confusion. We're on the road to being back together again. What else is there to discuss?

"The manager's position."

"Oh." He'd mentioned it, but my brain had forgotten. "Have you made up your mind?"

"I'm about sixty percent of the way there." He shoves his hands into his pockets. "But the most important factor to me is you. If I took it, would moving to Scottsdale be something you'd consider in the future? I know you want to continue skating with Dreams on Ice."

I want to say no. I want everything to stay as it is and have him continue living in Sequoia Valley. But I'd be a hypocrite if I told him that when I'm living out my own dream job. If he wants to be with the Sloths again, I won't hold him back. Considering my next words carefully, I offer, "Only you know how badly you want that job."

"Gemma, you're avoiding the question." He chuckles.

"Yes. If it would make you happy."

He lets out a sigh of relief, and I immediately know I've given him the right answer.

"That's a big weight off my shoulders." Tim flashes me a million-watt grin. "I have a trip to Scottsdale lined up in two weeks. I haven't been back in a couple of years. There's a brand-new state-of-the-art facility Mike's built, and a rehearsal hall, and . . . "

I smile and nod, only half paying attention. My heart may not be in Arizona, but I can learn to enjoy it as long as it means being with him. I thought I'd lost him once, and I'm not willing to lose him again.

Chapter Twenty

"Good job, Gemma, give me two more," Mel calls out.

Beads of perspiration drip down my forehead. My quads quiver from exertion. I use every ounce of strength I can muster to give Mel a few more reps with the leg press machine, then collapse against the padded backing. I ache, but it's the good kind of pain. I know what we're doing is strengthening the muscles around the injury, and it'll pay off in the very near future.

"Nice. That's one more than yesterday."

"Do you want me to work on the balance board today too?" I say, crossing my fingers we can actually skip it.

"No, we'll end the session with this. You're planning to skate today, aren't you?"

I sigh internally with relief. My body is exhausted. I've been back a full week and a half, and jumping right back into skating in shows has taken all my energy. I've been putting in extra PT and Pilates sessions with Mel, on top of doing longer warm-ups and cooldowns.

"Yeah." I sit up and wipe my forehead with the back of

my hand. "Fernando and I are going to skate in the intro and the Princess Melody. I'm not ready to jump back into my Cinderella program yet."

"Got it." She nods. "Well, based on how you did today, I'd say that strength-wise, you're improving from where you were a month ago."

"You can thank Frankie for pushing me."

"How's the pain right now?"

"A four and a half?"

Mel grimaces. "Still higher than I'd like, but I'll take it."

I was at a six on the first day back. I'm thrilled we're trending in the right direction.

"If we stick to the routine, and you're careful if you experience any flare-ups, I don't see why you wouldn't be able to make it through the remaining three weeks of the season. Dr. Zhang's report was encouraging."

I fist pump. "That's what I'd hoped you'd say."

"With any luck, by the time management receives my report and actually reads it, you'll have had surgery and will be doing your recovery PT."

"Fingers crossed." I gather up my mobile, earbuds, and water bottle, then wave goodbye and head to Fernando's dressing room.

The door is propped open a crack. As I peek through it, I see Fernando curled up, fast asleep on the couch. His snoring is loud, reminding me of a roaring bear. I giggle. He lets out an even louder snore. If Fernando had a super-power, it would be sleeping. He has the uncanny ability to sleep on demand. It's something Frankie and I have always been jealous of.

Discreetly taking out my mobile, I push the door open a little wider and angle the device so I'm in the frame and snap a photo. I'll use it for something fun later on. "Hola, Fernando. Time to wakey-wakey." I gently shake his body.

He lets out a loud groan. "Dos minutos más. Two more minutes."

"No two more minutes." He burrows under the cover. I tug it away. "Up now. We're on a schedule, Señor Alvarez."

"Fine," he mutters. A puff of dark brown hair appears at the top of the blanket. "I'm up."

"I'll be in my dressing room getting a start on my makeup. When you're ready to warm up our lifts, come find me."

Fernando stands, yawns, and waves me off. The blanket remains draped around his shoulders like a cape. It reminds me of Tim. My face falls. "Gemma, what's that look?"

I quickly glance away from my skating partner. "Nothing."

He frowns. "You're thinking about him again."

"Maybe?" I can't hide it from him. I wrap my arms around myself. "He's in Scottsdale today. I've gotten a couple of photos and texts from him showing me different parts of the city. He's so excited."

"Why don't you tell him the truth—that you don't want him to move to Arizona."

"I can't do that."

"Why not?"

"It's complicated."

"That's not a valid answer."

I unlock my mobile screen and swipe through my messages with Tim until I find an image of him posing next to the Sloth mascot with a flaming bat. "Look at the goofy grin on his face. He reminds me of a cartoon character. You don't want me to spoil it for him, do you?"

"You're too nice, Gem." Fernando folds the blanket and crosses his arms. "This is why I'm happy being a bachelor. All I have to worry about is me, myself, and I."

"You can't mean that."

"I do."

"Fernando, come on, you've got to admit that sometimes being single is lonely."

"Nope." He shakes his head.

I don't know the full story, but I know Fernando's had a girlfriend in the past. Every time Frankie and I have brought up the idea of setting him up with someone, he's shot the idea down. We think he must either still love his ex, or he's had his heart broken one too many times.

"What about when you and I have gone out to dinner, and I've caught you staring longingly at some of the attractive women sitting alone? Or the dating app I know you have on your mobile."

"I don't have any dating apps installed," he says a little too quickly.

I snort. "We're friends on more than half of them. I can see when you're online."

"What are you doing on dating apps? Aren't you in a relationship?"

"Fair point. I only logged on once recently, and it was to remove my credit cards from my profile before I deleted the apps."

I sigh. Fernando's always been a good friend to me. And the best skating partner. I know the right woman is waiting for him. I mean, how could you not love someone who's a prince? Albeit a fictional one. I want him to find his happy ending, just like me. As soon as I have my life figured out, I'm going to move on to helping him. That's what friends do.

"Anyway, don't worry about me," he says. "I'm good. Let's get to work. We need to prove to everybody that you're back and better than ever."

Fernando grips my hips firmly and rotates me around in a circle. The arena is dark, but still lit with soft pale-pink lighting. The neon glow-in-the-dark necklaces and bracelets the audience members wear pulse with the beats of the music. I can see all the way up to the top of the bleachers. Although I can't make out any faces clearly, I can still see little hands clapping and eagerly waving to me.

As I change positions and sit on top of Fernando's hand, I stretch my arms out and give my best princess wave. That's when I hear the voices.

"Cinderella, you're my favorite princess!"

"Cinderella, try not to lose your slipper and watch out for your sisters, they're evil!"

"Mom, look, she waved to me! Mom, did you see that?!"

Hearing the high-pitched, excited tones of the children is why I'm here. Seeing them light up with excitement is the reason I'm pushing myself to skate through the pain. I remember being five or six years old myself when my parents took me to my first ice show. It was the closest my sister and I could get to seeing my favorite princesses and heroes come to life. We were never able to afford a trip to a fancy theme park.

I want all those children who are like me to be able to get the same experience I did out of seeing Dreams on Ice. I want them to walk out of here talking about one thing—

how much fun they had at the show tonight. Who knows, maybe I'm even performing in front of a few future skaters.

Fernando sets me down on the ice. We skate one more lap, then disappear backstage. "Somebody has extra energy today." He laughs.

"I don't know. I just feel so inspired. I had a good session with Mel, and when we were out there just now, I had this flashback to when I was little, watching the mermaid battle the evil sea witch."

"Aww, you sound like Frankie. She got her start in skating by watching a show, too."

"I didn't know that. Funny, I know pretty much everything about her except that."

As we step off the ice, a tech hands us our skate guards.

"I'm going to grab a snack before the finale. Can I get you anything?" Fernando asks.

"No, but thanks. I'm just going to stretch and take my time changing."

"Great. Meet back here in an hour?"

"Yes, sir." I mock salute him. He laughs and disappears down the hall.

Pulling open the door to my dressing room, I remove the blond wig and pat my hair. The wig cap is still firmly in place. It's always the first thing I check out of habit. I throw on my favorite jacket, then zip open the front pocket of my skate bag to feel around for my tablet.

A knock sounds at the door. "It's open," I shout.

The handle turns, and a woman dressed in a white dress shirt and gray pencil skirt strides in. Her heels click-clack against the ground. From how she carries herself, there's no doubt this woman exudes confidence. I angle my body toward her. "Hello, can I help you?"

The woman tucks a clipboard under her arm. "Ms. MacLeod, I'm Annette Wilcox from HR."

"Oh hi," I say, confused about what she'd want in the middle of a show. I extend my hand. "Nice to meet you."

The woman's hands remain on her clipboard. Her gaze appraises me from head to toe, as if I'm being X-rayed. The hairs on the back of my neck stand up. Something about her screams evil stepmother. "Yes, well, let's cut right to the chase, shall we? I have a few details to confirm with you." The woman brings the clipboard up to her eye level. "It says here that you've been diagnosed with a partially-torn labrum in your right hip. Is that correct?"

"Yes," I say slowly. Has she read Mel's report already?

"And your preferred course of treatment is a combination of physical therapy and rest."

"Yes, that's right." I bob my head up and down.

Ms. Wilcox nods sharply and scribbles down a few notes.

"I don't know if it's been added, but Dr. Zhang, the team doctor of the Jasper Ridge Jaguars, is treating me. He's an ortho—"

"Yes, I have it here."

"Oh."

The woman tucks the clipboard back under her elbow. "May I ask, who was it who directed you to go see Dr. Zhang? Was it the physical therapist, Melanie Rosewood?"

I fidget. Yup, evil stepmother is the perfect way to describe her. Something about the way she's asking questions is raising a red flag. Technically, it *was* Mel who recommended I seek a second opinion. She didn't seem to trust the company doctor. Just as I don't trust Ms. Wilcox. "I did it all on my own. Dr. Zhang is a friend."

Ms. Wilcox pinches her lips together. "Were you aware

that when you did so, you breached the terms of your contract?"

My mouth drops open. "No, I wasn't," I sputter.

"Section five, subsection four, paragraph one, line three, notes that all employees of Dreams on Ice and its subsidiary companies may only seek treatment from the preapproved list of medical practitioners."

How on earth does she have that memorized? "I . . . I'm sorry, I didn't know. I don't, er, remember it being in my contract. It was an honest mistake."

"And whose fault is that?" Her eyes narrow at me. "When you signed your present contract, you stated that you had read and fully understood that any breach of its terms would subject you to potential disciplinary action. Based on this, and the lackluster skating skills I witnessed today, I've decided that you'll be released from the company effective immediately."

My breath hitches. "Excuse me?"

"You'll receive the written confirmation of your termination following today's performance."

My heart races. I shake my head in disbelief. I heard what she said, but I can't comprehend it. "You're firing me?"

"We are. Unfortunately, you're a liability. You've disregarded the company's rules. Dreams on Ice takes the health and safety of its employees seriously. It's all for your own good."

I clench my fists. My insides feel like they've been thrown into a teakettle at the point of whistling. "I'm sorry, but are you even qualified to judge how I skated today? Do you have any knowledge about skating?"

"It doesn't matter. It's clear to anyone with eyes that you struggled today. I have video proof as my evidence.

My decisions have never been questioned by my superiors."

I cross my arms. "The only thing I didn't do in the opening number was the throw double Salchow. How does that constitute struggling?"

"Paragraph eight of section nine, line seven, states that a figure skater employed by Dreams on Ice must perform the show's choreography as was intended. We can't have our skaters alter the opening number as they see fit. We have certain standards, not to mention brand integrity, to maintain."

How does she know what was supposed to be performed? She just admitted she doesn't know a thing about skating. Has somebody put her up to this on purpose? My nostrils flare. "This is all bollocks. I demand to file an inquiry into your findings."

"I'm sorry, Ms. MacLeod. It doesn't work that way. My decision is final. Dreams on Ice doesn't employ second-rate skaters past their prime."

"I've been with Dreams on Ice for eight seasons. The least you could do is let me finish the year."

"No. That would be too risky. Who knows if you'd even make it that far." Ms. Wilcox walks to the door and adjusts her glasses. "I'll have your final paycheck cut for you as you leave the building. Your medical insurance, as of the end of the day, is also terminated."

I sink down into my makeup chair. The reality of the situation is beginning to take hold. The job I've loved and given my blood, sweat, and tears to has been ripped away from me. "What about the hotel and transportation home?"

Ms. Wilcox flashes me a greasy smile. "As a gesture of goodwill, we'll allow you to stay at the hotel tonight on us.

Your transportation, on the other hand, is up to you. Have a good day." The woman sees herself out.

I slam my fist against the makeup table, and the contents clatter to the ground. I hold my head in my hands. "What a bloody mess." I scrub my eyes with my hands, momentarily forgetting I have a thick layer of show makeup on. My hands are covered in black eyeliner, mascara, and blue eyeshadow. "I don't want to work for this rotten company anyway. Good riddance."

Locating my mobile, I open a text message and start to type to Tim. I'm shaking so badly, I have to switch to voice to text.

Gemma: I know you're flying home and have work first thing tomorrow, but if you see this, can you ring me? Anytime is fine. I need to hear your voice.

Chapter Twenty-One

"They did what?!" Fernando and Mel exclaim simultaneously.

Other skaters stare at the three of us quizzically as they dash to their rooms to change. Stage technicians rush to pack sets, props, and other pieces of equipment away into their appropriate wooden crates. The next show is in less than twenty-four hours in a different city.

"I was made redundant. Fired. Let go. Terminated. Whatever you want to call it." I cover my blade with a plastic skate guard. "I'm too beat-up and too much of a liability to the company. And I also wasn't supposed to see a doctor outside the company network."

"That's BS. The company has *never* actually enforced that rule. Not to mention, I wrote in the report that your body had made a better-than-expected recovery from the three weeks of rest you took. Did they even bother to read it?"

I shrug. I have no energy left.

"Gemma, you have to fight this," Fernando urges. He looks angry, his face a splotchy red. "They can't do this."

My shoulders sag. "It's too late. The HR worker already gave me this"—I hold up a manila envelope—"the moment I stepped backstage. She didn't even wait for me to return to my dressing room to change."

"May I see that?" Mel asks.

I pass it over to the PT. Fernando wraps an arm protectively around me. "If you're going, I am too. I'm tired of skating the same old crap anyway. Time to try coaching full-time."

"Fernando, I appreciate you saying that, but you might as well finish your contract. Earn the money while you can. Besides, didn't you just book your parents on an around-the-world cruise for their Christmas gift?"

"I did, but this is more important than money."

"Gemma, the date on this letter is from last week," Mel suddenly interjects, "before you were officially back with us. And before they got my report."

"What?" I grab the paper from her hands and skim its contents, my jaw clenching. "It is."

"That's the only way they would've known the full extent of the injury. I had you down as on leave, but I marked the reason as personal," Mel says.

"That means the company had already made its decision on me before I was even back." I swallow hard. "Maybe there *is* a way I can fight this."

Mel and Fernando nod.

"It's worth a shot. I'll start looking up a couple of different lawyers tonight when we get into the hotel," she says.

"Lawyers?"

"Yeah. It's going to take a legal heavyweight to be able

to fight a company like DOI," Mel emphasizes. "Especially with how this new management group has treated you."

I see dollar and pound signs floating in front of my eyes. It's probably going to be a long, drawn-out process. That's not something I'm willing to take on. The fight leaves my body. Taking a deep breath, I look at Mel and Fernando. "No, I'm done with DOI. It's not worth the time, energy, expense, or heartbreak. I doubt it'll even make a difference. I'd rather cut my losses, make a clean break, and just figure out what comes next."

Fernando hugs me tightly. "My little Gemma-rella has grown up. That's the most adult thing I think I've ever heard you say."

"Are you sure, Gem? You probably won't be the first or the last person DOI decides to ruthlessly cut like this." Mel lowers her voice. "There's definitely something fishy going on behind the scenes. I don't know what it is, but I don't like this at all." She pinches her lips together. "It's my fault you went to see Dr. Zhang. I could go and set the record straight," she offers.

"Mel, I appreciate it, but no. It's like you said, nothing will change their minds. This is bigger than me." I take a moment to gather my thoughts. "If you catch word of any other skaters who are put in the same situation as me, let me know and I'll consider taking legal action, but until we know more, I'd prefer not to do anything else."

As I walk through the hotel lobby later that evening, the sound of Burl Ives' classic rendition of "Rudolph the Red-Nosed Reindeer" plays over the sound system. White, green, and pink Christmas trees trimmed with colorful lights and baubles fill the space. I should be angry, but instead, I'm eerily calm.

As I turn the corner to take the lift to my room, I stop to admire the sight of families queuing to meet Father Christmas. Children bounce up and down on their toes, anxious for their turn. Seeing the excitement on their little faces instantly lifts my mood. There are still some places in the world where magic exists.

Suddenly, there's a gentle tug on one of my sleeves. "Cinderella?" a girl with wide blue eyes asks.

How does she . . . never mind. My eyes travel down to my clothing. I'm still dressed in a light-blue dress with a black jacket thrown over it. I was so distracted, I forgot to change before leaving the arena. I'll have to have somebody sneak my costume back tomorrow. I can't risk having the company accuse me of stealing.

Seeing the little girl, my heart melts and I kneel down on one knee. "Hi, there. What's your name?"

"I'm Mia."

"Mia, that's a lovely name. It sounds like the perfect name for a princess like you."

The little girl giggles. "I told Mommy that I saw you, but she didn't believe me. I had to come and tell you that you're my favorite princess."

"Well, I'm so happy to hear that." Noticing suddenly that Mia is alone, I ask, "Where is your mum?"

She points to the end of the queue for Father Christmas. A woman with a rounded belly chats with another woman with a double stroller ahead of her. She hasn't noticed that her daughter, who has to be about five years old, has gone missing.

"How about we tell your mum you found me and then maybe we can take a photo together."

"Yes, princess."

Holding my hand, Mia walks me over to her mother. I soak in the last few moments I'll be able to be Cinderella.

"Do you really have glass slippers? Mommy said they're only make believe."

"I do, but can you keep a secret?"

Mia nods solemnly.

"My fairy godmother keeps them for me," I whisper in her ear.

Her little eyes widen.

"Mia!" her mother exclaims. "Did you run off after I told you not to?"

She pouts, reminding me of Richelle. "But Mommy, look, I found Cinderella!"

"I can see that, but it's more important that you know better than to run off and talk to strangers," Mia's mother huffs. Her gaze turns to me. "Thank you for finding her and bringing her back to me. I hope she wasn't too much trouble."

"She wasn't," I promise. "I was just on my way up to my room."

"We just saw you skate today. You were lovely."

"Oh, thank you so much." A blush creeps up my cheeks.

"Mommy?"

Her mother and I both glance at her. "Yes, Mia?"

"Can we take our picture together?" she pleads.

Mia's mother shoots me a "would you mind" look. I signal for Mia to come stand next to me.

"On the count of three. One, two, and three." Her mother snaps the photo. "What do we say?"

"Thank you!" Mia says, then launches her arms around my legs. "Is your prince around here too?"

I wish he were. I want nothing more than to be held by Tim right now. But that's not who Mia would see as a prince. "Oh, um, I don't know. I'll have to send one of my mice to see if they can find him."

Mia giggles again. "Or maybe you can send your fairy godmother."

"That's a brilliant idea too." I wink. "Don't forget our secret."

"I won't."

I smile, then turn to Mia's mother and exchange a few words with her as the clock in the lobby chimes seven times.

"Wow!" Mia suddenly exclaims. "Cinderella, is that your carriage? I thought it was made of glass. Can I have a ride? Are the horses really mice?"

We stop talking. Looking out the glass doors of the lobby, I notice a horse-drawn carriage stopping in front. A bride in a flowing white ball gown steps out, followed by a groom.

"Mia, that's not hers. Do you see the woman in the wedding gown? She's getting married."

But I don't hear the rest of what's being said. My attention is focused on the tall brown-haired man in a tan overcoat, pulling off a pair of gloves as he enters the lobby. Under one arm, he carries a large bouquet of flowers. He checks his mobile. Maybe there is a little magic in the air! "Tim," I call out, awkwardly half waving my hand.

His head shoots up. Smiling, he returns my wave and walks toward me.

"Boyfriend?" Mia's mom asks.

I nod, my eyes not leaving his person. I've forgotten just how handsome he is since the last time I saw him. The overcoat fits his body like a second skin, hugging him in all the right places.

"We won't keep you, then. It looks like you two have plans. Come, Mia, it's almost time to meet Santa. Say thank you and goodbye to Cinderella."

"Bye, princess. And thank you again!" Mia and her mother move up in line. "Mommy, did you bring the cookies and milk? And my letter?"

"I brought cookies and your letter, but remember, we aren't giving Santa any milk in case he's allergic. Don't forget, last year he told you he was lactose intolerant."

As Tim makes his way toward me, a group of hummingbirds flutter their wings so quickly in my chest that it reminds me of performing a spin on the ice. "Hi," I manage as he stops right in front of me. "You're . . . here."

"These are for you." Fumbling with the flowers, he shoves them in front of me.

I accept the bouquet of pink, red, and white roses and sniff them. The smell reminds me of an expensive bottle of my favorite Jo Malone Red Roses perfume. "These are stunning. Thank you so much."

"I'm sorry, I didn't see your text message until just now."

"You just received it?"

He nods.

I rub the nape of my neck. "Then how did you know how badly I needed to see you?"

"I didn't," he says slowly, frowning. "It's just a coincidence. I flew into Toledo this afternoon to surprise you. I can't believe I haven't seen you skate sooner. What you can do on those tiny metal blades is just amazing. You were hands down the best skater on that ice. I'd planned to meet you at the stage door at the arena, but you never came out. Is everything all right?"

"It is now." I sigh. He wraps his arms around me, and I

take a deep breath as he rubs circles on my back. "I had one final treatment with Mel, our PT. I was one of the last skaters to leave. I must've just missed you."

"That's what I figured when I ran into Fernando. He told me where to find you."

I release him and my face falls. "Well, I'm glad you were able to see today's skate. It was my last."

"Huh?"

"It's kind of a long story." I glance over my outfit. "Um, tell you what, let me put these flowers in my room and change. I'll meet you back down here in five minutes."

"Okay." Tim nods. "What do you think about going for a walk? It looked like there were some charming festive lights on Main Street we can check out."

"I'd like that."

Rising up onto my toes, I kiss him, then leave for my room.

Chapter Twenty-Two

It isn't cold enough to snow, but there's still a brisk chill. I pull the zipper of my black puffer coat up higher. Despite being from Scotland and a figure skater, I'll never be a fan of cold weather.

As I walk with Tim through Promenade Park, an area across the street from the hotel, the distant sounds of a brass band playing classic carols fill the air.

"The hotel concierge mentioned that the tree lighting is at nine," Tim says. "If you can spare some time, I thought maybe we could stroll past the market stalls, grab a bite to eat, then circle back here to watch it?"

"That sounds brilliant. I'm a free woman. I have all the time in the world."

"Gemma?"

I rest my head on his shoulder. "Dreams on Ice terminated my contract this afternoon."

He abruptly stops walking. "What?"

I lower my chin, staring at the sidewalk. I resist the urge to start crying again. "I'm a skater who is, in their words, 'past their prime.' They don't have a use for someone who 'can't meet the standards set by the company.'" Saying those words aloud leave a bitter taste in my mouth.

"How can a person who is only twenty-eight be past their prime? What cockamamie person told you that?"

"A woman from HR." I sigh. "In a way, she was right. Most skaters peak before they turn eighteen."

"That's the stupidest thing I've ever heard." Tim's nostrils flare. "What about people like Frankie and Charlie? They're not teens. They're both mature skaters in their early thirties."

My gaze travels to Tim's face. The lines around his eyes and brow make him appear more distinguished. He's adorable when he's angry on my behalf. "They're both an exception to the rule."

"I don't understand. You were under a contract with them through the end of the year. And you'd already signed your next one. It's the second week in December. How does it make any sense to let you go now? What about giving you notice?"

I explain how the situation was exacerbated by my visits to Dr. Zhang and how the date on my termination letter had been preset.

"That doesn't sound right."

"Mel and Fernando didn't think so either."

"Do you want me to phone one of the lawyers the Sloths use? Mike wouldn't mind. He owes me a favor."

I shake my head. "No. I'm staying as far away from DOI as possible. I'm angry and beyond frustrated, and it'll just be easier for me to move on without opening Pandora's box."

Tim pinches his lips together and envelops me in a hug. The scratchy fabric of his overcoat rubs against my cheeks. "You're too good of a person."

As he releases me and we continue our walk, the enticing smells from a cart selling mulled wine, hot chocolate, and popcorn catch my attention. "Do you mind if we stop for a hot drink? I need something warm."

"Whatever my Gemma-rella wishes." We join the queue.

"How did you get extra time off? I thought you had to be back on Monday?"

"I called in a favor from my school principal. He's subbing for me through Wednesday. Let's just say, I'll be heading the school's event-planning committee for the foreseeable future."

The future. I suddenly have nowhere to be and nothing to do starting tomorrow. Where am I going to live and what will I do now that I'm suddenly unemployed? What about my relationship with Tim? When will he make the move to Arizona? "The end of the school year will be here before you know it." I blink a few times. "Then I guess you'll be packing up your place and settling into life in Scottsdale."

"No, I won't. I'll be staying right where I belong . . . in Sequoia Valley."

I gasp. "But the manager's job—that's your dream job, isn't it?"

"At one point it was." He shoves his hands into his pockets. "But that ship has sailed. I was about sixty percent sure I didn't want it. I needed to visit Scottsdale to be totally certain. You're the first person I've told."

"What tipped you over the edge?" I ask as we advance a bit in the queue.

"The vibe. It was like I'd entered a time warp. The current group of guys on the team are all young and eager. They wanted to go out every night and stay up into the early hours of the morning. That isn't my idea of fun. I wanted to go back to the hotel, enjoy a night in, and call you. I'm a grandpa—I like to be in bed by ten. The trip made it clear that I'm in a totally different place in life than I was when I played for them. If I took the job, I'd be miserable."

"Hearing you say that makes me relieved." I look away from him. "I wasn't really a fan of moving to Scottsdale, but I would've done it for you."

"Gemma," Tim admonishes. "Why didn't you say anything?"

"I didn't want to plant any seeds in your mind."

He groans. "We really need to work on our communication."

I couldn't agree more.

We make it up to the front. "Hi there, folks, what can I get you tonight?" the cart vendor asks.

I order a hot chocolate and Tim a mulled wine.

"So . . . you have three days off, and I also suddenly have a bunch of free time on my hands. Any ideas on how we should play this?" I ask.

"How do you feel about a visit to New York? It's the perfect time of year to see the city all decorated and dressed for Christmas," Tim says.

A date with my boyfriend in one of the most romantic places in the world during the holidays? Count me in! "I'd say that sounds brilliant. I've never been to New York."

His eyes widen. "You, a world traveler, have never been to New York? I find that hard to believe."

"It's true. I was supposed to take my first trip to the city with DOI this year, but, uh, that plan's been tossed into the rubbish bin."

"Order up!" the vendor calls out. "I have a mulled wine and a hot cocoa. Do you want whipped cream on top?"

"Yes please," I answer.

Collecting our drinks, we step away from the cart and continue along the pathway illuminated with life-sized candy canes. As we chat about New York, my heart swells at the thought of never have to go through a long-distance relationship again. The chapter of my life with Dreams on Ice might've come to an abrupt end, but there are still plenty of other things in life to pursue outside of skating.

"If we're deciding between driving or flying to New York, I vote for the plane. Do you think we'd have time to see the Rockettes at Radio City Music Hall?"

"Yes. We can do anything my Gemma-rella's heart desires." Tim stops walking. A wide, brimming smile fills his face. "Do you see what I see?"

Following his line of sight, my eyes travel up. "Mistletoe."

"You know what tradition calls for."

"A kiss," I whisper.

Carefully taking hold of my drink, he places it on the ground next to his. Our eyes lock. My breathing quickens. Wrapping one arm around my back, he pulls me in closer to his body. "Happy early Christmas, Gemma." He moves a few stray hairs out from my face and cups my cheeks. A smile tugs at the corner of his lips. "I love you."

My eyelids flutter as we kiss. Around us, a light dusting of snow begins to fall. It's as if I've stepped into a scene straight out of *The Nutcracker*. We're transported to a dark, enchanted forest, surrounded by dozens of dancing snowflakes. I smell the evergreen and the spices of the mulled wine. The holiday music playing in the background changes, and I hear the haunting echo of the celesta.

As we break apart, Tim doesn't let go. "I love you, too," I tell him.

He traces the outline of my lips with his thumb, seeming to savor the moment before we kiss a second time.

As I stand in Tim's arms, filled with deep emotions of love, I can't help but feel that we're headed down a path toward finding our own happy endings. It isn't a path that needs to be traveled quickly, but one that can be taken at whatever pace we want. After all, everything about our relationship is done in our own way in the sloth zone.

Epilogue

ONE MONTH LATER

"You can just drop me off here," I say as my rideshare enters the downtown area of Sequoia Valley. I mutter a word of thanks as I climb out and gaze into the window of a shop filled with brightly colored comic books and cardboard cutouts of superheroes. Before I know exactly what I'm doing, I enter The Caped Crusader's Corner. A bell chimes.

"I'll be right with you," a man's voice calls out from behind a black curtain.

"Okay," I reply.

Taking a moment to figure out what I'll say to the clerk, I glance at my surroundings. The shop is definitely a place where Tim would feel at home. Each wall is covered in floor-to-ceiling shelving, but to my surprise, there aren't only comic books. There are also several rare vintage toys, stuffed animals, and DVDs, and a small coffee bar is set up in the corner. A handwritten sign indicates that drinks are free, but donations are appreciated.

"How curious," I mumble to myself as I feel something rubbing against my legs. Glancing downward, I spy a black-and-white tuxedo cat studying me with large yellow eyes. Its fur is long. Its tail wags side to side, like an excited puppy. "Hello . . ." I glance at the collar. "Ivy. That's a very pretty name." On cue, Ivy begins to purr and butt her head against my hand. "Aren't you a friendly feline."

"Ivy? How did you get in here?" says a man with salt-and-pepper hair, thin wire-rimmed glasses, and a blue striped shirt. I stand and brush stray cat hairs off my jeans. "You're supposed to be napping in the back, not exploring the front where you can knock things over."

Blinking slowly, Ivy arches her back, scratches the carpet, and hops up onto the glass counter next to the register. She tucks her paws in as if to say, "I know I'm not. But I'd like to see you try and get rid of me now that I'm here."

The man sighs. "All my life, I've been a dog man. Then I let my wife talk me into getting a cat, and now Ivy runs our lives." He absently scratches the cat's head.

"She's lovely."

"She is. My wife and I can't help but spoil her. She's the daughter we never had." We stare at Ivy for another moment before the man turns his attention to me. "I'm sorry about not being here when you walked in. How can I help you today? Is there anything in particular you're looking for?"

"I'm not sure. I saw the shop and thought it could help me take my mind off some things." I scratch Ivy's forehead. "The bloke I'm dating loves comics and said they're the best way to escape the world. I'd like to see if I can find a series I'd be interested in reading. And maybe something special for him too." I stare at the packed shelves. "I have no idea what he already owns, or where to even start."

"I can try and offer you a little guidance." The man adjusts his glasses. "I'm not as up to date with the new comics these days, but I'm well-versed in the classics like *Superman* and *X-Men*."

"Your secret is safe with me."

"Let's take care of you first. What types of tropes do you enjoy reading about?"

"For tropes, my favorite stories are romances with enemies to lovers, secret identities, or grumpy-sunshine couples, but I don't think that would be of much help with finding a comic book."

"You'd be surprised." The owner chuckles. "I find that asking a person about what tropes they enjoy is more effective than asking what types of characters they like." Walking along the rows of shelves, we stop in front of a section of books that are thicker than an average comic book. "Have you ever read any of the *Sailor Moon* manga?"

I shake my head. "No, but I've heard of it."

"Let's try this one—and oh, this one." Staring at the shelf a moment longer, he adds one more to my pile. "Those should tick the enemies-to-lovers and secret-identity boxes. Now to see about a grumpy-sunshine book."

Following him around the store, I can't believe how many different titles they stock. They carry just as many as a traditional bookstore. It isn't long before I have a stack of eight titles.

"Your boyfriend might be a little trickier. You said he's a collector?"

"Yeah, he's a fan of anything featuring self-made heroes, but Batman tops his list." My cheeks burn. "You don't happen to know if there's a sloth character, do you?"

The man lights up. "A sloth?"

"Uh-huh, my boyfriend also has a fondness for them."

"That wouldn't be Timmy, would it?"

"Yes, it would."

"He's one of my best customers. No sloths, but there's a villain who's named Penguin in the *Batman* series." The man opens a glass case and runs his finger over a few books kept in plastic sleeves. "This comic is the first issue he appears in."

He hands it to me. "December 1941? I hadn't realized the series dated back that far."

"Yes, off the top of my head, I think May 1939 was the first printing."

For something so old, the colors on the comic appear to still be bright and vibrant. The paper is pristine, and there are only a few creases on it. My eyes bulge, however, upon seeing the orange price tag on the corner of the plastic sleeve. "Nine thousand dollars?" I carefully set it on the shelf with two hands and take a step back.

"That's the same reaction I had when my nephew explained the value of certain issues to me. We have a few *Superman* and *Spider-Man* comics that are worth just as much." The man's eyes crinkle in amusement. "I can't say I understand it, but he's the one who stays up to date with the market and pricing. If it were up to me, I'd say these books are supposed to be enjoyed, not stay in plastic their entire lives."

"I agree with you," I say with a nod. "Do you, er . . . have any more reasonably-priced *Batman* books you'd recommend, or another series?"

The man strokes his chin. "I'll see what I can find, especially if it's for Timmy. Somebody just came by this morning and donated a bunch of comics that were sitting in their attic. Give me a few minutes to go through what's inside."

"Take your time."

"Help yourself to some coffee." He disappears behind the curtain.

I sit in one of the oversized chairs in the corner of the shop, crack open the top book in my stack, and begin to skim through the pages. I become so engrossed in the reading that when the man returns, he startles me.

"It's easy to get lost in a good story. I'm glad you found something that piqued your interest. Feel free to leave the ones that don't appeal to you here and I'll restock them later." He gestures to the counter. "I managed to find something special. Here, have a look. If you think Timmy will enjoy it, I'd be happy to give it to you free of charge."

"Free?"

"Yes," he confirms. "This isn't in our inventory, and if it's going to the home of a comic lover, I'm sure my nephew won't mind."

"Oh my goodness, thank you so much." I shoot him a bright smile. "I don't know what to say."

The man walks behind the counter. "Just tell that boyfriend of yours to come on down to the shop with you again soon. It's been too long since we've had a good chat."

"I will. And I'd like to buy all of these. I can see myself enjoying each one for a different reason."

"Of course." The man rings me up and places the items into a paper bag. It feels good to support a local business.

"Thank you so much again for everything today . . . er, what's your name?"

"I'm Hank."

My lips twitch as we shake hands. "Gemma. Nice to meet you."

In the distance, I hear a woman's voice call out to him.

Hank sighs. "Looks like my wife needs some help. Is there anything else you need?"

I assure him I don't and wave goodbye to Hank and Ivy, my spirits much improved.

THREE MONTHS LATER

Tim pushes me along in a wheelchair decorated to resemble a medieval spinning wheel. "This is hands down the craziest seventy-two hours of my life," he says. "I can't believe we saw Frankie and Charlie medal at Worlds in Liverpool three days ago. Twenty-four hours ago, we were in London . . ."

"And now we've hopped across the pond and are back in sunny Los Angeles." I yawn. "This has indeed been one for the books. I'm exhausted thinking about it."

"You're the real star, Gem. How are you holding up? If it were anyone else, they'd be resting in bed."

I had surgery much later than I'd anticipated. It worked out best for Dr. Zhang to wait until the hockey season was over and for Tim to be on spring break. I had my labrum repaired this past Friday. Being an early-release day meant it worked out well for both of us. Since it was an outpatient procedure, Tim dropped me off on his way to school and picked me up on the way home.

I blink my eyes lazily. "Everything is pretty sore." Tim opens his mouth. "But before you say anything"—I glance over my shoulder—"I'm *not* willing to spend the day in the hotel. I want us to keep sailing full-steam ahead. We need to put every spare moment of your time off to good use."

"I'll say we've *more* than done that." Tim stops pushing

the chair momentarily. "Do you need some meds? You didn't take any when you woke up."

"No." I shake my head. "I'm tired of them playing games with my stomach. I'm an athlete, I can handle the discomfort."

"If you change your mind, I have some ibuprofen in my bag. Dr. Zhang thought you might need some over-the-counter stuff just in case. I picked some up at the airport store."

"You did?" Tim's mask makes it difficult to read his expression.

"Yup."

We got in so late that I didn't even notice he'd gone out. He's definitely a keeper. I tuck a loose strand of hair behind my ear. "I'll, er, take one, then."

Tim fumbles around under the chair. I hear the sound of him rummaging through my backpack. "Here's a water bottle and the pills."

"Thank you." I pop the cap off and take two, downing them with some water, then hand the items back to him.

"What's your pain on a scale of one to ten right now?" he asks in a hushed tone.

"A five. It's a lot better than it was on the plane."

He nods. "If it gets worse, let me know immediately and we'll head back to the hotel."

Okay."

He starts pushing the chair again. As the pain starts to dull to an ache, I relax and begin to soak in more of the details of those around us. A *Star Wars* stormtrooper, a Sailor Moon, and a Captain America walk past us, each of their costumes more detailed and impressive than the last. How do these people have the time and resources to put outfits like this together?

"Sleeping Beauty, Batman, great costumes!"

"Thank you," we call out in unison.

"Maybe next year, I'll be able to get you to wear a costume that's a little bolder, like a Catwoman suit, or maybe even Poison Ivy."

For the first time since we've started dating, I get the reference! "We'll see. Just wearing this is a big step for me."

"And aren't you glad you did? It makes the experience even more fun."

I don't want to admit he's right, but he is. I change the subject. "Which multiverse is Poison Ivy from?"

"Batman. She's one of his archenemies. Not as much as someone like the Joker, but Ivy is definitely up there."

I frown. "Wait a moment . . . Ivy . . . that's the name of the cat that lives in the comic store. Do you think Hank named her after Poison Ivy?"

"It wouldn't surprise me. All cats are evil."

I lean back and look at Tim's masked face. "They are not."

"Yes, they are. Every time I get within ten feet of a feline, they try and scratch me or hiss at me."

I huff. "I find that hard to believe."

"Believe it or don't." He shrugs. "I'm a sloth person. Not that it matters—I'm not planning to get any pets unless it's a Chia Pet."

We'll see if he changes his tune when we visit the animal shelter next week. I bet I can convince him to adopt a cat. I love dogs, but I've always grown up with cats. I need one in my life again. If I adopt one, by default, he'll become a pet guardian too.

As we enter the main exhibitor hall, I have to blink several times to soak in just how many different booths there are selling everything from comics and vintage toys to full-on life-sized garden statues of characters. It reminds me of the Lake Wakahanra antique market I visit with Suzy. "Wow, there is so much stuff here."

"I know!" Tim's voice jumps up an octave.

"Just remember, whatever you buy has to fit in the car." I snigger.

"I'll keep that in mind." Tim suddenly slows his pace, his head turning from side to side. He's itching to stop and shop. This is his happy place.

I sigh. "Why don't you drop me at the booth Hank is running and come find us in an hour?"

Tim hesitates. "Gemma, this is your first convention. I want you to get a little taste of everything. I can shop later."

I press my lips together. "Tim, we have all day to poke around. It would be more efficient if you got your shopping out of the way now. Plus, I haven't seen Hank in a few weeks; it would be nice to catch up with him."

"Are you sure?"

"Positive."

As if I'm riding in the Batmobile itself, Tim flies down the aisles at lightning speed to one of the largest vendor booths. Hank waves to us. "Hey, Tim, Gemma. If it isn't two of my favorite people," he jokes. "It's good to see you guys."

"Hey, Hank. Right back at you. Looks like a good turnout this year," Tim says.

"It definitely is."

"Is your lovely wife around?" I ask.

"She'll be here later with our grandkids. They're spending the morning at Universal Studios."

"Sounds like fun."

A customer calls for Hank's attention. "I'll be right back," he says.

I brush Tim's arm. "You can set me over there. Then go shop."

He parks me next to a box of T-shirts with various telly show logos. After promising he won't be more than an hour, he pecks me on the cheek, then power walks down the aisle, his cape flying wildly behind him. I grin. The shapely, formfitting costume is a good look on his powerful frame. Maybe I should ask him to model some of his costumes around the cabin.

I recall just how quickly the last few months have flown by. So much has happened. I've moved to a cabin in Sequoia Valley, overcome my past demons and become a coach, and fallen deeper in love with Tim. Although it hasn't always been easy, I'm finally beginning to find my stride. Fernando will soon be moving to the area too.

At the start of the new year, Dreams on Ice started finding ways of getting rid of its more veteran skaters. I count myself lucky to have escaped when I did. News eventually broke that the new management team of DOI was going to be rebrand the company and all its shows to be more relevant and in tune with current trends in the market.

Frankie, Fernando, Mel, and I lamented that it marks the end of the family-friendly company we'd once known. With all the large lawsuits being tossed at the company for how they've handled letting us skaters go, I doubt it'll survive the year.

"Sorry about that Gemma," Hank says as he straightens a box of comics. "Did Tim rush off already?"

"He did. I could tell he was chomping at the bit to get out there and see what was on offer at different shops."

"I hope the kid doesn't overspend." Hank chuckles. "Last year, he dropped three grand on a collection of limited-edition light sabers, and he doesn't even care for *Star Wars*. I ended up buying them from him for the shop. He gets it in his head that something is limited edition and suddenly he has to have it."

That's his inner child for you. "Oh no." I laugh. "He promised he wouldn't go too crazy."

"If you think that's bad, you should hear about one of my customers who's crazy for dinosaurs."

"Dinosaurs?"

"Oh yes. His name is Lucas, and we met at a *Jurassic Park* convention a couple years back."

Later that afternoon, after enjoying a panel with some of the actors slated to be in a remake of a popular spy film, Tim and I sit outside enjoying a snack.

"I meant to ask you earlier, did you have a good haul? You only came back to the booth with two bags." I lick the top of my strawberry soft serve.

"It was all right. I picked up a couple of comics and a Sloth bust of that character from *Zootopia* for the garden at your place. The selection was a little disappointing this year."

"Were you looking for anything in particular?"

"Not really. I mean, I'm always on the hunt for vintage *Batman* books, but most of the good ones are outside my price range. I try to keep my big-ticket purchases under five grand. I keep hoping that someday I'll get lucky and find something that was produced early, like a number-ten comic, in lousy condition. I'd be happy just to have a rare book in my collection. I'd actually be able to read it and enjoy it as opposed to keep it locked away and protected in a plastic cover."

My lips twitch. "And what would you say about number one or two?"

"Yeah, that's not going to happen anytime soon." Tim laughs sarcastically. "One of those costs as much as a house."

Sitting taller in my seat, I gestured to my backpack. "I know your birthday isn't until next week, but there's something I want you to have."

"Gem, you didn't have to get me anything. Just you being here at the convention with me is plenty."

"I didn't buy it. Your gift kind of just fell into my hands." I point to the big zip pocket. "Just make sure your hands are clean before you open it."

Tim finishes his ice cream, then excuses himself to go wash his hands. I sit giddy, excited for what's to come. I've been waiting for just the right moment to surprise him, carrying around the comic in my bag for the last few months.

When he returns, he sets his Batman mask on the table and retrieves the package wrapped in sparkly red Christmas paper. He raises an eyebrow.

"What? I had a lot of paper left over." I have my hand behind my back with my fingers crossed.

Tim makes quick work ripping off the paper. As he peels back the wrapping, he inhales sharply and leans forward. "No way! *Batman* number two?!" He turns it over in his hands, his fingers stroking the edges. "This has to be a grade seven! I mean this is . . . this is . . ."

"A good gift?"

"Better than good." His head snaps up. "It's better than

anything I've ever received. Where? How?" His voice comes out strained.

Warmth spreads throughout my body. "Thank Hank." I explain how I'd received it all those months ago after looking for a gift for him.

"I don't believe it." He laughs. "Gemma, you are amazing. I mean you could've sold this and made a huge profit, but you didn't."

"A gut instinct told me it was intended for you, and I knew you had to have it. I just didn't know when that time would be."

He leans forward in his seat and kisses me. "I'm so lucky you've come into my life."

"And I'm lucky you're in mine, too."

"I have something small for you, too."

I wonder what exactly he could be carrying. His suit is formfitting. There are no pockets. Is the item in my backpack? As he reaches down into his boot, I realize he has a small zippered compartment.

Oh, that's where he keeps his ID, credit cards, and phone. I'd wondered about that.

Pulling out a small black velvet box, he places it on the table and slides it to me. "Open it."

My heart races. "Tim?"

"Open it," he repeats.

My hands close around the velvet. Inside is a dainty gold necklace with a Celtic knot charm.

"Tim, it's beautiful." I carefully take it out of the case and place it around my neck. "Thank you so much."

His lips twitch. "Mom helped me do a little research about Celtic jewelry. This particular knot is supposed to signify growth. I thought it was perfect to symbolize just how far we've come as a couple."

I touch the knot and squeeze it in my hands. "This is perfect."

"I love you, Gemma, and I hope that with time, I'll continue to fall even deeper and more madly in love with you than I already am. Not that I need an occasion to give you gifts, but happy seven-month anniversary."

"Happy seven-month anniversary to you too. I love you," I whisper.

As we kiss again under the golden sun, I imagine a bright future for us built on love, laughter, and happiness. Oh, and maybe filled with a sloth or two, too. Life can't get any more brilliant than this.

Dear Reader

Thank you for taking the time to read "The Sloth Zone."

You can find the bonus content for this book here:
    https://tomitabb.com/the-sloth-zone-bonus-content/

If you enjoyed this book, please take a moment to leave a review on Amazon, Goodreads, Bookbub, or whatever platform you may have discovered this book on. It helps Tomi connect with readers like you!

Love her books? Become a part of her treasured community here.

Stay connected with Tomi by scanning QR code, or by visiting her official website.

Https://TomiTabb.com

258

Acknowledgments

Writing a book is by no means a singular process and there are many, many people working behind the scenes who have helped to bring Tim and Gemma's story to life that I'd like to extend my heartfelt gratitude towards.

First, I'd like to thank my amazing editor and friend Joanne Lui. A year ago, you inspired me to write a figure skating book because we were tired of seeing stories with so many of the same age old cliches. I never imagined that Frankie's story would grow to become a full series! Thank you so much for not only your brilliant editing work, but also for letting me bounce ideas off of you, and for opening my eyes to the world of exhibition baseball. I truly could not have done it without you.

To Brooke Gilbert. What can I say, you are another person that I am so very proud to call a friend. You're always there to provide me encouragement, especially on a particularly difficult day. Without your prodding, I never would've been brave enough to take on designing my own covers. Thank you so much for all that you've done.

To Charity, thank you so much for your keen eyes. You are my proofreader extraordinaire!

To all of the teachers who have shaped who I am, thank you. Although you have each been wonderful, I'd like to single out two individuals in particular—my 6th grade English/History teacher, Mrs. S, and my 10th grade World History teacher, Mr. K. You two have been the single greatest influences on my life and are the reason I am pursing an advanced degree in history. I know there are countless other students you have inspired over the years too. On behalf of everyone whose walked through your classroom doors, thank you.

To all of the teachers around the world, I'd like to express my gratitude toward you all. It takes a special person to become a teacher and in my opinion, you are all among the hardest working people in the world. Society tends to undervalue and under appreciate you, but I want you to know that I see you! Coming from a family of educators, I know exactly what goes into teaching. You are real-life superheroes. From the bottom of my heart, thank you!

To the Savannah Bananas baseball team thank you for revolutionizing how the game of baseball is played. Your dedication to your fans has not gone unnoticed.

Lastly, to my family and friends, thank you all for your continued support as I continue my writing journey. This last year has been tough and I am so thankful that you are there to remind me that being an author is a marathon journey. Not a sprint. I could not do what I do without you.

To my wonderful treasured community of readers, thank you for your support. It means the absolute world to me that you are there and enjoy my work. I literally would not be here if it wasn't for you.

About the Author

Tomi's publishing journey began in 2020 with the release of her debut novel, *Dancing With a Royal*. Although she's always loved writing fictional stories, Tomi's background is in academic writing. She holds an MA degree in History and is currently pursuing her doctorate degree in the same subject.

In her rare free time, Tomi enjoys figure skating and hunting for new pumpkin flavored foods to try. It's one of the many reasons fall is her favorite season.

Tomi is a California native where she resides with her family and one very spoiled cat.

Website: TomiTabb.com

Also by Tomi Tabb

The Unexpected Royals

-Dancing With a Royal

-Jiving With a Royal

-Designing for a Royal

-More Than a Passing Shot

Friends of the Unexpected Royals

-Designs on Love

-Engineering Love

Novellas Related to the Unexpected Royals Series

-Pointe Shoes and Sugar Plums

The Skaters of Sequoia Valley

-The Rules of the Rink

-The Sloth Zone

-Caught In a Loop

The Royals of Isola Nostrum

-The Great Austen Adventure

-For the Love of Dinosaurs

Historical Romance

-The Mysterious Mr. Marcellus